Joi and Payne

A Contemporary Christian Romance

Novel by

Sheila L. Jackson

Virtuous Books

ALSO BY SHEILA L. JACKSON

Non-Fiction

The Enemy Within

Perfectly Normal

Contemporary Christian Romance

Where Was God

Where Was God Book II, coming in January 2018

Joi and Payne
Virtuous Books
Copyright ©2016 Sheila L. Jackson
http://www.sheilaljackson2.com
SJ@comcast.net

Cover Photo by: BookCovers.com/Lori
Interior Design: Sheila L. Jackson

ISBN-13: 978-0692656860
ISBN-10: 0692656863

For Worldwide Distribution
Printed in the U.S.A

Dedication

To my reading audience, your reviews and positive comments are what give me the inspiration to continue writing books that entertain as well as spiritually edify the soul.

Acknowledgements

Thank you, Lord, for without Your anointing, penning Joi and Payne would have been impossible.

To my family and friends who continue to encourage and pray for me, your support means a lot.

I am grateful to Debra Kavanaugh and Ivy Woodard at the Shreve Memorial Library in Shreveport, Louisiana. Whenever there is an event in the area, you ladies make sure that I am a part of it.

To the bookstores, who never failed to house and set-up my book signing events, thank you so much for your hard work.

I am humbled and grateful to the many readers who purchased my books throughout the years. Your e-mails and posts on social media have inspired me to continue to write uplifting material.

Many thanks to those in the ministry, who prayed and encouraged me along the way; this has indeed been a long, hard, and lonely journey. But your interceding for me, gave me the strength to persevere.

Prologue

The subdued faces of the two policemen standing outside of Joi Campbell's door spoke volumes to her overactive nerves.

Her heart pummeled against her chest as their stern demeanor rendered her speechless. Struggling to see behind one of the officer's wide physique, she'd noticed her parents speeding into the driveway almost on two wheels. Her mother got out of the car before her father came to a complete stop. Charging toward the house, she ran upon the porch, pushed past the officers, and grabbed hold of her daughter. Like a movie playing in slow motion, the scene wasn't going to turn out well. Especially when her father made it into the house, gasping for air as he clutched his chest. Now, Joi had reasons to panic.

After finding her voice, Joi addressed one of the officers who had partnered with her husband on The Shreveport Police Department. "Where is Michael, Jacob?" Her hands began to shake out of control as she continued to question him. "Where is Michael?" She screamed louder, knowing that policemen only made personal visits to families of fellow officers killed in the line of duty. Jacob and Michael had partnered for ten years and now the day she feared, had come. Joi held her breath and waited for the officer to give her the dreaded news.

Officer Jacob Winn tried putting on a brave face, but no words formed. It was apparent that whatever he had to say was not good, leaving the escorting officer to be the bearer of bad news. Joi's stomach clinched as she braced herself for the words she had hoped to never hear.

"Mrs. Campbell," The agony shone in his poignant blue eyes, as his chubby cheeks quivered. "Your husband and kids were killed this afternoon in a car wreck involving a teenage driver, texting behind the wheel. The young lady ran a stop sign, causing her to crash into your family's vehicle." His words caught in his throat as he struggled to keep his taut posture.

Joi stared into the officer's sorrowful eyes as he delivered the worst news no wife or mother ever wanted to hear. As she tried wrapping her brain around losing her husband and ten-year-old twin boys, Jayden and Kayden, her airwaves seemed to have closed, making it difficult to breath. The realization of his statement had become too much for her to process. Her brain felt as if it had short-circuited and like the flip of a switch, everything around her went black, causing her limp body to collapse into her father's arms.

Chapter One
Two Years Later

Joi knelt beside her husband and twin boys' graves, still mourning their deaths. True, two years had passed, but for her, it seemed like yesterday. Her parents by her side helped to ease the pain and loneliness of visiting the cemetery on the anniversary of their passing. Her parents kept a watchful eye on her. If not, she'd visit everyday.

Her life consisted of church and work. She had no social life. The thought of dating made her cringe. She was thirty-three years old, widowed, childless and alone. After their funerals, she moved back home with her parents. Joi sold the house she once shared with her family for her sanity's sake. It had become cold, and the memories deafening. Her sons' laughter and fighting over the television remote control had faded. Michael, shouting from the bedroom for her to help find his badge that he had misplaced for the umpteenth time, became nothing but bitter sweet memories. A year later, she moved out of her parents' home and found a place of her own to start over. Those words sounded foreign to her.

Her father rested his hand on her shoulder. "Joi, c'mon. It's time to go. We've been out here quite a while."

With the palm of her hand, she wiped at a tear threatening to spill from the corner of her eye. She stared up at her father and mother. "I thought it would get easier," she gulped, hoping to suppress the pain. "Each time I visit, I find it harder to leave."

"I know baby," her mother said, stroking through the layers of Joi's short hair. "Michael wouldn't want you to live the rest of your life grieving over him and the boys. You can find comfort in knowing that they are with the Lord."

"Knowing that doesn't ease the pain." "I want to move on, believe me, but it's hard."

Her father helped her to her feet.

"I didn't say it would be easy." Her mother gave her one of those, *this-too-shall-pass*, kind of smiles.

Joi dusted the grass off her knees, took a deep breath and said, "How am I going to face the future, when it's lying here in three graves? My heart aches for them daily, Mom." She didn't want to fall apart in front of them. If she did, they would talk her into moving back in with them. That was the last thing she wanted to do. She valued her privacy.

The three strolled over to a vacant bench. Joi sat in the middle. Taking in all that had been said, she didn't want to worry her parents any more than she already had. So, she hid her agony to keep from hearing another one of their lectures about, "God, putting no more on her than she could bear." She had heard enough of that from her pastor, and frankly, she was tired of hearing it. Joi had lost the love of her life and her sons because of some irresponsible teenager whom she thought had gotten off easy for reckless driving. It wasn't fair that she had to go on without those she loved while a criminal got away with manslaughter.

"What are your plans for the rest of today?" her mother casually asked. Changing the conversation was something she'd always done if the subject was depressing.

Pathetically, Joi answered, "I have no plans. I'm going to watch a *Lifetime* movie, microwave a TV dinner and call it a night." Why take the time to prepare a meal when there was no one but her?

"TV dinner! *Lifetime* movie!" Her mother shouted, while her father scooted to the edge of the bench, looking at her as if she had said a curse word. "Child, those movies are depressing. Either someone is being killed, stalked, dating a psycho or committing adultery. Why don't you join your father and me for a good home cooked meal?" A hopeful smile smoothed the worry lines that had formed across her mother's forehead.

Her father shook his head in agreement. "That's a great idea." He gently squeezed Joi's hand. "You know your mother always cooks too much food for the two of us."

"I'm going to pass on dinner. It's been a long day." She yawned, hoping her tired act would cause them to back off. If she accepted their dinner offer, they would try to get her to sleep over. "I just want to go home and relax before going to work tomorrow. You know how it is in the hospital's ER, never a dull moment." She faked an exhausted smile.

Over the past ten years, Joi worked as an emergency room nurse. She loved her job. The thought of making a difference in others' lives gave her a sense of purpose. Working at Blessed Memorial Hospital saved her in more ways than one. It kept her busy and sane, until she arrived home after a long, grueling day, then silence greeted her at the door.

"Yes, I do remember," her mother said. "I don't envy you at all. People don't know the pressures that go along with being a nurse."

"Well, my beautiful ladies, it's time to head back into town before nightfall." Her father stood to his feet. Helping her and her mother up from the bench, he escorted them to the car. Once inside the backseat, Joi craned her neck out the window to get one last look at the cemetery as her father drove away. She wanted to run back to their graves and scream until she could not scream anymore.

*****

Later that night, Joi wandered over to the fireplace mantle lined with photos of a once happy family. She picked up one and cradled it in her arms. How she wished she could see their smiling faces and hear their laughter again. She and Michael had been college sweethearts. They were inseparable until fate had torn them apart.

Their deaths could have been avoided if only Rebekah, the teenage driver had kept her eyes on the road, instead of her cellphone. Her parents hired the best lawyer money could buy, getting her off with no more than a pat on the hand. The judge sentenced the teen to do five years of community service. Her family lives meant nothing to the justice system, which told her money and power still ruled. When the girl's sentence was handed down, Joi wanted to scream. Was she the only one in the courtroom that thought the sentence was too lenient? Joi wanted to yell at the injustice of the entire proceeding. Surely, it had to be a terrible mistake. Before she got the chance to voice her complaints, her parents and in-laws hauled her out of the courtroom.

Whoever coined the phrase, "Time heals old wounds," lied. Her wounds were still fresh. No scabs had formed to start the healing process. Joi placed the photograph back onto the mantle, and called it a night.

In her mind, she wanted to move on, but her heart said differently. No matter how many prayers she prayed or tears she cried, none of it had brought her family back. She wanted to live again, but didn't know how. Grief consumed her constantly, even in her dreams. Escaping it was getting harder to do, especially during those long, lonely nights when there was no one to share her bed with. Michael was the only man she had known intimately. How could she let another man into her heart when her deceased husband still claimed it?

For now, she sought solace through the memories of much happier times. That had to do for now. The dating scene today was downright scary and dangerous, especially when television shows reenacted dates and marriages that had fatal endings. The thought of it, terrified her.

Lord help!

Dating was on the bottom of her list of things to explore. She shivered at the thought as she lay in her empty bed wishing Michael was there with his strong arms to hold her through the night. Instead, she snuggled up with a pillow and cried herself to sleep as she had done for the last two years.

Chapter Two

"Have you considered my offer of taking an all-expense paid trip to the Caribbean, Joi?" Tara Givens, a fellow nurse and friend waved a flyer wildly in Joi's face. "And don't try to weasel your way out of it. We both know you don't have any plans."

"I'm not interested in sitting on an island just so you can chase behind half-naked men flexing their muscles." Joi said while writing in a patient's chart.

"The way I see it, you haven't been interested in much, lately." She snapped her head around at Joi. "Besides, what's wrong with wanting to see God's gift to women show off what they have to offer on a hot, sandy beach?" Tara flashed a wicked smile at Joi.

"Humph. Don't try to justify your lustful ways by bringing God into it." Joi stopped writing and gave Tara a scolding eye. "Girl, there are more sexcapades between the tourists and islanders, and who knows what else goes on at those resorts."

"You're just saying that to keep from going." To get her attention, Tara gently placed her hand down on the patient's chart that Joi had been writing in. "It's time for you start living again. Life is too short not to enjoy it, and the Caribbean's is a beautiful place full of history. So, you can leave the men for me while you go discover the ancient landmarks of the island."

They both laughed as they busied themselves behind the nurses' station in the emergency room.

Why was everyone pestering her to start dating again? Who were they to tell her what she needed? She didn't want to date. Her life was just fine.

Liar!

Her daily regimen consisted of work, eat and sleep. She wanted to be left alone, but her family and friends continued to stick their noses into her personal business. Dating had become overrated. Who needed the drama that came along with it, surely not her? Michael had treated her like a queen and she'd never accept any less than that from any man.

Her loved ones meant well, but had become a bit intrusive into her private life. Her Mr. Right was gone, taken away from her in the prime of his life. No man could ever take his place. The sooner they accepted that fact, the better.

Like a song she once heard playing on the radio, "Love Don't Live Here Anymore," it had left her a long time ago. She was empty, tapped out, void of any passion of the romantic kind.

"No, I'm not." Her voice turned defensive. "The thought of a man coming on to me is hard to digest."

"Are you listening to yourself?" Tara's hazel-brown eyes widened. She tossed a handful of braids off her shoulder and said, "So, you're going to live the rest of your life without feeling the pleasure of a man's touch?" Resting a hand on her slender hip, she shot an annoyed look at Joi. "Girl, get real."

Joi considered her friend's advice. The thought of never experiencing the gentle touch of a man, scared her. She missed Michael and their date nights; they would leave the boys with her parents one weekend out of the month. It helped them to reconnect as a couple. Her body ached from missing his strong, firm hands caressing her. The thought of another man touching her that way, made her felt like and adulterous. True, she had been a widow for two years, but starting over with someone else did not feel right. She was married to the same man for ten years. Jumping back into the dating scene wasn't going to be easy. Her heart just wouldn't let her.

"Tara? Don't you have patients to take care of, instead sticking your nose into my business?"

"Right now, your business is my business." Tara brows arched as her full lips grew into a smile. "I'm leaving, but trust me when I say this conversation is far from being over. We will continue it at lunch."

Shoots!

Joi placed the patient's chart in a slot with the others, and then faced Tara. By the look on her face, Joi knew that she meant every word. "We?"

"Me, Becky and Albre," she said. "The three of us will see you at lunch. Don't pretend that you're busy. Or we will come and hunt you down."

The three of them ganging up on her would make it nearly impossible to say no about the trip. Nevertheless, she was determined to stand her ground and not allow them to back her into a corner. If they wanted to flaunt their half-naked bodies on the Caribbean beach, they would do so without her.

She and Michael had met in college and married soon after graduation. Back in those days, men used more tact when asking a woman out on a date. Now, the first thing a man wanted to know from a woman was her occupation. Or, they wanted to have sex on the first date. She had no plans to be the next featured story on, *Unsolved Mysteries*. Adding the horrors of online dating to the mix made her want to lock herself in her house and never come out. The image of some pervert stalking them on their trip made her flesh crawl.

"I'm not ready to date, Tara," Joi said, trying a more stern approach, but, Tara saw straight through her.

"That's what your mouth says during the day. I know your body says differently at night. You are human." Tara winked, flashing a knowing smile, and then turned on her heels to leave before Joi could respond.

*****

"Ms. I-Don't-Need-A-Man has graced us with her presence." Tara teased as Becky and Albre giggled in the background when Joi neared their table in the hospital's cafeteria.

"Don't start with me. Today is not the day. The ER is standing room only and it's only noon," Joi warned with her eyes as she placed her tray on the table. She blew out a deep breath and flopped down into one of the vacant seats. "I can only image what the rest of the day is going to be like."

"We've had a busy morning, too. That's why we came down to the cafeteria to unwind," Albre said, twirling her long raven hair with her finger. The frustration shone in her epicanthal folds.

"Speak for yourself. I can think of better places to go to unwind than a noisy, overcrowded hospital cafeteria," Becky added, tucking a stray blonde curl behind her ear.

"Look, we are not here to talk about the hospital's scenery." Tara jumped in. "We need to discuss our trip to the Caribbean, which is three months away."

Joi rolled her eyes at Tara. She wanted to grab her tray and move to another table but she knew better; they would follow her. Tara's persistence was driving her crazy. Her friends did want what was best for her; however, neither had experienced losing their entire family in the same day. It was hard to pick up the pieces and move on. She was stuck, and found it difficult to pull herself out of her rut.

"I told you this morning, I'm not going." Ever since Tara discovered the flyer on the hospital bulletin board advertising the trip, she had been bugging Joi to go. How could she enjoy life without Michael and her boys? The thought of them lying in some cold, dark grave tugged at her heart. They were the ones who should be taking the trip with her.

Albre squinted at Tara, which made them appear tighter than usual. "Stop pressuring her, Tara. Give her time to decide if this is right for her," she said, her Asian accent sounding thicker with each word she spat.

"I agree," Becky added. "Neither one of us has ever been married nor suffered tragedies like Joi." The color depleted from her fair complexion, causing her to appear paler than normal.

"Thanks for understanding." Joi relaxed back into her seat. "I'm not trying to be a fun-sucker. I miss my family." Her words caught in her throat. "It should have been Michael and me going on this trip."

"I'm sorry for being so pushy," Tara said, with a little too much excitement in her voice.

Confused, Joi wondered if her friend was apologizing or making fun of her. "What's with the stupid grin?"

"Look over there to your left, at the last table." Tara used her eyes as a guide. "Men alert."

"Oh-my-goodness," Albre sang.

Becky pulled her compact mirror from her purse and applied foundation to her ghostly skin. With her fingers, she combed through her flaxen blonde mane and added color to her plumped lips. She was the queen of plastic surgery.

"If the three of you are going crazy over the guys at the table, I can only imagine how you're going to behave in the Caribbean." Joi took a sip of water to put out the flames threatening to erupt inside her. The men were gorgeous, but she would never voice it aloud.

"You need to be like *Stella*, and get your groove back," Tara joked, faking a Caribbean accent while eyeing the men over at the next table. "And the best place to get it back is on an island filled with exotic men." She swung her braids wildly, putting on her best sexy act.

Joi had eyes. There was one man sitting at the table that stood out from the others. His physical characteristics reminded her of why she had fallen in love with Michael. If her friends had any inkling of her thoughts or desires for wanting to be held, touched or loved, they would kidnap her and haul her off to paradise.

This trip doesn't sound like a bad idea. The more I think about it… the more I'm contemplating going.

Chapter Three

As a newly divorcee, Wyatt Payne spent his days sulking over his ex-wife's deception. He came home from a hard day's work to discover she had packed up and left. Thankfully, no kids were procreated during their union. Although, it wasn't from his lack of trying, Trina lied that she had stopped taking her birth control pills. Only later to discover, that she had tucked them away in the back of her drawer. When he confronted her about it, she told him that she was not ready to start a family. But truthfully, his yearly income as a firefighter for The Shreveport Fire Department had waned on her, causing her to want out of their union.

When he applied for a chief position in another district and failed to make the cut, Trina vanished. Later, having the gall to send him a disheartening text message, stating that she left him for a man with a more prestigious and lucrative career...a doctor.

"Of all the places to eat in this town and you drag us to a hospital cafeteria for lunch on our day off," Jett said, taking a hearty bite out of his fried chicken.

"I know you're not complaining about the food considering the way you are tearing into that drumstick." Wyatt joked as Jett stuffed his face. "I needed a break from those fast food joints. I heard Blessed Memorial Hospital serves great food, and by the way you guys are chowing down, I see it's true."

"Amen to that," Paul added, scooping up a spoon full of peas.

"At least a single man can look forward to eating three meals a day down at the fire station when on duty," Seth said, running his tongue over his lips.

The men grunted, agreeing with Seth as they continued to stuff their faces.

"Not only does Blessed Memorial Hospital serve great food," Jett added, his attention focused on more than the food on his plate. Wyatt trailed Jett's eyes to where four attractive women were seated. "They also have some delicious looking women working here as well."

Wyatt blew out a deep breath. He knew where his friend's mind was headed. "Jett, can you keep your mind out of the gutter for one second?"

"Man, my mind is never in the gutter." Licking his lips like a hungry wolf as his eyes widened on the prey he spotted across the room. "It's on those lovely nurses."

Jett's appetite for women had a way of getting out of hand. He never took no for an answer. Wyatt feared that Jett's cocky attitude might someday land him in serious hot water. His conceited behavior toward women would be the cause. No, meant no, to most men, but in Jett's self-centered mind, 'no', was a word women used to tease him with their feminine wiles. Jett's boyish good looks had gone to his head. He thought every female wanted him; whether, in his work uniform or everyday attire, women were drawn to him.

For Wyatt, he never cared much for the attention as Jett had. After the boulder his ex-wife had dropped on him a year ago, his trust in women was at an all-time low.

"Can we for once enjoy our lunch without you going into your attack and conquer mode every time we are out in public?" Wyatt asked, trying to keep his cool, which at times was hard to do with Jett's impulsive behavior.

"Speak for yourself, man. Not all of us are bitter against women," Seth added, joining Jett in stalking the ladies with their eyes.

"Bitter?" Wyatt yelled in a hush whisper. One thing he hated was drawing negative attention on him in public places.

"Yeah. You heard right. Bitter. Ever since Trina left you for that doctor, you have become a drag to be around," Paul said, turning to face Wyatt.

By then, Wyatt had begun fuming under the collar at his friends' attacks.

Seth continued to stuff his face, shaking his head in agreement with Paul.

"I'm not going to waste another minute listening to the three of you trying to counsel me on things you have no knowledge of." Wyatt had had enough of his friends' tongue-lashing. Trina hurt him deeply. Neither of them had ever been married or in a serious relationship to know the pain and scars her deception had left on him. Jumping back into the dating game at the present moment was not a priority of his.

"Well, you can stay in denial if you want. But like the saying goes, 'the truth will set you free, my brother,'" Jett said with a halfcocked smile.

Wyatt shook his head at Jett, knowing he was telling the truth. His ex-wife had pulled a fast one on him when she mysteriously left without warning. Only later to discover she had left him for another man. She claimed her new beau was loaded with money. He wanted to get back into the dating game, but he had to resolve his trust issues first. No need for him hooking up with a woman if he was going to be suspicious of her every move.

Paul pointed out one of the women at the table. "Wyatt, the nurse sitting at the end of the table is your type." Lowering his brows at Wyatt, he knew he'd struck a nerve. Paul then, turned his attention back onto his plate and devoured his lunch.

"What's my type, since you know me so well?" Wyatt felt the veins in his neck began to bulge. He liked hanging out with the fellas, but sometimes their jokes went a little too far.

"Man, live a little." Seth ceased chomping long enough to comment. "And stop taking everything so personal."

His friends continued to stare over at the nurses' table as Paul described which one was perfect for Wyatt. "Okay, Mr. Over-Sensitive. The lady sitting next to the one with the braids is your type. She seems reserved. Uh…well, more like guarded, unlike the other three, and beautiful, which they all are. Her honey brown skin is smooth and flawless, and she's short and slim. You know how you hate tall women."

"Check, check and check," Wyatt smiled, rubbing his chin in agreement.

"So, I got them all right, huh?"

"Yes, you did. Now go back to eating your lunch. I'm tired of you trying to psychoanalyze me."

Blind, Wyatt was not. He'd already spotted the woman Paul had picked out when he and his friends entered the cafeteria. Still he wasn't ready to date. What if she was already spoken for? Sneaking around was not his thing. He didn't believe in sharing his woman.

Once the pain lessened from his ex-wife's deception, maybe then, love would find its way back into his heart. He just could not handle that kind of rejection a second time.

Jett slapped Wyatt on the arm, alerting him that the women were headed their way. The men's overactive hormones ruled their minds, except for Wyatt's. They behaved like schoolboys when the women passed their table to put up their trays. Wyatt wanted to hide his face in shame. *They are firefighters for goodness sake. Why are they acting so immature? They are trained to save lives in the face of danger, but, someone needed to protect them from themselves.*

"Hello, beautiful ladies." Jett, of course made sure the nurses noticed him as they passed their table giggling and looking sexy as heck.

"Hello, yourself…handsome." A dark skinned beauty with braids and the most beautiful set of hazel-brown eyes, responded. The other two smiled, while the lady that Paul said was Wyatt's type acted uninterested.

"Excuse my forwardness, but are the four of you nurses?" Paul asked, squaring his shoulders in a dignified manner. Watching him with that silly grin smeared across his face made Wyatt's food nearly lodged in his throat.

Duh-hh-hh! Yes, they are nurses. Stop with the stupid act.

"Yes, we are," the lady with the beautiful hazel eyes said.

"You don't know these men, Tara." The reserved one slapped her on the arm, whispering something in her ear.

"Stop being so old-fashion, Joi."

"Joi-ii-ii," Seth sang. "What a beautiful name, isn't it Wyatt?" He nudged Wyatt in the side with his elbow.

Wyatt shot him a scolding glance. "Let these ladies get back to their jobs. They have lives to save." He wanted to smack the crap out of Seth for putting him on the spot.

"And we don't?" Seth asked, gesturing with his eyes for Wyatt to chill out. "Hi, I'm Seth. These are my friends, Wyatt, Paul and Jett. We are firemen at station three down the street."

"Nice to meet you all." Tara proffered her hand, flaunting a beautiful smile as she swung her micro braids off her shoulders. The other ladies followed.

Wyatt could feel the reservation in Joi's handshake. Either she thought they were going to attack her, or, she was like him, forced to be cordial due to his friends' pushiness.

Tara was an attractive woman, but she was not his type. Now Joi, on the other hand, caught his attention at first glance. Knowing his luck with women, she probably was married. She appeared more reserved and poised than the other three man hungry ladies accompanying her. *All the good ones are always taken,* Wyatt, whined in silence.

The men greeted the women in return. If his colleagues' had tails, they would be wagging right about now. Wyatt thought maybe it was time for him to start hanging around a more mature crowd, but for some reason, he always found himself drawn back to this womanizing bunch. Though they lacked maturity at times, they were like his younger brothers. Maybe he needed them more than he realized. He just hated when they dragged him into their— seek-and-conquer games— when it came to the opposite sex. Wyatt used a more tactful approach with women, especially the ones he was interested in.

"It was nice meeting you ladies, too," Paul said, in his *Keith Sweat* voice. Wyatt wanted to get up and leave the table. His friends played the same games with every woman they met.

Wyatt stood up, signaling to his friends that it was time to leave. "Ladies, it has been a pleasure talking with you." He nodded his head, but for reasons unbeknownst to him, he could not take his eyes off Joi. Her flawless skin and stunning liquid brown eyes had lured him in. "But, we have to go."

"Speak for yourself," Jett said after being shockingly quiet throughout their entire conversation.

"No problem," Tara interrupted. "We have to get back to the ER."

From the look that Jett was giving Wyatt, he wasn't too pleased with him.

The ladies said their goodbyes.

Wyatt did not know how long he could keep his composure in front of Joi. She was like a gentle fresh breeze, causing him to realize what he had been missing.

Maybe one day, the Lord will see fit to send someone special into my life. A woman I can have children and grow old with. Hanging out at the station is fine, but it doesn't compare to having a woman.

He left Blessed Memorial Hospital with new hope of seeing Joi again. Maybe their meeting was more than coincidental. *What if meeting her is God's divine plan?* He tossed the thought out his mind. God had better things to do than concern himself with his love life.

Chapter Four

Joi thought they were going to enjoy a girls' night out. When they arrived at the restaurant, she'd learned that Tara had set her up without her permission with a clone of the nineties rapper, *Master P.*

Everyone knew Tara did not have the greatest track record when it came to matchmaking or men. Her and Joi's taste were vastly different as night from day. The over-aged wannabe rapper sitting next to her had a mouth full of gold teeth, which blinded her each time he opened his mouth to speak.

Where did Tara find this one...at a rap concert? She moaned inwardly, sneaking a sidelong glance at him. Joi wished someone would slap her out of this nightmare.

She made a mental note to kill Tara for setting her up with a man she had no plans of seeing again. This, by far, was the worse date ever. Usually, she knew the men Tara was trying to hook her up with and had the chance to graciously decline, but this one was a sneak attack.

Tara's dates were always tall, dark and every woman's fantasy. The man she picked for her tonight wore boots with heels to make him appear taller. Joi could see the top of his head and she stood five-foot-five. He seemed to have the small man's complex. During their conversation, he bragged about his accomplishments and stretched his torso, as if it would miraculously give him height. He had no shame when it came to asserting himself. What he should have done was take out those gold teeth and put on a shirt that fitted. The muscle shirt he so proudly wore exposed his flabby abs.

"Joi, you haven't said much ever since we arrived," Tara whispered to keep the men from overhearing her.

"Just wait until we get out of here," Joi said through clenched teeth, faking a smile at her date from another planet. "I'm going to put a serious hurting on you." Joi wanted to flag down their waitress and ask her to pour her something stronger than a root beer soft drink. She needed something to help alter her vision, in order to look at her mercy date across the table from her.

"I know he's not much of a looker, but he has a decent job."

"As what?" Joi presented a serious look at Tara while the men talked amongst themselves. "A reject of the "Ying Yang twins?"'"

"You must keep an open mind." Tara tried making light of the situation.

Her date was the best looking man in the restaurant, while she sat next to one of the seven dwarfs from *Sleeping Beauty*.

"An open mind. Are you serious?" She questioned with her eyes. "No thanks, I prefer to keep it closed, if this is what I'm going to see." Joi turned her attention back to their dates, hating to be caught up in another one of Tara's tricks to get her out the house. She wanted to call it a night before it ever started. What was Tara thinking? Better yet, she wasn't thinking at all, just looking at the hobbit of a man made her eyes twitch.

Her date or whatever it was, opened his mouth to speak. And like a vampire shielding his face from the light, Joi had to take cover from the glare reflecting off his teeth. "Uh... Joi, I didn't get a chance to run by the bank today to cash my check. So, I hope you have some cash on you to pay for our meals."

You got to be kidding? After he has bragged about his accomplishments and finances, he has the nerve to expect me to pay for his food. This scam may have worked on other women but not on me. I have no plans of paying for his dinner. He better glove up and head to the kitchen to pay for his meal.

"Say what?" Joi craned her neck in his direction to see if he was kidding. The serious look on his razor bumped face caused her to turn and look at Tara. "You better handle this."

Tara let out a fake laugh and said, "Don't worry, I'm treating." Her date appeared to be short on cash as well, from the way his face lit up when he learned that she was paying.

Leaning in close where only Tara could hear her, Joi whispered, "Oh you gon' pay, in more ways than you can imagine."

"I'm sorry, Joi." Embarrassment crept up her face.

The men were in good spirits as they chatted and bumped fist, but of course they would be. They had just eaten over a hundred dollars' worth of free food.

Joi refused to say another word. She snatched up her purse from the table, leaving the three of them there with their mouths hanging. The audacity of him thinking that she would pay for his meal took her aback. Of all the scoundrels Tara tried fixing her up with; this idiot was by far the worst. If she stayed a second longer watching him pick his teeth, she would have screamed.

As she high-tailed it for the nearest exit, Wyatt, the man she'd met at the hospital's cafeteria, entered with a woman, Joi supposed his wife. When her eyes locked with his, something spiritual transpired between them. Or maybe, it was the way his polo shirt and jeans loosely cradled his physically toned body. Fireworks ignited inside her.

She wanted to kick herself for feeling such a way about a married man. True, she was lonely, but not desperate enough to fool around with a man who belonged to someone else.

He called out to her as she tried dodging past him and his wife. "Joi?"

She stood frozen in place. "Y-Yes," she hesitated. The sound of her name coming from his lips sent joyous ripples up and down her spine, which angered her. *Get a hold of yourself. He's married,* she scolded herself.

Does that mean she had betrayed Michael because she felt such a sensation from this man's voice? Shame riddled her heart, knowing that the man standing before her inflicted such desire within her.

"You don't remember me...do you?" He stood before her wearing a silly grin.

How could she forget a man like him? He coined the phrase, sensuality? "No-oo-oo... should I?" She tried playing dumb, lying through her teeth. She knew full well who he was. The woman hanging on his arm wasn't too happy about him talking to her. Joi thought it was rather rude of him not to introduce his wife. The woman snatched away from him and stormed into the restaurant. Joi decided that Mr. Wonderful might not be so wonderful after all.

"At the hospital cafeteria, yesterday." Wyatt continued their conversation. Either he was insensitive or hadn't noticed that his wife had stormed off.

"Oh, yeah. Now I remember." Her blind date had been a nightmare and to top the night off, Wyatt was not the man she'd envisioned. What man would treat their spouse in that manner? She wanted to leave, and quickly. The exit door was just a few steps away, but he kept on talking.

His wife returned. Her fury could be felt. This was Joi's cue to leave. One thing she wasn't—a home wrecker. "Look, I came here to eat and have some alone time with you," the woman spat as she turned her neck with an attitude.

Joi jumped in, "Well, you two have a lovely dinner, Sir."

"Wyatt," he said with the same look on his face that she wore earlier on her blind date— the need to be rescued, but she wasn't his savior. He had to save himself.

"Wyatt, you and your wife have a pleasant evening, excuse me." She pushed past them and left, but not before getting out of earshot of hearing the woman reprimanding him for not introducing her.

Good girl.

*****

"Note to Joi," she said to herself after arriving home. Thankfully, she had driven her own car. "Never go out on a blind date again, especially if Tara arranges it."

She grabbed the photo of her family off the fireplace mantle and pressed it close to her chest. Joi closed her eyes, letting her mind drift away to happier days. Each time she arrived home from another foiled evening, it made her miss Michael even more. The single life was not for her, but here she stood in a home, alone. She wanted her old life back. Why did God have to take the only man who ever loved her? Her entire family wiped out by one teen's stupid mistake to text and drive.

If every man out there was like the imbecile she had left at the restaurant tonight, then she would rather spend the rest of her life as a single woman. With the picture of her family snuggled close to her bosom, she believed that she could feel their presence. How she missed putting bandages on scrapes and bruises when her boys fell off their bikes. Or, how Michael thought it was the end of the world when he wasted coffee on his uniform. She'd save the day by handing him a fresh one. Her mind had to be playing tricks on her. She could smell his cologne throughout the room.

Her fantasies had become so real. She believed that she could feel her husband's touch. *Why do I continue to torture myself each and every night?* When she opened her eyes, like a puff of smoke, his image quickly faded.

Tears chased each other down her cheeks. Joi missed their romantic date nights. Michael would post love notes throughout their home. She'd retrieve the last one off the bedroom mirror, listing what their night would consist of. Now, she only had precious memories. Memories she'd cherish for the rest of her life. Sadly, they weren't enough to chase away the longing of a man's touch.

Chapter Five

Joi took a late lunch today. She needed to clear her cluttered mind and regroup after treating several trauma victims. As she sat alone in the cafeteria, enjoying her garden salad and romance novel, she wished that she could vanish into the pages to escape her humdrum life. A man's deep, delightful voice prevented her from taking a quantum leap into the world of make believe. She closed her book to investigate to whom the alluring voice that intruded on her me time, belonged to. Joi hoped it was not another male employee trying to hit on her or ask her out, especially after her date from another planet last night. Her eyes trailed up at the tall figure, hovering on the opposite side of table.

What does he want? Instantly, her breathing had gone from cruise control to downright reckless when she took all of him in at once. *Let the church say amen, to this gift to women standing before me.* Trying to steady herself, to keep from looking foolish, she grabbed a napkin from the table to wipe the beads of sweat that had formed on her upper lip.

"Hi, Joi. I don't mean to impose, but do you mind if I sit here?" Wyatt asked with an unsure smile. "I would have sat someplace else but every seat is taken."

"Sure." Joi did not want him at her table. The only other place for him to sit was on the floor. She couldn't flat out say, no. This stranger had awakened parts of her that she thought were impossible to resurrect, and it scared her to death. She knew nothing about this...Wyatt. But looking at him sure made her insides happy. She hadn't experienced this type of happiness in a while.

"Thank you, I promise not to disturb your reading," he said, without ever taking his eyes off hers as he sat across from her.

Why is he staring at me that way?

"I was just getting ready to leave." Her legs were shaking underneath the table. Wyatt was gorgeous. How could she continue reading her novel and pretend that he wasn't there? She had to get herself together. For crying-out-loud, the man had a wife and possibly a houseful of kids, she had to think rationally.

"You hardly touched your salad," he said, looking over into her plate. "Don't leave on my account."

Joi had worked up an appetite after the busy morning she had in the ER and wanted to finish her lunch in peace. From the look on his face, she knew a conversation was brewing behind those insatiable lips of his.

"I was hoping to have a couple of minutes *a-lone* before returning to the ER." She placed emphasis on alone.

"Well, I'm sorry that I interrupted you." He stood, grabbing his tray to leave as he looked around to see had anyone left one of the other tables.

"No…don't leave." The words flew from her mouth before she could stop them. "There is nowhere else to sit. Stay." Joi felt like a heel for being so rude.

"Thank you." He placed his tray back onto the table and began to eat.

Joi tried focusing her attention back on her novel before Wyatt had invaded her space. She figured he must have ditched his immature friends she had seen him with the other day. They looked like the type that traveled in packs. Well, who was she to judge, she and her girlfriends did the same.

The irritating sound of Wyatt clearing his throat told her that a conversation would soon follow.

And it did.

"What type of nurse are you, if you don't mind me asking?"

Closing her book, she focused her eyes on his full, masculine lips. They moved in such a way that her eyes followed their motion as he chewed his food. Guilt sucker-punched her overactive imagination as Michael's face flashed before her.

Ashamed of her feelings, her eyes made their way to his. Then, his laid back demeanor put her to ease. Because the last thing she needed or wanted was a married man to come on to her, especially at Blessed Memorial Hospital. Rumors had a way of spreading fast and she did not want any to be about her. Surprisingly, he didn't seem the type, which helped her to relax—a little.

"I work in the trauma unit in the emergency room." Joi wanted to keep their conversation as light as possible.

"That's a lot of stress." He finished the last of his vegetables, washed it down with a glass of water, and gave her his undivided attention. Her heart palpitated out of control underneath her scrub uniform. Although, the cafeteria was filled with people, he made her feel as if they were the only two there.

Just as she thought when he first sat at her table, he had no plans of letting her enjoy her lunch in silence. "Yes, it can be at times." Another short answer; she wasn't going to allow their talk go any further, because it may expose the way he was making her feel.

Since he had no plans of going anywhere, she might as well entertain his questions, within limit of course. If they turned personal, then, she'd have to cut him off and end their lunch.

Resting his elbow on the table, he said "I guess we both have challenging careers."

"I guess we do. What are the odds of that?" Making small talk was not her forte'. With men these days, a woman couldn't be too careful, especially when he chose not to wear his wedding band. The tan around his ring finger gave him away. As long as he kept the chitchat light there would be no problems, but if he crossed the line, she would just have to set him straight. One thing she learned from her mother, never step over into another woman's territory.

Her friends teased her that half a man was better than no man. She disagreed with their philosophy. There was no way a woman could burn down another woman's house and expect to build a mansion from the ashes.

"Being a fireman is a stressful job," he said, rubbing his hand against the side of his chiseled face. "I chose this profession because my grandfather and dad were firemen, but, I never imagined the strain that came along with it, until I joined, The Shreveport Fire Department."

With his good looks, he can easily model in one of those calendars for firemen. I can see him as Mr. July. The month of hot, sizzling summer fun and I would be the first in line to get my copy. Stop it! She reprimanded herself. Her thoughts had gone into a forbidden zone.

Joi understood his plight. Being a nurse in the ER had its downside. Watching patients brought in on stretchers with parts of their limbs detached from their bodies was a lot to digest. She learned to channel her emotions in order to do her job effectively. When someone's life was at stake, falling a part in front of them could be disastrous for both parties.

"I agree, Wyatt." His name slipped from her lips before she realized it.

"So… you remember my name, huh?"

"Yes." The tight smile she wore since he sat with her, loosened. "Your friends made sure of that," she snorted. "So, what brings you back to Blessed Memorial's cafeteria?"

"You," he said matter-of-factly.

"Right." She blushed under his intense stare.

He didn't elaborate. She guessed his straightforward statement had taken him aback as well. Instead, he went in on his friends' behavior. "You have to overlook those guys. They are young and impulsive," he chuckled. "They see a group of beautiful ladies and they go wild."

Joi had to laugh. Wyatt demonstrated confidence in her presence, unlike the men, Tara had set her up with; having a decent conversation was out of the question.

"I know what you mean. My friends are the same," she added. "Especially Tara, she's the matchmaker of the group.

Lord knows, I've been her guinea pig on more than one occasion."

"Guinea pig? A woman as beautiful as you, need fixing up on a date?" His eyes lit up in surprise. She was not sure if that was good or bad. "You can't be serious?"

The temperature rose up a notch in the cafeteria or she thought it had. Joi covered her mouth to conceal her silly grin. Wyatt had caught her off guard with his compliment. Now, she was glad she allowed him to sit with her. Their conversation had been light, which made lunch with him quite pleasant. After Michael's death, she found it hard to trust the men around her. Wyatt's gentle nature advised her not to lump all men in the same category.

"Thank you," she said, feeling the heat rush to her face.

"I take it that you are married?" he asked, raising a curious brow.

"Widowed," she answered. His question hit a sad note for her and wondered if he heard the pain in her voice.

"Sorry, I didn't mean to..." his voice trailed off.

"That's okay. How could you've known?"

"I kind of know how you feel."

Joi stared over across the table at him. She hoped he wasn't going to lie about being married. The discoloration around his finger gave him away. "You're a widower too?" She waited for his story or rather, his lie.

"No. My wife left me for another man." A look of shame shone on his face.

"Ouch! What a slap in the face." Joi ears could not believe what they were hearing. What woman in her right mind would walk out on this man? Unless, there were major defects

In his character that she hadn't noticed until after the honeymoon.

"Ouch is right," he said. "And do you want to hear why she left?" His eyes told her that he needed to vent his frustrations to someone. Maybe he needed a sympathetic ear that his friends had lacked.

Although she did not know him well enough to intrude into his private life, curiosity had gotten the better of her. Without waiting on her to respond, he began his tale of rejection.

"She said that she couldn't live the life she wanted to on a fireman's salary. I didn't make enough money for her." His shoulders slumped in defeat. How was she to respond to that? And comforting him was out of the question, especially in the cafeteria where people were looking for the latest gossip to spread.

"Wow, that's a low blow." Now, she understood why he wasn't wearing his wedding band. "Did she know how much you earned before she married you?"

"Yes, but she was hoping that I'd eventually make chief."

Forgetting what others thought; Joi extended her hand across the table, resting it on top of his massive ones. She assumed that divorce was just as devastating as death. Their loss was different, but they shared the same pain. Neither one of their significant others were a part of their lives.

Chapter Six

Wyatt entered Better Body Gym, where Jet and the others awaited his arrival. As usual, they were up to no good. He'd noticed one of the female gym members, waving her finger in Jet's face, mouthing something. The creases in her forehead told Wyatt their talk wasn't good. He had a problem figuring out his friends. Female issues were always the brunt of their troubles. He thought by taking them under his wings would help them to mature. It seemed that his counseling and talks had gone unheard, more so with Jett.   Needless to say, his old school methods weren't working on his new school buddies.

As he approached Paul and Seth, Wyatt vented his frustration concerning their womanizing ways. "The three of you are bordering on harassment." They grinned, but Wyatt was dead serious. "If I was a woman, I wouldn't waste my time on you barbarian."

Jet escaped his finger lashing from the female he'd ticked off and made his way over to Wyatt. He threw his gym bag down next to the bench press, and said, "Wyatt, I don't want to hear your back in the day, how men treated women foolish talk." He straddled the bench press, pointing to Seth to place several weights on the bar as he laid back.

"Don't worry, I'm not," Wyatt said as he began to stretch before hopping on the treadmill. "But don't come looking for me to bail you out of jail when one of your female friends come after you."

Paul added his take on their conversation, and said, "Why do you have to be so serious all the time, Wyatt? It's just innocent fun."

"Fun? Is that what you call it? The appalled reactions on the women faces, says differently."

"Wyatt is right. Sometimes we do take our pursuit of women too far," Seth said while spotting Jett as he lifted weights.

Wyatt changed places with Seth. As Jett strained to lift his last set, Wyatt grabbed the weights from his hand and placed them on its cradle.

Snatching a towel from off his gym bag, Jett stared at Seth and Wyatt, and said, "So, the two of you are ganging up on Paul and me?"

"No, I'm looking out for your best interest." Wyatt gave a friendly slap across Jett's sweaty shoulder. "We work for the public. I don't want some money hungry female dragging any of you into court, trying to sue, because a couple of Shreveport Firemen couldn't keep their hands to themselves."

"I'm grown." Jett wiped the sweat from his brow as he turned to face Wyatt. "I don't need you watching me. You're not my daddy." Jett leapt from the bench, standing eye level with Wyatt.

Wyatt tried his best to be a positive male figure for the three rookies, but there was only so much he was willing to tolerate, and disrespecting women was not one of them. Since working for the fire department, he'd seen men lose their jobs for nonsense that could have been avoided. He was trying to keep his friends from falling into the same pattern. If Jett's arrogance continued to dominate common sense, then he'd have to learn the hard way.

"Jett, you are like a little brother to me. I have seen others lose their jobs behind something that could have been prevented." Wyatt kept his stance, hoping his words penetrate through their thick heads.

"We're not ganging up on you, Man," Seth said as calmly as possible. "But you need to get that temper of yours under control."

"Speaking of under control." Paul changed the conversation, when he noticed the way Jett's moist hands had balled into a fist.

Wyatt was relieved when Paul spoke up, because Jett looked as if he wanted to punch something or somebody.

Paul continued, "Wyatt, I noticed when you entered the gym doors, you had a silly grin on your face and whistling. What was that about?"

The men turned on cue to face Wyatt.

"How did our talk turn to me?" Wyatt asked.

"I know you Dude. It doesn't take a genius to figure out something is up with you." Seth added, brushing a hand through his short, blonde hair.

"When you guys ditched me earlier today, I decided to have lunch at Blessed Memorial Hospital." A smile as wide as Caddo Lake flowed across his face. "And I had the pleasure of eating with Joi."

"Do tell... my brother." Jett said, sobering up from his anger. The mention of women had that calming effect on him.

"We had lunch...the end. There's nothing else to tell, only that I found out that she isn't married. She's a widow."

"Are you going to pursue her?" Paul asked, but Wyatt hated the hidden message behind his words.

"No...I believe she's still grieving the loss of her family."

"You learned all that about her at lunch?" Jett asked, twisting his lips up in doubt.

"Jett, I'm going to say this to you only once." Annoyance seeped its way in Wyatt's words. "Then, I'm going to finish working out. There will come a day when you're going to run your game on the wrong woman. And yes, I can tell Joi is grieving."

Wyatt learned a lot about his beautiful lunch mate today. She was his type. Joi had the total package. He'd learn more about her in half an hour, than he'd known about Trina in their two-year union. He prayed that they would meet again.

After Wyatt and his friends' conversation, he hoped they'd take heed to his warning when it came to women. Every woman wasn't going to play by their rules or thought that their unwelcomed advances were flattering. Their horse playing went a little too far at times and they probably expected him to do the same with Joi. As for him, he'd plan to let things happen in God's timing. He'd finally met a woman who fascinated him and had no plans of scaring her off.

Chapter Seven

With a cup of coffee in hand, Joi relaxed on her living room sofa. She let out a deep sigh, thankful that the week had passed quickly, as she stared out the large bay windows. Two days off with nothing to do sounded heavenly after working twelve hour shifts in the ER. Today, she planned to catch up on some much needed housework before the dust bunnies began to take over.

The steam flowed from her cup as she sipped and watched the neighborhood kids play hopscotch, joggers run alongside the curb and landscapers manicure their lawns.

A faint smile lined her face when one of the little girls playing outside noticed her through the window and waved. Joi returned the friendly gesture. Her thoughts immediately turned to her boys, Jayden and Kayden. They would have been twelve years old now. Their innocent faces flashed before her. Her heart ached at the thought of knowing there would be no first girlfriends, no proms, graduations or weddings for them. God had left her with nothing but memories— memories that tortured her daily. On days when Joi was at her lowest, she'd wished that she had been killed in the crash along with her family. However, the protective hands of God kept her strong when those dark moods overwhelmed her. The agony of their absence at times made her bitter. Why was her family taken from her? Michael was in the prime of his life. Her kids hadn't begun to live. They had plans. Why did God have to come and interrupt her perfect life? Why? She lamented, never taking her eyes off the kids playing outside her window.

As quick as those dreadful images had come, pleasant ones of Michael holding and caressing her emerged. The memory of his calming voice rescued her as they always had when she felt troubled. In her mind, the images were real. She escaped reality and sank into her fantasy. A fantasy so real that Michael seemed to have smothered her lips with his kisses. In a robotic motion, Joi touched his face, hoping this time it was true. Yearning for his love, a moan escaped her wet, hungry lips. Just when she eased into the comfort of his strong, muscular arms—poof—like a cloud of smoke, Michael had faded into a world where she could not enter.

Joi sat on the sofa, disappointed when reality called her back into her lonely existence. She had to get herself together before she found herself strapped in a straitjacket.

There had to be a man out there for her somewhere. With all the crazy stories on the news, Joi thought it best to pray that God send the right man for her. Subconsciously, she whispered, "A man that finds a wife; finds a good thing. God, if there is a man out there for me, then he will find me. I'm not going to look for one and he turns out to be a psycho."

Joi arose from her hopelessness, cleaned her house from top to bottom and spent some much needed time in prayer. The last two years of her life had flown by. She had no plans of ending up an old lady with no one to keep her company but a house full of cats.

Her parents kept telling her that it was time to move on. Well, she didn't know exactly how. She just knew that she had too.

Lord, show me how to live again. I've been walking around lost and confused. Teach me how to love again. You gave me Michael and the kids for a short time. Why, they were taken from me so soon, only You can answer. I have faith that in time; the right man will find me.

She remembered the fun times she and Michael had on weekends when they did their weekly cleaning. Joi would turn on the CD players, pop in their favorite up-tempo song and clean the house from top to bottom. Just one simple thought had changed her somber mood as she got up from the sofa and reenacted those days. Joi danced, sang and dusted with a new sense of purpose.

*****

Later that evening, Joi met Tara at a local restaurant for dinner. She was in such a good mood that she failed to see the frustration on Tara's face.

"What have you been up to today, Missy?" Joi asked, unfolding her napkin and placing it on her lap.

"I had planned to sleep in, until you called, pestering me to have dinner with you." She ran her polished finger up and down the menu before placing it down on the table, and asked, "And you?"

"Boring stuff."

"Like?"

"Housework. Girl, it looked as if a tornado had blown through my house, leaving dust in its aftermath."

"You know what Joi," Tara sighed, resting her chin on the ball of her fist. "Sometimes working in the ER can take its toll on a person." Tara took a sip of water that the waitress had placed before her. "I mean, watching those people fighting for their lives makes me put my life in perspective."

"I understand how you feel, completely," Joi remarked. The same waitress returned with their orders as they continued to hash out their complaints. "It's hard when you are trying to do your job while some irate family member is cursing you out when they think you're not doing all that you can for their loved ones," Joi continued.

Tara huffed, shaking her head in agreement. But, she was not the type to ignore their rude comments. She had been reprimanded for using a few choice words at some of the patients' rude family members.

"I hate that I brought up work. I don't want to waste my day talking about that job," Tara said with annoyance in her voice as she began to eat her smothered chicken and rice.

"Well, what do you want to talk about, then?" Joi asked.

"Those fine firemen we met on our lunch break the other day." Her eyes danced in her head as they usually did at mention of the opposite sex.

The spunky girl Joi knew had returned. Any subject relating to men had that effect on her. Joi swore Tara had men on her brain twenty-four/seven. "Is your head still spinning over them?" Joi remarked.

"And yours not?" Tara stopped eating and stared up at Joi as if she had a third eye in her forehead. "I was checking out the one named, Wyatt. I think he likes you."

"How do you know that?" Joi played the dumb role. Wyatt was an attractive man and in her age range, but, he probably had women falling all over him because of his occupation. A man in uniform had that effect on most women, and she wasn't most women.

"I know men, Joi." A sly grin curled up her mahogany painted lips as she winked at Joi. "I consider myself an expert when it comes to them."

"Don't be so sure. There is always a penalty to pay when it comes to the affairs heart." Joi dipped her stuffed shrimp into a bowl of tartar sauce and took a big bite, while watching her friend's confused look.

"Affairs of the heart? Girl, all I want is to get my hands into one of their bank accounts."

"Tara, you make good money."

"Yeah. But there's nothing wrong with wanting more." Her eyes flashed with dollar signs.

"Don't get caught up in greed, Tara. Trust me, nothing good will ever come from trying to play a man."

"Why do you always have to be such a downer? Men take advantage of women every day. Maybe if you loosen up a little, you will find you a man with fat pockets," Tara advised, wearing a silly smirk.

"No thank you. I'm looking for a man that loves God. And if he does, then he will know how to love me."

Wyatt was a handsome man. Tara had that correct for sure, but his job was a strike against him. Joi did not want to be with another man with a dangerous occupation. Although technically, Michael wasn't killed in the line of duty, but if he had survived the car wreck, the possibility was always there. She believed God had a plan and purpose for her life— but what? She shook Tara's comment out of her head. Wyatt had no interest in her. With his towering height, muscular built and lips that could possibly give smoking, hot kisses, finding a mate were the least of his problems.

Joi thought it best to wait on God. She had no intentions of getting burned by the fireman.

Too late.

He had already begun to reignite a fire she thought had fizzled out with the loss of her husband.

Chapter Eight

Wyatt handed the attendant behind the counter of the bowling alley his shoes, in exchange for a pair of bowling shoes. As he sat on the vacant bench to put them on his feet, Joi's beautiful, diamond shaped face entered his mind. She was the type of woman any good man would take notice of and he had definitely taken a liking to her.

He was growing tired of the same old routine of hanging out with his boys—Jett, Seth and Paul. At the age of thirty-five, he had no desire for the nightlife. With his rigorous job and schedule, getting his rest was a must. His friends were young and wild; they wanted to hangout until the wee hours of the night, not realizing that the community depended on their alertness and ability to do their jobs effectively.

Life after divorce for Wyatt consisted of work, church and keeping his ex-wife off his back, even though they were no longer together. What baffled him the most about Trina, if her new boy toy was loaded, then why was she calling him to borrow money every other week?

Sticking her nose into his private life had become a nuisance. Trina left him. She had no claims on him anymore. If Wyatt didn't know any better, he'd think that she was still trying to keep her claws into him. For what reason, he had no clue.

When Trina began comparing him to other men with money, something smelt fishy. Like a lovesick puppy, he thought that she just needed some space, so he gave it to her. Then, when she started to cut off all forms of communication with him, the alarm went off in his head. Unfortunately, it was too late; she had packed her things and left him with not so much as a goodbye.

A firefighter's salary couldn't afford her a dream home in Knobb Hills—Snobb Hills was more like it— but it definitely could have afforded a nice comfortable middle class home in Western Hills to start a family. His applying for the chief position had been her entire conversation. When that dream flopped, she hauled tail, leaving him broke and emotionally distraught. Trying to pay for her expensive taste had worn him out.

Quickly, he shook the images of his broken marriage from his head. She was not deserving of a man like him. The next woman God send into his life, Wyatt would be sure that they both wanted the same things. His thoughts drifted back to Joi. She seemed to have a good head on her shoulders, but so did Trina, until the spell she had cast over him wore off. When he finally came to his senses and saw the real woman he had married, her head was spinning around like *Linda Blare* in the *Exorcist*. He would think twice in the future before he lost his mind behind the next pretty face or curvaceous figure that strolled his way.

A slap on the back rescued him from the tortuous memories of life with Trina. "Why are you looking so bummed out, Bro?" Jett asked as Wyatt scooted over to make room for him on the bench.

"Waiting on your late behind," he said. "And where are the others? I swear the three of you are going to be late to your own funerals."

"We're not like you, old man," Jett joked, slapping him on the back again. "You are the only one that has no life."

"I got your old man." Wyatt balled his hand into a fist and shook it at Jett."

Seconds later, Paul and Seth walked in, hi-fiving each other, which meant one thing, women. Wyatt swore, sooner or later the right woman was going to lock the three of them down.

"What's got you two so excited?" Wyatt asked, knowing the answer.

"Only one thing, my man, can put on a smile on my face like this," Seth said, wearing a goofy grin. Paul sat beside the others to tie his bowling shoes "I finally scored a date with the Honey at Jackie's Bakery. You know how long I've been going over there, pretending to like those disgusting donuts they serve?"

"So, she finally caved in to your smooth charm...huh?" Jett added, giving his approval with hand shake.

"Yeah man. I knew eventually, I'd wear her down."

"Don't be so sure." Wyatt said as he stood to make sure his bowling shoes fitted comfortably.

"Man, keep those rain clouds over there," Paul sounded off.

Wyatt threw up his hands, leaving the three to search for a vacant lane to bowl. His advice about women fell on deaf ears anyway. One day, the three will appreciate his wisdom.

"Are you guys coming?" Wyatt called out over his shoulder as he headed to one of the vacant lanes. The three mumbled something amongst themselves; Wyatt assumed they were discussing him.

"We're coming," Jett yelled back. "But keep the unwanted advice to yourself. I already have a daddy."

The others agreed and snaked over in Wyatt's direction.

*****

"Are you going on the trip or not, Joi?" Tara asked along with Albre and Becky. They cornered her before she had the chance to clock in. "We need your answer today." The three stood with their arms folded, waiting for her to answer.

"I suppose... I don't know." Joi scratched the side of her head, trying to decide. Mixed feelings crowded her mind as she stared at the three. The last thing she needed or wanted was for some old geezer rubbing up on her on the island. The visual picture made the bile rise to her throat.

"You suppose!" Tara shouted. "Yes or no. What's so hard about that?" Her braids swung back and forth.

"Come on Joi, the four of us do everything together," Albre whined.

For the record, they never did everything together. Their minds were always on the opposite sex. She lost count of the men they have dated and those they had broken up with. No longer in their twenties, it was time for her girlfriends to think about settling down.

Tired of their whining and pressuring her about the trip, Joi caved in. "Yes... I will go."

Joi hoped that she had not agreed too fast before thinking it through. Maybe, her going would get her parents off her back, especially her mother who continued to remind her that her biological clock was running out of time.

As long as no sleazy, scum-bag tried brushing upon her in the Caribbean, everything would go well. On the other hand, if some toupee wearing, Casanova runs up in her face, things might not end on a good note in paradise.

"It's about time you live a little," Tara cheered. "Today is the last day to put in our vacation dates for the year, so don't go changing your mind, Joi." Tara gave her the evil eye and wiggled her fingers as if she was casting a spell over her. What her friend had not learned was that her Voo-Doo incantations did not work on her. She better take that superstitious stuff back to New Orleans. The blood of Jesus was more powerful than the powder she carried around in her purse to scare the other employees with.

Becky jumped around like a hyper cheerleader, her blond hair bounced around her narrow face. "You know what this mean, don't you?"

The three laughed at Becky's awkward happy dance moves when Albre shouted, "Shopping spree!"

Joi hoped Becky would brush up on her dancing skills before traveling thousands of miles away from home. If not, the islanders would think that she was having a seizure with her jerking and twitching moves.

She decided to put her reservations aside and planned to have the time of her life. If the girls began to stalk or chase after gorgeous men, like those she had seen on the brochure, she promised not to become an old Mother Hubbard and spoil their fun.

If Tara wanted to keep any man's attention for more than a second, she had better quit it with her mumbo jumbo crap. If it really worked liked she swore it did, she would have had a steady man by now. Instead, she scared them off when she began mouthing strange things about putting a spell on them if they ever left her, which caused them to run for the nearest exit.

They agreed that a shopping spree was in order. The last time Joi wore a bathing suit, she and Michael had vacationed in the Florida Keys the summer before the fatal crash. Now, her hair and wardrobe screamed makeover. Spoiling herself was a must; this trip was just the thing she needed to get her feet wet and test the waters of life. Still, a permanent relationship was out of the question. The memories of Michael and the love they once shared continued to be a sore spot for her. Moving forward with someone else was unthinkable.

Chapter Nine

Joi eased her tired body down into a chair in the visitor's area at the hospital. After desperately trying to save a young boy's life earlier, she had to steal away to regroup. Although she'd witnessed tragedy on a daily basis, getting used to it was hard. Today had been an emotional rollercoaster, and the trip Tara and the girls had planned was the outlet she needed to get off her ride of despair.

With force, she pulled herself out of the chair and headed down the hallway. Her tired eyes widened when she recognized a familiar face heading her way.

Wyatt!

Only, he wasn't wearing his normal work attire, but a navy blue shirt and pants. He was dressed as a paramedic and looked as exhausted as she did.

He spoke first, flashing a smile that made her forget about her bad day. "Hello, Joi," Wyatt greeted. "You look beat." They moved against the wall to keep from blocking the flow of traffic on the hallway.

Those were not the words she had hoped to hear from this gorgeous man. Joi jaws dropped. Did she really look that bad? She rubbed a hand against the side of her face.

He must have sensed that his comment had hit a sour spot and tried to fix it. "I mean, not that you look bad are anything." She watched as he chose his next words carefully. "You just seemed a little tired, that's all."

"No need to defend yourself." She mustard up a weak smile and then ran her hand through her hair. She had passed tired. Joi was downright beat and ready for her shift to end.

Three kids were rushed into the ER. Their injuries came from starting fires. Neither incident had adult supervision. As one boy struggled to breath, she saw her sons' faces when she looked into his terrified eyes. A panic attack nearly caused her to lose control, but her training as a nurse kicked in and she help to save the child's life.

"Let me treat you to a cup of coffee," he suggested, his hands fidgeting in his pockets. "You need a moment to catch your breath."

How was she going to catch her breath when his tall, lean body stood so near? What should she do? Should she head back to the ER or accept his offer? Without thinking, the words raced from her mouth. "I can use a cup of caffeine right about now." Did she just say that? Not only was she tired but apparently delirious as well. Wyatt seemed like a nice guy; she hoped he did not read much into her accepting his offer. Firemen and paramedics, they were the same in her book— skirt chasers.

"I know what you mean. I can drink an entire pot and then some after the day I had."

The two headed toward the cafeteria. Once inside, finding a vacant table was easy. The lunch crowd had thinned out, allowing them plenty of places to sit. Wyatt purchased the coffee and made his way back to Joi.

"Powdered lactose free creamer or milk?" He placed both in front of her as he stirred his. "I didn't know which you prefer."

"Powdered is fine, thank you." She ripped the creamer package open and poured it into her coffee, taking in a hefty sip. "Mmm mmm, just what the doctor ordered." *Or fireman/paramedic.* "Thank you."

"My pleasure."

To her surprise, Wyatt slid in the seat beside her, causing her to wonder about his intentions. His closeness made her uncomfortable. Trying to be discreet, she scooted her chair to give them some space. Joi enjoyed his company and prayed that he would not ruin it by making a pass. She also questioned him showing up regularly at the hospital. The food was great, but not that great to show up three days out of the week.

As he played with the stirrer in his cup, Joi stole glances of his massive biceps. Her thoughts ran to his ex-wife who left him for another man. If money was the only reason for her leaving him, she had to be insane. Any decent woman would appreciate and love to have a hardworking man. Whether that was the real reason for his wife's departure or not, she had no right to judge. There were always three sides to every story—his, hers and God's.

Her eyes had a mind of their own. She did her best to keep them from roaming in places they had no business. From the length of his powerful legs, right up to his chiseled face, this man had the total package—on the surface. Maybe his personality had flaws. Looks could be misleading. There had to be something wrong with him that caused his wife to run into another man's arms.

"You work as a paramedic too, huh?" Joi had to say something before her eyes got her into trouble. *Yes, the man is a paramedic, get a hold of yourself.*

"Only part-time." He sipped his coffee, never taking his eyes off hers.

Her insides squirmed. Wyatt was checking her out also. Too young to experience hot flashes, but the intensity of his stare was turning up the heat. If he did not take his eyes off her and soon, she would be in need of a paramedic to revive her. Why did she agree to have coffee with him? A rush of guilt swept over her. The thoughts she was having of the man sitting next to her, made her feel dirty and low. Here she sat, enjoying the company of another man, while Michael lay in his grave.

"Did I say something wrong?" He touched her hand, which caught her off guard and she snatched it away, placing it in her lap. He eased his hand back to the side of his table.

"No, nothing is wrong." She spoke in a hushed whisper due to the awkwardness his touch had caused. "I was thinking about something that I had to do later." She lied. *Yes, Wyatt, something is wrong. I feel as if I am cheating on my husband.*

"If you are uncomfortable with me sitting beside you, I can move," he said, but his body language told another story.

"No, no, no… that's not it," she rushed to add. She wanted him to stay put. His presence made her realize just how lonely she was for male affection. The more she glanced into his adorable brown eyes, the more she assumed his ex-wife had to be crazy. What woman in her right mind would walk off, leaving a man like him up for grabs? But money does have a way of blinding most women. Her bad decision may be another woman's blessing. Sadly, Wyatt and his band of brothers' used their profession to flirt with women. She would hate for the first man she'd taken an interest in since her husband's death, lead her on, knowing he has no plans of sticking around.

"Do I make you uncomfortable, Joi?" he said with concern.

Her eyes shot up, meeting his. Yes, she was uncomfortable, downright terrified. It wasn't everyday a handsome man asked to buy her coffee. Instead of lying, she stated the truth. "Yes."

"I don't bite…you know. I offered to buy you coffee because you looked as if you needed a break." He picked up his cup from the table and made a swirling motion with it. "I'm not trying to make a move on you, if that's what concerns you."

A shameful grin lined her face. "I feel so foolish."

"No, you're not foolish." He turned in his chair to face her. "It's called being cautious, which I fully understand." Just when she thought he was finished, he said, "A beautiful woman like you have reasons to be leery of a man vying for your attention."

Joi did everything within her to steady her hand now wrapped tightly around the Styrofoam cup. His words made her feel warm and giddy inside. She tried her best not to act like a silly teenager, but that was how his words made her react.

What did she really know about him? He was a fireman who came to Blessed Memorial Hospital for the lunch, he claimed. For all she knew, he could be feeding that same tired line to other women at the hospital.

"Trust me. I know how to protect myself from smooth talking men."

"That's good to know."

Playing with a strand of hair that fell against her brow, she could not help but be intrigued with the man sitting next to her. His manly aura made her remember what it was like to feel like a woman. Those desires had died with Michael. For the first time in two years, a man had come along whom she was certainly interested in; if only she could get past what he did for a living.

Chapter Ten

"I was going to hook you up with my cousin, Roscoe. But when I saw you earlier with that fine fireman in the hospital cafeteria, I changed my mind," Tara said, tapping her foot on the ceramic floor, giving Joi a questionable look.

Joi stocked her tray with medical supplies, ignoring her colleague's comment. If men were made into a pill, she would overdose on them. Tara came into the world with men on her brain. Seconds later, Joi gave in to the gossip her friend craved. "I see you have resorted to spying?" She placed a box of bandages on her tray and turned to face Tara.

"For your information, I stopped by the cafeteria to get a snack to tide me over until my shift ended. Instead, guess who I saw smiling and flirting with one of those sexy firemen we met the other day?"

"Are you crazy?" she shouted, forgetting her surroundings. When co-workers turned and stared in their direction, she quickly lowered her voice. "We had coffee and for your F-Y-I, I was not flirting with him. Besides, when did drinking coffee with a handsome man became a crime?"

Tara continued to dig her claws deeper into Joi's business. "I have twenty-twenty vision. I have not seen that glow on your face since..." Her voice trailed off, realizing she had gone too far.

"Don't go there." Joi snatched up the tray she was stocking. Her chest swelled with anger. Tara's words had the impact of a sucker punch. If anyone should have understood her pain, it was Tara. Throughout the entire horrible ordeal of losing her family, she was her anchor. Now, she was dismissing her feelings by trying to hook her up with a man. "You know my family's deaths are still a sensitive subject for me, and you have a lot of nerve comparing this so-called glow you're seeing on my face to what I had with Michael."

Tara grabbed her by the arm to prevent her from leaving the small, closet size storage room in the ER. "Are you listening to yourself? I'm not comparing anyone to Michael, I'm stating a fact." She looked Joi squarely in the eyes and continued her lecture. "Joi, you looked happy. And there's nothing wrong if it's because of a man."

Joi dropped her head. She allowed her anger to get the best of her. Tara was only concerned about her well-being. For the first time in a long time, she was happy. However, she fought the notion that it might be because of Wyatt.

Tara released Joi's arm and stepped back. "Maybe you need to talk about how you feel. One day you are on top of the world, and then the next you're down in the dumps. Life is passing you by. You are in the prime of your life. Don't you miss the touch, the smell and the love of man?"

"Stop it," Joi lashed out again, dropping the tray down onto the table. "You will never understand how I feel."

"Then, help me understand." Tara folded her arms, showing no signs of backing down. "Every man that has tried asking you out, you shoot'em down before ever giving them a chance."

The storage room wasn't bigger enough for both of their strong personalities. Tara's had already filled the small space. Turning her back to her friend, Joi wrestled with the tears threatening to spill down her face. She wanted to break out of her grieving shell, but each time she tried, guilt pulled her back in. How could she start over, when Michael and her kids could not? Her conscience had become her worst enemy. Sure, she wanted a man to come home to cuddle up with and to love her; each time she'd tried, the images of her deceased husband ruined any chance she had of starting over with a new man.

As if paralysis had taken over her body, Joi stood, unable to will her legs to move. Warm liquid flowed down her cheeks. How long would the memories of her family haunt her, controlling every aspect of her life? She tried wiping the tears away with the back of her hands. Tara was right. She needed to admit to herself that she was holding on to the past. Every man she had met, she compared him to Michael and when they failed to measure up to her expectations, she found a reason to send them packing. A second date was out of the question.

Joi turned, facing her friend. "I'm trying to keep the faith Tara, but some days I feel as if God has forsaken me. I'm angry and I'm bitter."

Tara strode over and gently touched Joi on the shoulder. She led her to the nursing lounge. Once inside they took a seat on the most ugly green leather couch ever designed. Blessed Memorial Hospital had to purchase their furniture from the lowest bidder.

"Everything is going to be alright. God knows your pain." They took a seat. Both their tempers had simmered. "I may not understand what it feels like to lose someone that close to me." Tara reached for a box of Kleenex off the table next to them. "That's why getting away from this atmosphere will be good for you. It will help you to put things in perspective. Maybe, even find a love connection," Tara joked, nudging Joi playfully.

Tara always had a way of making her see the brighter side of things. She wiped her nose and patted her eyes with the tissue and said, "I hate when these depressing moods come over me. My entire life changed because of one irresponsible teenager. Her failure to wait until she got to a stopping point to text is the reason that I am in this situation." Joi paused and shook her head. "Losing Michael and the boys tore me apart. Then, when I found out that I was six weeks pregnant afterwards, it gave me a small sense of joy, but, I lost the baby because I was unable to eat or drink anything. My grief had consumed me. I lost the last connection I had to Michael and the boys."

When Joi complained of having severe cramps, her parents immediately rushed her to the hospital. The pain had become so intense that she passed out; awaking to doctors giving her the bad news of losing her baby. That information had sent her into rage. She tried her best to be careful to carry the baby to full-term, but her body wasn't strong enough.

Unable to cope, the physician ordered her to be restrained and sedated for her own protection. Spending a month under the supervised care of her doctor, it helped her to snap back into reality. Although, she considered herself a walking zombie after her release, she put on a brave face, trying to move on with life as best as she knew how.

She remembered how her parents treated her with kid gloves when she moved in with them after her family deaths; certain conversations they avoided to keep her calm. No matter how they tried, the vault of tears she fought to hide always managed to break free.

Her parents had taught her from a child on up that God never puts more on a person than they could handle. From the way she saw it, God had put a boulder on her shoulders and left her to carry it alone.

"That's a lot for any one person to carry." Tara shook her head. "I'm sorry for what I said earlier."

"It was the truth. I needed to hear it."

They sat in silence until Albre and Becky walked into the room gossiping about something.

"There you two are. We wondered where you guys had run off to," Albre said. Her cheerful face had dropped when she looked at the two on the sofa, holding tissue in their hands.

"What's going on with the two of you? Who died?" Becky shot them with a load of questions as she opened her locker to retrieve her purse.

"Joi needed a shoulder to on cry and mine was available," Tara added. "No need to worry, everything is okay."

Thankful for her supportive girlfriends, Joi mood lighten. The three had been her rock since that fateful day. If it wasn't for them sticking by her side on moments like these, she might have lost her mind.

Albre and Becky joined them on the couch as they embraced in a group hug. Thank God for friends who had her back. No matter how they fussed or fought, their bond only grew stronger. They were the sisters she never had.

Chapter Eleven

Wyatt clocked in at the station, chitchatted with fellow firemen, and then headed outside to wash and inspect his fire engine. From the hose, tires and siren, every nook and cranny had to be checked for proficiency. Failure to be thorough caused delays, which put fire victims in greater danger. Wyatt took pride in doing his job right the first time.

With the sun blazing down on his sweat-drenched body, he prayed for a cool breeze to blow his way. As he scrubbed the fire engine, thoughts of Joi sent a smile to his fatigued face. Although she was shorter than most women he had dated— five-feet-five— she left a huge impact on him.

He rounded the truck, satisfied with his handy work. He wiped the sweat from his brow, and leaned against the ladder to relieve his aching back. Wyatt considered himself a perfectionist. Whenever his turn came to wash the truck, clean the station or cook the meals, he gave one hundred percent. Mediocre wasn't in his vocabulary.

Wyatt was lost in the moment when Jett appeared out of nowhere, startling him. A wicked grin laced Jett's face, which meant it involved a woman. Wyatt prayed for the day when the right woman would enter Jett's life and change him from his playboy ways. Women flocked to him like bees to something sweet and savory. Jett's youthful good looks and muscular built were like a magnet as far as women were concerned. Being a firefighter on the Shreveport Fire Department only heightened their attraction to him even more.

"What's with the smirk?" Wyatt inquired, hoping his friend hadn't come outside to get under his skin, as usual.

Jett continued walking toward Wyatt, dismissing his question. Now standing next to him, Wyatt couldn't help but wonder what his friend was up to.

"I went over to Blessed Memorial Hospital today to see if that sweet little nurse, Tara was on duty and guess who I spotted in the cafeteria?" Jett asked.

"I'm sure you're dying to tell me." Wyatt folded his arms as he continued to lean against the ladder.

"Man, don't play me. I saw you in the cafeteria talking to one of Tara's friends." Jett folded his arms, waiting on Wyatt to respond.

"You saw right." Wyatt did his best to play down his and Joi's coffee break, because in Jett's mind, two people of the opposite sex couldn't just have an innocent encounter together without something going on. In truth, he enjoyed his time with Joi. "We were having a cup of coffee. Satisfied?" Wyatt strode near the fire truck and began packing up his tools and brushes, ignoring Jett's probing eyes. The last thing he planned on doing was justifying his actions with Jett. He knew nothing about having a pleasant conversation with a woman.

"Are you purposely keeping me in the dark about your next prey?" His hands flew up in the air.

"Prey? Man, when has sharing a cup of coffee turned into a hunting game? Or in your case, a stakeout." Wyatt's blood started to heat up. He liked Joi. She was the first woman he had shone any real interest in since his divorce. Jett, implying that she was some type of loose woman, angered him. Jett believed women were put on earth for his pleasure and nothing more. His mother abandoning him as a child has distorted his image of women.

Wyatt knew Jett was looking out for his best interest. He'd witnessed firsthand some of the horrible things Trina had put him through, but he wasn't going to tolerate Jett interfering in his love life.

Wyatt found Joi's strength, after facing tragedy, attractive and courageous. Having a nice body and making her own money made the fascination that much stronger. Lord knows, his ex-wife never worked a day in her life. She chased after men whom she thought had money. When she didn't hit the jackpot she had hoped for when marrying him, she left.

Wyatt spent the first three years of his marriage trying to please her. The more he strained to give her the finer things in life, the more she wanted, which sank him deeper in debt. The pressure she laid on him to become chief added more fuel to their already failing marriage. When he came home and told her the bad news, she called him a failure. Her words stung, which was the beginning of the end of their marriage.

"Tell me, you're not developing feelings for this woman?" He stepped away from Wyatt as if he had a contagious disease. "You barely know her."

"No," he said, adamantly shaking his head. His mouth said one thing but his heart said another. Wyatt tried to sound convincing, but Jett was no fool by any means. The man should have had a doctorate degree when it came to reading him. Blood brothers they weren't, but Jett could always see straight through him. He didn't want his friend to bring up what happened with his ex-wife, so he denied his feelings for Joi.

"Good." He breathed a sigh of relief. "We have a trip to prepare for. Starting up a new relationship with that nurse will only ruin things. There will be plenty of women to sink your paws into soon." Jett eyes widened like the wolf that he was. Morning, noon and night, women were never too far from his mind, and Wyatt couldn't wait for the day that cupid shoot an arrow straight through his womanizing heart.

"Her name is Joi, not 'this woman.'"

"Yeah, whatever." He dismissed Wyatt's correction as he pulled a brochure from his shirt pocket. "Now this is what you need to be focusing on." Jett handed him the brochure filled with women in bikinis and drinks in their hands.

He ran his hand across his face, studying the brochure. He twisted up his face and said, "I don't know about this." Wyatt handed it back to him.

"Don't go changing your mind. We have been planning this trip for months. Plus, the four of us have already put in our vacation time." The veins in Jett's neck bulged, which caused Wyatt to become alarmed. His immaturity emerged when things did not go his way.

"Why do I continue to let you talk me into things?"

"When has taking a trip to paradise become a problem?" Jett asked.

Wyatt knew there was more hiding behind his words. "Don't allow a trip to paradise to cause you to come back home with something you cannot get rid of." Wyatt slapped his friend on the shoulder and they broke into laughter.

After getting what he wanted, Jett left Wyatt and headed back into the station. Wyatt scanned his surrounding for any tools he had overlooked. A prayer escaped his lips for his young friend. Each time he invited Jett to a weekly men service at his church, he declined. Wyatt believed that if Jett hung around men who were more grounded and family oriented, that it might help him, but Jett had no interest in church. His mission was solely satisfying the flesh.

One thing Wyatt learned from his mother and sisters, a scorned woman was a dangerous woman. Sooner or later, Jett would find that out. Wyatt hoped that his friend's life lesson with women wouldn't cost him his job or his life. He'd learned at an early age that if a man played with fire long enough, he was sure to be consumed in it."

Chapter Twelve

Joi's girlfriends dragged her from one department store to the next, each trying to find the perfect outfit for their trip. Tara, notorious for her provocative clothing, tried on the most revealing apparel in the swimsuit area. Mixed emotions regarding their trip began to overshadow Joi's jovial mood, but she kept her thoughts to herself. Who knows, the trip could turn out to be the best thing for her. She just might have fun. Nevertheless, searching for Mr. Right had to take a backseat, until she heals and process her losses. Any strange pervert attempting to come shaking his groove thing in her face better be prepared to get the taste slapped out of his mouth.

Being with the girls brought back so many memories. She forgot how much fun they had when they were together. Nothing had changed. Giggling and chattering about their upcoming trip as they mauled the clothing racks, were like old times. Albre held an animal print, skimpy bikini close to her rail thin body, and of course, Tara wasn't the one to be out shined. She found a barely there bikini, which they threatened to leave her at home if she wore.

"I will behave in a Christian manner on this trip." Joi said as they stood in between a rack filled with assorted bathing suits. "And I suggest you ladies do the same." She reprimanded them with her eyes.

"Oh... we will," Albre stuttered; glaring nervously in Tara's direction, as if they knew something she didn't.

Tara chimed in. "What does it matter? Christians or non-Christians, if you have the body, I say flaunt it." Her eyes zoomed in on the flora one piece bathing suit Joi had draped over her arm.

"I may not work out as much as you all, but I still have a nice body." Joi looked to the others for support, but neither said a word in her defense. She stared down at the hideous bathing suit and placed it back on the rack.

"See, this is exactly what I'm talking about, Joi," Tara added. "You need to loosen up. Christians are allowed to have fun too." She licked her lips, shooting Joi a naughty grin. "But, I won't tell anyone if you act outside of your Christianfied self when our plane lands in paradise."

"What will the children at the church think about their youth leader getting buck wild in the Caribbean's, Becky?" Joi asked.

Pretending to be engrossed in her search to find the perfect swimwear, Becky acted clueless. She turned and asked, "What does this have to do with me. This is between you and Tara."

"You have been quiet throughout the entire conversation."

"Joi, relax. Who knows when we'll ever get this opportunity again?" Becky stopped thumbing through the rack of bathing suits to face her friends. "Yes, I'm the youth leader at the church, but I'm no monk either." Tossing her blonde mane off her shoulders, she then turned her attention back to search for a swimsuit.

Joi pointed her finger at them. "You all better not embarrass me with your choice in clothing. Because if some old geezer with no teeth approaches us in any kind of way." She balled up her hands into a fist and shook it at them. "The three of you will pay."

"Yes, old maid. We hear you, but cool your heels. This trip is supposed to be a nice, relaxing get away. Nobody wants to end up in the hospital with your fist in their mouth," Tara quipped.

They resumed their pursuit for the perfect swimwear and Joi vowed to keep her opinions about their selections to herself.

The last time Joi remembered shopping at the mall, she was with Michael and the boys. The outing with her girlfriends was the remedy for her blues. She felt refreshed and ready to take on the world. If only those good feelings tarried longer; one minute she was up and the next she would be bawling her eyes out.

Today had shown her that life was worth living. As the four strolled up and down every strip of the mall, Joi watched an elderly couple walked hand in hand, teens bobbing their heads to music, people walking, talking, laughing and enjoying life. Then, she wondered if she would ever find that happy place again.

The four found a vacant table at the food court to unload their shopping bags and rest their tired feet. Joi had a great time and realized that she had to do some major soul searching. She was blessed and it was about time she recognized it. This trip was about sisterhood and finding herself again. If a man came into the equation, then it was God's will, but she had no plans of going out to look for one.

"Whew! My feet hurt," Joi said; removing her heels to rub her aching toes.

"Why did you wear heals in the first place?" Becky asked.

"Crazy I guess. I'll remember the next time." She leaned back into her chair, relieved that her feet were free from agony. "When I receive my credit card bill, there might not be a next time," Joi groaned.

"I hear you," Tara agreed. "I just might have to find a second job when I come back from our vacation."

They laughed.

"So, are we all in agreement to catch the flight out of Ft. Lauderdale?" Becky asked, changing the subject. "I have the itinerary for our entire stay." She reached inside her large *Michael Kors* handbag and gave them each a copy.

"Yes," the others said in unison, grabbing a copy off the table.

"Everything looks good to me," Tara said.

"Joi?" Becky and the others gawked over in her direction.

"Ye-ee-ah", she agreed hesitantly.

"Okay, so, we're set for our trip to paradise," Albre said.

Joi sat up straight in her chair. After glancing over their itinerary, Joi wanted to question some of the events. She kept rehearsing in her mind to think positive. Because knowing those three, who knew what else they had on their devious little minds. She whispered a small prayer to herself and hoped she didn't end up in the pits of Hell for following them.

The four chatted for a while before heading out the mall and going their separate ways. Joi decided to pay her parents a visit before heading home. They would be happy to hear that she had made the first step in moving on with her life.

Joi felt as if she had aged five years since the loss of her family. She hadn't planned on living the rest of her life alone, but, if she continued the path she was on, that was exactly where she was heading. She had watched enough movies where the only companions most people had were their pets and she had no desire to be one of those people. She still had a lot of living to do.

In her rearview mirror, Joi glanced at a fire station as she drove. Her mind shot straight to Wyatt. Was he the perfect man to help her get back into the dating game? But her heart took a nosedive, when she remembered him at the restaurant with his date. She quickly erased him from her mind. She didn't want to confuse his nice gesture of buying her a cup of coffee into something more. Men and women had plutonic relationships all the time. However, they weren't friends; just two people who ran into each and shared a table and coffee together. Sure, he shared the details about his bitter divorce with her, but it doesn't constitute a friendship. She wanted to believe that, but truthfully, she desired to know more about the jilted fireman.

Chapter Thirteen

Joi pulled into her parents' driveway, turned off the ignition and hopped out of the car. Before letting herself into their home with her key, she stopped to admire the rows of azaleas lining their privacy fence. When it came to gardening, her mother had a green-thumb. That gene had apparently skipped her. The thought of being on her knees in the dirt and grass, turned her off. Working indoors was her specialty. Decorating had been one of her favorite things to do. She'd leave the love of gardening to her mother.

After taking in her mother's picturesque yard, Joi stepped upon the porch, placed her key into the keyhole, and let herself inside. She called out to her mother, announcing her arrival. It had been over two weeks since her last visit. Working double shifts at the hospital took up most of her time, leaving little for herself.

Placing her purse and key on the coffee table, Joi headed to the kitchen. The fresh smell of coffee and cookies brought a childlike smile to her face. Her mother still had a knack for making a house feel warm and inviting. Being an only child, she was spoiled rotten. Her mother made sure she always had a special baked treat waiting for her when she arrived home from school, and today wasn't any different. Her mouth watered from the delicious smell of fresh baked cookies as she followed the aroma through the house.

Entering the kitchen, she found her mother preparing dinner. "Hi, Mom," Joi greeted, placing a soft kiss on her mother's cheek.

"What took you so long, dear?" Her mother placed a lid on the pot simmering on the stove, and then returned her daughter's kiss.

Joi strolled to the kitchen table, which could seat six people and took a seat. Although, it was just her mother and father living in the house, her mother refused to downsize to a smaller one. "The girls and I went shopping at the mall," Joi said as she grabbed one of the chocolate chip cookies her mother had placed in the center of the table. "We stayed longer than 'I'd expected."

"It's good to see you out and enjoying yourself." Her mother walked over to one of her freshly painted shelves, removing two mugs and filled them with coffee. "I spoke with Tara the other day. She told me that a certain fireman seemed to have taken an interest in you."

Joi eyes rolled in her head as she bit into one her mother's moist cookies. *Why can't Tara mind her own business?* "That's news to me," she said, avoiding the question.

"Well, I think it's great."

You would, she thought.

"It's about time you start getting out and meeting new people. And speaking of new people, I heard about this social media site where Christian Singles can find others like themselves and go out on dates and stuff." Her mother gave her an under-eyed look.

"Mom!" she yelled, almost choking on her cookie. "Are you serious?" Her mouth flew open at her mother's suggestion. "Of all people, you want me to go on an online dating site to find a psycho or even a pervert. Please!" She sat in disbelief.

"What's wrong with a little help? Nothing else is working… I'm just saying." She took a sip from her mug. "You're at the hospital day in and day out and still haven't found that special someone." A sincere look adorned her face as she straightened the table matt in front of her.

"Now that's something I would expect Tara to say, not my own mother." A horrified expression crept upon Joi's face. Never in a million years had she thought her mother would say such a thing.

"Don't get me wrong, darling. I'm not saying to throw yourself on the first man that comes your way. I just want you to go out there and have fun." She arched her shoulders. "And see what life has to offer."

"Mom, pleas-ss-ss-e," she whined. "I don't want to discuss this."

As usual, her mother heard what she wanted to hear and dismissed her pleading.

"Now, back to the fireman. What's his name?"

Really?

Wyatt... Mom." She felt like an awkward teenager whenever her mother pried into her personal life.

"Huh. So, has he asked you out yet?" She exhaled. "Oh, let me guess. He has, but you turned him down?"

"No." She kept even-toned with her mom, but her probing into her non-existent love life was pushing her buttons. "He hasn't." Just the mention of his name, caused a rush of heat to run through her body. A woman had to be insane not to notice or appreciate a man as attractive as Wyatt. Although, she thought that he was charming, her anger quickly kindled against her best friend for giving her mother false hope. "I wish Tara would keep her big mouth closed. Wyatt and I were just enjoying a cup of coffee together."

"True love starts off innocently. Then, before you know it, you're exchanging wedding vows." Her mother gave her a wink.

To dignify her mother's remark with an answer was like walking into a trap. Her mom invented the word, *slick*. She knew how to get information out of Joi; however, today, Joi came with her game face on. Her mother had to try a lot harder to pry any incriminating evidence out of her. Her personal life was just that, personal. She wasn't in the mood for sharing.

"Enough, Mom!"

"You know I'm right."

Joi shook her head. The conversation had given her a splitting headache. Her mother wasn't the type to give up.

Lately, their talks surrounded the topic of finding a man, dating or marriage. She didn't care to discuss neither. Why would Tara tell her mother about Wyatt when there was nothing to tell? And why was Joi concerned about the female he had on his arm at the restaurant, who appeared all wrong for him?

Women loved a man in a uniform and Wyatt wore his perfectly. The day he offered to buy her a cup of coffee, she caught him sizing her up, but that didn't mean he was interested in her. All men eyes tend to roam the length of a woman's body. She supposed women did the same when it came to a good-looking man. His outward qualities hadn't escaped her wandering eyes either.

Never once had she envisioned herself being thirty-three and single, and to be thrown back into the dating pool terrified her. The entire dating scene had changed drastically since her college days. Men and women were more aggressive. When she and Michael had met in college, things were simple. He approached her like a lady and not a piece of meat. Today, men's words and stance were hard and possessive. She witnessed it on several occasions at the hospital, how the male employees flirted with the female employees. Thank goodness for the Sexual Harassment Law.

Joi's mother continued to rail on her about her lack of love life, and like a defiant teenager, she wanted to take her fingers and plug up her ears. The last thing she wanted to discuss with her mother was sex. *Ewe wee!* She cringed inwardly, feeling the urge to gag. Could they just skip the subject? She'd told herself; the next time she visited, she would make sure that her father was home. Her mother tended to express herself a little too freely in his absence.

"Are you listening?" her mother asked. "I'm trying to help you."

"Yes, Mother. I hear you." What Joi wanted to do was haul tail it to her car and burn rubber out of there. She thought listening to her high school teacher talk on Sex Education was uncomfortable, but her mother's illustrations and gestures had topped it. When it came to relationships and sex, she thought that she was an expert. Then again, maybe she was. Her parents had been married for over forty years.

"Your father and I wouldn't have lasted these many years if I didn't know what I was doing." Her mother flexed a proud smiled, and then snapped her fingers, swaying her body to music that only she heard.

Joi let out an uncomfortable laugh.

Her mother was always high-spirited. She could never remember a time that a smile wasn't on her flawless face. Age hadn't diminished the twinkle in her eyes or the beauty she always possess.

She rose from the table to wash her cup, when a letter addressed to her on the countertop grabbed her attention. "Mom, what is this?" She held the letter in her hand, inspecting it.

"Oh, I was busy talking about finding you a man that I forgot to tell you that Rebekah is trying to contact you again." Her mother now stood from her seat. "Baby, I think it's time to talk to her." She rested her hand on her daughter's shoulder.

"For what?" Her tone turned cold. "She's living her life while my family is lying in their graves." Joi toss the letter back where she found it.

"We raised you to forgive. This anger you're holding onto is making you bitter." Now standing eye level with her daughter, she tried reasoning with her. "She's hurting too."

"She should hurt."

"Joi? Don't speak that way. What if God stop forgiving us of our sins?"

"I never killed anyone." She groaned through clenched teeth.

"Sin is sin. Your unforgiveness is just as sinful. What happened to Michael and the kids was an accident. The child never set out to kill them."

"She was texting while driving, Mom. She made her decision that day. She had a choice and she chose to text."

"I'm going to say this to you, and then you can do with it whatever you want. Rebekah knows that she made a terrible mistake. She has to deal with taking the lives of three people. Her parents have told me that she's been in and out of rehab because she cannot cope with what she's done. And to make it worse, she has tried reaching out to you for two years and you've ignored her calls and letters."

"Mom!"

Her mother threw up her hand to silence her daughter. "Hush and let me finish. The only way you're going to get on with your life is talking with Rebekah. I don't want her doing something to harm herself."

Joi stood quietly, taking in her mother's advice. One thing she had never done and that was talk back or disrespected her parents. But at the moment, facing the girl that destroyed her life was out of the question.

"I miss Michael and my grandbabies just as much as you." She grabbed hold to Joi's hands. "We are taught to forgive. I will never get the chance to spoil my grandsons. But, I can't allow it to stop me from living and going on with life. And that's exactly what you've done.

"I'm not there yet, Mom; as a matter of fact, I don't think I will ever be; Rebekah will just have to sleep in the bed she's made. She has to face the consequences of her sins."

Chapter Fourteen

Wyatt pulled a portable table from his hallway closet for an evening of dominos with the fellas. He dragged it into the spacious living room, placing it in the middle of the floor. It had been a while since the four played the competitive game at his house, and Jett was the reason. Wyatt kept his fingers crossed, praying that Jett left his hot temper at home. His friend often lost his cool without warning. One minute, Jett would be laughing and joking, and the next, he'd fly off the handle; about what, remained a mystery.

The three barged through his front door, startling Wyatt as he fixed the table. Fed up with their horse playing and lack of manners, he shot them an austere look. "Does anyone knock anymore?"

"Since when have we knocked?" Paul asked, unloading the bags of snacks onto the kitchen island.

Ignoring Wyatt as usual, Jett strolled over to the card table where he stood. He pulled their plane tickets from his jacket pocket and sang, "I got four tickets to paradise." He continued singing and waving them in the air, until Wyatt snatched them out of his hand.

"Be careful with those tickets, Bro," Jett yelled. "You will have to stay behind if one gets damage." He grabbed them back from Wyatt and inspected them.

Being left behind may not be as bad as it sounds, he thought. *Who knows what the three of them might get me into once we leave American soil?*

After preparing the chips and dip, Seth and Paul poured their drinks and took their seats at the table. Wyatt and Jett did their usual, arguing and challenging one another to a butt whipping in dominoes.'

"Can the two of you lower your testosterone level long enough to play a civil hand of dominoes for a change," Seth said, furrowing his brows at the feuding buddies.

There was no such word as a friendly hand in dominoes. If there weren't any trash talking or slapping them down on the table, what was the purpose in playing?

"Seth, you better go to the library if you want silence." Jett added, ready to get the game started. "Man up and stop acting like a Mama's Boy."

"Oh, I got your Mama's Boy," Seth barked as he gnawed on his chips and dip.

It was game time. The trash talking had begun. Wyatt teamed up with Paul, leaving Jett to pair up with Seth, which ticked Jett off. Swirling the dominoes on the table, Wyatt watched his friends go at each other, but Jett seemed to take it a little too personal. He had some maturing to do.

Jett's short temper was the reason he never stayed in a long-term relationship. When his evil twin appeared, the women headed for the nearest exit. A good woman wanted more than a handsome face. They wanted a man with common sense, which Jett seemed to lack at times. He couldn't figure out why none of them stuck around and was too stubborn to listen when Wyatt and the others tried telling him.

Wyatt tuned out the noise from the dominoes and his friends' loud voices when images of Joi overpowered his ability to stay focus. Although, they only had a few encounters, he wished that she was the one going on the trip with him, instead of his friends. She had a smile that brightened any man's cloudy day. She was intelligent and able to carry on a decent conversation with him. The few women he'd dated after his divorce came up short in that area. When he'd ask questions about politics or their favorite movies, some giggled, while others had no clue.

A break from women was the logical thing for him to do, especially after his mercy date. All she did was whined about her no good ex-boyfriend and how sorry men these days were. Wyatt wanted to pay for dinner, leave a tip on the table and burn rubber getting out of dodge. His date had played the jealous role when they ran into Joi, then when they were alone, she turned into whining Wanda.

"Wyatt!" Jett called, slamming his hand down on the table. "It's your move. Get your head in the game, man."

"Sorry." Was all he could say, as he stared at the dominoes in his hand; Joi seemed to pop up in his mind when least expected. The petite beauty had infiltrated his heart.

The fellas continued to play round after round of dominoes. Each serving up their share of trash talking, except Wyatt, his mind had long left the game. He tried concentrating, but Joi's beautiful face continued to invade his thoughts throughout the night.

Jett, the bloodhound, sensed that something more was going on with him. As he played his hand, he subtly gave Wyatt a sidelong glance; Wyatt acted clueless. Any mention of the nurses at Blessed Memorial Hospital tend to send his egotistical little friend testosterone into overdrive.

If he told his friends that he was falling for one of the nurses, he would never hear the end of it. So, in the meantime, he preferred to keep his secret to himself. Paul and Seth were the understanding type, but Jett didn't have a tolerance bone in his body when it came to love. The *L-word*, he claimed wasn't in his vocabulary.

Wyatt tried being a positive influence in Jett's life since he had no positive male figures growing up, but he began to question his efforts. He'd tried the best he knew how to guide him. Even with all his trying, Jett had a mind of his own and did what he wanted to do, regardless of what others had to say. Trying to figure him out, took up too much brain space. So, Wyatt prayed that whatever his friend's problem was, that he would get help for it, and soon.

Without warning, Jett leaped from his seat and shouted out in anger. "See, this is the reason I hate playing with you guys."

Wyatt had been zoned out for some time, now. He sat and watched the others with a blank stare, trying to figure out what was going on.

Paul and Seth looked at each other in confusion, and then back in Jett's directions. Before either had the chance to utter a word, Jett flipped over the card table and stormed out the door. Seth broke the pregnant silence in the room. "So, you guys still think it's a good idea to take Jett on this trip with us?"

Rubbing his hand across his face, Paul took a deep breath and said, "What is it with this guy?" He stood from his seat to help Wyatt gather the dominoes that went sailing across the room. "One minute he's laughing and joking and the next, he is acting like the *Tasmania Devil*."

"I'll get to the bottom of it." By Seth facial reaction, he was still trying to process what had just transpired.

"No," Wyatt cautioned. "Let me. He's always thought of me as an older brother. Maybe I can get to the bottom of his sudden mood swings."

"Maybe he has PMS," Paul joked.

"Man, only women get PMS." Seth bit down on his bottom lip and shook his head.

"Like I said," Wyatt stressed. "I'll talk with him one on one. Now help me clean this mess up before the two of you leave me alone to clean up your filth." He tried making light of the situation, but deep down he was worried about Jett.

They began searching the four corners of the room for the dominoes Jett's antics sent flying everywhere. Approaching Jett about anything of importance, lately, caused alarm. Wyatt knew he had to get to the bottom of what was bothering Jett before he found himself in serious trouble. He prayed that the trip would diffuse the time bomb erupting inside him.

Paul and Seth found and placed the twenty-eight dominoes into its casing, said their goodbyes and left for the evening. For the most part, tonight had been an enjoyable one, until Jett had to go and ruin things.

As Wyatt locked up when his friends left, his mind went cruising back to Joi. Her delicate features and a beautiful personality to match caused him to want to know her more. Once he returned from his vacation, he planned to ask her out on a date. The last thing he wanted at this point in his life was to jump back into a relationship, but a woman like Joi was worth taking a chance on.

Chapter Fifteen

Second guessing herself as she half-heartedly packed for the first vacation since she had found herself widowed and motherless; she folded her wardrobe into her suitcase, and then began taking them back out. Indecisiveness claimed her judgment. Was it a good idea for her to go on the trip of a life time with good friends? Or stay at home and hide away like a hermit? Michael wouldn't have wanted her to live her life that way, but that was actually what she was doing.

For one thing, she needed to stop watching those, *Fatal Attraction* and *Dates from Hell*, shows. Whenever a man spoke to her, she'd assumed that he could be a stalker or psycho. Her imagination seemed to run rampant when approached by a stranger. If she doesn't loosen up and get a grip, she could let a good man get away.

Even if she did found Mr. Right, she'd just run him off. After sharing her life with Michael, no man could ever hold a candle to him. He was the type of man every young girl dreamt of marrying when they grow up. When she'd brought him home to meet her parents, they fell in love with him at first sight.

Michael was a great husband, provider and father. What if by chance, and that was a slim chance that she married again? Would her new husband be the superman, she had known Michael to be? Or would her standards be too high for him to obtain?

Instead of driving herself crazy about the, what ifs, she continued packing. This trip with her girlfriends was making her crazy. Neither of them had ever been married. So, teaching them how to restrain themselves around men, especially good looking ones, posed a challenge.

Joi stepped inside her walk-in closet. Each shelf was filled with shoes she'd bought over the years and barely worn. She made a mental note to donate them a local women's shelter when she return from her trip.

One pair in particular caught her eyes. The black, Oxford chunky heels were the must have shoes back in the nineties. She retrieved them from the shoe rack Michael had built for her and held them gently against her chest. He'd surprised her for her twenty-fourth birthday. Back then, every woman rushed to the mall to snatch up a pair. He knew how bad she wanted them, but their personal finances at that time, did not allow room for them to splurge. They could only afford the bare necessities. Purchasing a pair of expensive dress shoes was out of the question.

To her surprise, Michael had sent the kids over to her parents to spend the night. He'd taken the day off to prepare dinner for the two. Candles were lite throughout the house and soft music played through the surround speakers. Next, she spotted a breathtaking centerpiece that adorned the table, which he had confessed later that his sister helped him to arrange. Extending his masculine hand, he led her to the dining room.

When they finished dinner, Michael began fishing for something underneath the table. What was so important under the table that it took his attention away from her? Within seconds, her question was answered. Michael held two Dillard Department store shoe boxes in his hands. Screaming out of control, Joi shot from her seat like a rocket and propelled into his arms.

She squealed, jumping up and down as she opened each box of shoes. Joi ran back into Michael's arms, thanking him for working overtime to make her birthday special. To verbally thank him wasn't enough. She plastered kisses all over his face and led him to their favorite place, the bedroom.

Back to reality, Joi found herself surrounded by clothes and shoes. A deep breath she didn't realize she had been holding, escaped her lips. "Lord, show me the way." The chucky heels were still clutched against her chest as her mood darkened.

It seemed strange how she could be happy and excited one minute, and then sad and gloomy the next. She wanted to be set-free from the stronghold of depression. Maybe, if she had listened to her friends more and got out of the house, she wouldn't feel so trapped in her despair.

Work was all she had. She'd never been a fan of going out to nightclubs. Dinner and a movie sounded great, but she didn't want to go alone or with a group of women every time. She figured, God knew exactly what she needed, and in time He would heal her aching heart.

She discontinued her search for the perfect pair of sandals to compliment her wardrobe for the trip, and placed them back on the shelf. She started rummaging through the closet for anything that reminded her of Michael. Although, she should have given all of his clothes to the Salvation Army, she kept one of his shirts. Remembering how her eyes filled with desire each time he wore it.

Protected by plastic, draped on a wooden hanger in the back of the closet, she caressed her hands over it. Joi stared at it as if Michael would magically appear and ask her to iron it for him. She eased the plastic off, and caressed it against her cheeks.

With shirt in hand, she backed out of the closet. Though, it had been taken to the cleaners, Joi inhaled it, trying to pick up any lingering scent of Michael. She knew it was a bad idea, but she did it anyway. Heading to the bed, she spread the shirt neatly on it and snuggled up against it.

"Please, Father in Heaven, help me to heal from this pain," she said, tears rolling down the sides of her face and onto the shirt. She had lost her desire to pack. Instead, she sought comfort in lying next to her deceased husband's shirt.

As her vacation date neared, Joi began to feel a certain amount of guilt. Wasn't she allowed to be happy? Or, to smile again? There were so many questions swirling around in her head. Wyatt made her insides smile after years of hiding, and the brave decision to go on a trip with good friends made her happy. So, why was she feeling so guilty?

She prayed for guidance from above. If falling in love and sharing her life with someone else was meant to be, she would be given a sign, Joi hoped. She had no plans on spending the rest of her life smelling her husband's shirt for comfort; or, living and surviving on old memories. It was time for her to get out and begin making new ones.

Joi raised her head and stared down at Michael's shirt underneath her and asked for his spirit to release her. How was she going to move forward with another man, if she couldn't stop thinking about him? His spirit seemed to possess her. Giving her mind, body and love to another might prove to be difficult. It had been two years and she wasn't back to her fun-loving self. She was once outgoing and up for anything, but now, she hardly recognized the person she had become.

Turing over on her back, Joi spread the shirt on top of her body and sobbed. For the first time, since her husband's death, she felt like a fool. If Tara and the others knew how severe her grieving had become, they would suggest she tried talking to another grief counselor, which was out of the question.

Feeling silly wrapped in her husband's shirt, she tossed it aside, hugged herself and continued to cry. She had to find a way to get over her pain before she ended up old and alone. Her life wasn't over. She could remarry and have kids, but each time she tried convincing herself of that fact, guilt reared its ugly head, telling her that she would forget Michael and the boys if she did.

To forget them, meant she never loved them. No new man or babies could ever erase the love she has for her family. Her next husband would have to be a strong man and secure in himself to accept the fact that she wasn't willing to let go of her family memories. If he couldn't understand that, then he wasn't the man for her.

Chapter Sixteen

Reservation churned in the pit of Wyatt's stomach as he packed for his trip to the Caribbean. What concerned him most was the drastic change in Jett's behavior. It had weighed heavily on his mind since last night. Wyatt thought a night with the boys before leaving Shreveport was a good idea; then, the unthinkable happened. Jett lived up to his name and flew off the handle. Who knew what his behavior would be like once they arrive on the island. What Wyatt wanted most, was to have a week of fun and relaxation with great friends, but having to baby sit Jett wasn't part of the plan.

He zipped up his suitcase and placed it by the door in the living room. Wyatt was meticulous that way. When he packed, everything had to be in one general location, unlike his ex-wife, Trina. She waited until the last minute to do everything; then, had the nerve to holler at him when she'd forgotten something. How did they ever manage to hook-up, knowing they had nothing in common? Their conversations always began and ended with how much money he could make when he applied for the next chief position that came available at the fire department. At that time in his life, he wasn't ready for that type of responsibility. He had enough on his hands trying to keep her under control. How in the world was he going to manage a crew of testosterone driven men?

He headed back toward the bathroom for a 'once over' before his friends picked him up. The last thing he wanted to do was leave something behind, only to be charged through the wazoo at the hotel for it.

Their flight would take them to Fort Lauderdale, Florida and on to Kingston Jamaica for seven days filled with glorious fun.

He hoped.

With Jett's brewing temper, who knew what they were in for.

Before leaving Shreveport, Wyatt wanted to have a serious talk with Jett about his behavior. The last thing he wanted was to end up in jail in paradise because of his friend's explosive temper. He wanted to suggest that he get a psychiatric evaluation, but knew that his proposal wouldn't go over well with him.

Their jobs were stressful, and Jett had seen his share of tragedies as a young fireman. Post-Traumatic Stress might very well be what his friend was dealing with. Wyatt scratched his head, trying to come up with some logical answers for Jett's sudden change in behavior.

One thing Wyatt did know for certain, that as soon as he landed back in Shreveport, the first thing on his agenda was to ask Joi Campbell out on a date. It was time that he let down his guard when it came to women. His ex-wife really did a number on him when it came to trust. He prayed that God would help him in that department. Wyatt had gone to great lengths to ask his pastor to keep him lifted up in prayer, concerning the issue.

Joi was an interesting woman with exotic features, which attracted him to her the first time he'd laid eyes on her at Blessed Memorial Hospital. He sensed, like himself, her cautious nature. He desired to get to know her, to see where fate would take them.

Being set-up on a date wasn't his idea of fun. He loved and valued his friends, but clearly their taste in women weren't the same as his. Seth liked the bookworm type, Paul dated only blondes, and poor misguided Jett loved them all.

He placed his shaving kit into his bag, and muttered, "Well, that seems to be everything."

*****

Wyatt and his friends boarded the airplane for Fort Lauderdale, Florida. Once they found their assigned seats, they did as the stewardess commanded and buckled up their seatbelts. Wyatt wasn't a drinking man, but the rough take off had him wanting something strong to knock him out until they arrived in Florida.

Paul and Seth sat behind him and Jett. This seating arrangement gave him the opportunity to chat with Jett regarding his behavior. Wyatt stirred in his seat, thinking of ways to approach the situation without offending his young friend. The last thing he wanted was to spend a week together with bad blood between them.

"You seem to be in a good mood today?" Wyatt asked as he paid close attention to Jett's demeanor. When the stewardess passed them for the second time with drinks, he came close to snatching one off her tray. If he was having this conversation with one of the other guys, it wouldn't have made him so antsy.

"I'm okay. Why?" He turned and gave Wyatt a bewildered look.

The calmness in his voice put Wyatt at ease to further dig for clues concerning his uncontrolled anger. "I was just concern about you…that's all." He took small breathes and continued, trying hard not to use any words that might set him off.

"Why are you concern about me?" Irritation shone in his body language.

"Because we're like brothers and if something is bothering you, then it bothers me." Wyatt's voice remained even toned.

"Since you brought it up, what do you think is bothering me?" Surprisingly, Jett voice remained quiet, but his wrinkled up face told another story.

"I don't read minds, Jett. But last night when you flipped over the card table and stormed out my house, caused alarm."

"That was nothing. I just had a lot on my mind." He straightened back into his seat, trying to make light of the incident.

Anger began to rise up in Wyatt. As usual, his friend tried to down play the situation. "No one acts that way without cause."

"I got it under control, so you don't have to walk on egg-shells around me on the trip." Jett put on his shades, earphones and then leaned back in his seat to let Wyatt know their conversation was over.

Wyatt cocked his head at Jett, giving him one of those, "Are you serious," looks. He tossed up his hands and stared out the window. He made the decision that whatever trouble Jett found himself in on the trip, he would have to dig himself out of it.

Chapter Seventeen

Tara, always the one to cause a scene, screamed! "We're in Florida." She twirled and danced like a crazy woman. The tourists gawked in their direction, shaking their heads.

"Girl, act like you got some sense," Joi whispered, nudging Tara to stop whatever silly dance moves she was doing.

"See, that's what's wrong with the three of you." Tara stopped her outlandish behavior long enough to scowl them. "You don't know how to let loose and have fun."

"Fun is one thing, but acting a fool is another," Albre shot back.

"I'm going to let that comment slide, Missy, because I don't want to ruin my trip," Tara warned, cutting her eyes at Albre.

"Stop it ladies, it's time to board the plane," Becky shouted.

Joi shook her head at the two and headed up the ramp. She just wanted to find her seat and take a quick nap before landing in Jamaica. Anticipation filled her racing heart. She was proud of herself for making the first step to reclaim her life. On the trip, she hoped to find the adventurous, outgoing woman that disappeared two years ago. Life had thrown her a curve ball, but with the grace of God, she was more determined than ever to get back in the game of life.

Her husband and boys' lives weren't in vain. There had to be a reason why they entered and left her life so soon. Maybe one day she would learn why, but if not, she had found comfort in knowing that God knew the reason and was thankful that He allowed them to bless her life. No matter how short of a time it was.

She observed Albre and Tara putting their differences aside when a flock of handsome men entered the plane. Leave it to them, to stop their bickering long enough to spy out the opposite sex. Becky busied herself turning the pages of some magazine she'd brought aboard.

Joi read her brochure about the Caribbean for the hundredth time. Maybe it was nerves or her being anxious. Whatever the reason, she was ready to get this vacation started. Her mind wandered with interest of the many tourist attractions Jamaica had to offer. From the brochure, the ambience was breathtaking, like something Joi had never seen before. She could only imagine what the actual island would be like. Blue skies and beautiful weather, what more could a girl ask for. She'd seen television commercials advertising the Caribbean, but never in her wildest dream had she imagined traveling to a place of such beauty.

*****

When the airplane landed in paradise, they rushed off to board a shuttle van, taking them to their resort. Like teenagers left with no supervision, they chatted about the many places they wanted to visit while there. With their faces pressed against the van windows, their mouths hung open in amazement. The water was bluer than the heavens. The closest they had come to such beauty was on television, and to think, they haven't even scratched the surface. Joi could only imagine what the water would be like once they were on the beach.

Unpacking was out of the question, once they arrive at the resort. The four tossed their luggage on the floor and stormed out the room. Instead of having the shuttle van provided by the resort show them around, they decided to take a stroll around the area. They pulled and tugged on one another, trying to decide where to go next; needless to say; their excitement was over the top.

As they headed back to the resort, the pool area seemed to be screaming their names, and like any fun seeking vacationers, they had to answer. Joi's eyes bugged and her mouth dropped to her chest. "Tara, you didn't booked us at a nudist resort, did you?" she asked, turning to face her friend who played with her fresh braids. Albre and Becky snickered in the background.

"No-oo-oo," Tara sang with a smirk on her beautiful dark face.

Half-naked men and women showing off their magazine perfect bodies caught Joi off guard. Now, she understood why Tara wore a suspicious smirk on her face when they were shopping for bathing suits back home.

"TARA!" Joi screamed.

"Kinda sorta." With her forefinger pressed against her lips and twisting her body like a five-year-old caught red-handed. "It's a mixture of both."

Albre butted in. "Both of what, Tara?"

"You all are going to laugh when I tell you this."

"Tell us what?" Becky asked. To keep her from escaping, the three surrounded her.

"The reason we got the trip so cheap, is that they were running a mix and match discount at the resort."

"Say what?" The three said in unison as hot steam flared from their nostrils.

"What the heck is a mix and match discount?" Joi asked. "It's bad enough that we have to worry about men hounding us down. Now, we have to watch someone's naked butt each time we come to the pool area?" Joi slapped her hand against her forehead. "I knew this was a bad idea. I could feel it in my spirit, but I gave in to the begging and pleading of the three of you."

"It may not be as bad as you think." Becky tried lightening the mood, unsuccessfully.

"May not be that bad." Joi pointed in the direction where men and women were splashing and frolicking around half-naked in the pool. "It looks like Sodom and Gomorrah over there. We have fast forwarded past paradise. We have entered into Sin City."

Joi stormed off, heading inside the resort when she collided with a tall, handsome tourist with a rock hard chest. The direct hit from his firm torso made her vision fuzzy. When the imaginary birds stopped swarming around her head, she looked up and shouted, "Wyatt?"

She glared up at the giant of a man. The direct hit had made her delirious. Maybe it was wishful thinking on her part. Why would Wyatt be on the same trip as she? Could it be possible? The spell was broken when he spoke her name.

"Joi?" he asked, stunned as he looked down at her. "What are the odds?"

"I-I know." She found it difficult to speak. Although it was out of her character, she wanted to jump into his arms and never let go. She'd been fantasizing about this man day and night and now here he stood in the flesh.

"Are you here with someone?" he asked. If Joi didn't know any better, a glimmer of hope seemed to have formed on his chiseled face.

"Yes, I am." Disappointment lined his squared jaws. She wasn't ready to reveal that she was there with her friends. For all she knew, he could be there with the airhead she'd seen him with at the restaurant or someone new. Why get her hopes up, and then later get them crushed.

She assumed her friends had gone to do more site seeing. Or should she say "butt watching." If either of them knew she had run into Wyatt, they'd be all up in her business, and Tara would be searching for Wyatt's friend, Jett.

Not only did she have to worry about the no censorship at her resort. Now, she had learned that Wyatt was in the Caribbean. Things are going to get very interesting in paradise for the next six days. Joi felt it in her soul.

She wanted to ask him, did he come with someone, but she couldn't bear to hear the answer. Instead, she tried making a quick exit to her room. "Well, I hope you enjoy your trip." His closeness threatened to uncover feelings that she didn't want exposed.

He extended his arm, blocking her from passing. "It's still early. Besides, we're on vacation. Do you have to leave?"

She wanted to say, "I prefer to stay here with you." But she wasn't going to make a fool of herself, especially if his female traveling companion decided to show up. The last thing she wanted was to end up in a catfight in paradise over a man. The girls would never let her live it down.

Gently he touched her arm, sending waves of electricity throughout her body. Craning her neck to stare up at him, she said, "Yes, I have to go." She hated herself for lying, but like word vomit, she had no control.

"I understand," he said in a wounded voice and lowered his arm to let her pass.

Joi wanted to reenact the moves that "Gloria" did in the movie, *Waiting to Exhale*, when she turned to see if Marvin was watching her walk away. Without thinking, Joi turned and found Wyatt doing exactly that, watching her sashay down the walkway. Heat rushed to her face, causing her to feel light headed under the gorgeous fireman stare.

Chapter Eighteen

The word, *luck*, wasn't in Wyatt's vocabulary, but he had just hit the jackpot. What were the odds of him and Joi running into each other in the Caribbean? He couldn't believe his good fortune. Out of all the women to run into on the trip, thank goodness it was Joi. God had blessed him to fly the friendly skies to meet an angel. Now he didn't have to wait until he returned to Shreveport to ask her out. Distracted by the excitement of seeing the woman who had been invading his thoughts, he quickly remembered that she was on the trip with another man. Now how was he going to work around that?

He stood, staring out at the breathtaking island. Then, Jett came and stood in front of him, blocking his view. "Why are you standing out here alone when there are tons of single women out here to be claimed?"

With a blank stare, Wyatt moved back to put some space between them.

"Is that all you think about, Jett?" He asked, trying to keep his cool. "There is more to life than chasing after women who add no substance to your life."

"Substance?" He twisted up his nose, as if Wyatt asked him to eat a bucket of worms. "I'm not looking for a wife. I'm here to have a good time."

"I thought you booked this trip to get in touch with your spiritual side?"

"I did." A wicked smile lined his face. "My spiritual nature can't be happy if my physical nature isn't. And chasing after single, fine, young woman makes both natures happy."

He slapped Jett on the back, shaking his head. He wanted to tell his friend about running into Joi, but quickly changed his mind. Jett had a way of turning an innocent chance meeting into something sordid. And that was not his intentions with Joi. He wanted to know her on a deeper and spiritual level. He prayed the boys understood when he began ditching them to hang-out with her, but, it depended on whether or not she was there with another man. The thought of trying to sneak around for the chance to talk to her, sounded sleazy. For an opportunity to claim her heart, he'd jump into the deep blue sea to be with her.

"Take it easy." Wyatt pressed his hands against Jett's chest. "You led me to believe that this was a resort for Christian singles. Then, if so, we'll be attending workshops on how to handle ourselves as godly men around godly women."

"And you believed me?" He gave Wyatt a look of disbelief. "I told you that so you would come. You were being difficult, so, I had to tell you what you wanted to hear to get you to come."

"You what?" he yelled. "What the heck have you gotten me into?" The news of his friend's deception had him boiling with anger. Leave it to Jett. Wyatt knew he should have been the one researching and booking their trip.

"Relax, will you." In a manly stance, Jett put his hand on Wyatt's shoulder, looking him square in the eyes. "There are lots of single, lonely females here." He let out a disgusting laugh.

Wyatt slapped Jett's hand from his shoulder. "You know what, do what you want, but don't come running to me again when you find yourself in trouble." He cocked his head to the side with a stern look. "Remember what happened last year? I won't be there to bail you out this time."

"Then call us even." He brushed passed Wyatt and strolled into the dining area where a group of young women were seated. Wyatt turned and left in the opposite direction. The farther he distanced himself for his misguided friend, the better. Maybe it wouldn't be a bad idea when he arrived back home to cut all ties with Jett. Their friendship had become toxic.

Wyatt found an empty table near the pool area to cool down. He took a deep breath of fresh air and just when he exhaled, he spotted Joi two tables down, alone. He leaped from his seat and without thinking, he headed in her direction. The Lord was truly working things out in his favor. With no boyfriend in sight, he decided to seize the opportunity and hopped over to where she sat.

Easing up behind her, he poured on the charm. "Your boyfriend must be crazy leaving you defenseless around the slick talking men at this resort."

Her hand acted as a visor to block out the sun. She scrunched up her nose, trying to locate the person behind the voice. When she turned to face him, he was met by one of the warmest and inviting smiles he'd ever received from a woman.

"Hello again," she greeted, gesturing with her hands for him to have a seat.

Either, she wasn't on vacation with a man or she was the type to play the field. She didn't fit the profile of a two-timer, but, she didn't have to ask him twice. He slammed his butt so fast into the chair before she changed her mind. He gladly obliged just to be near her.

"Alone again... huh?" Really, was that the only line that he could come up with?

"The scenery is gorgeous. Like, something taken straight out of a movie." He watched as her glistening lips spat out every word. "So, I decided to ditch my friends and enjoy the view."

Wyatt's antennas went up at the mention of "friends." He knew then that she had to be talking about the three ladies he'd met at the hospital. They did travel in packs. At first, he had assumed that flying to the Caribbean with his friends was a bad idea. Now, things were beginning to look up for him. If everything worked out, he just might leave Jamaica with a new love, but, before he could get to that point, he had to win her over and allow her to see that he was a decent guy.

"The view in front of me is breathtaking also, and might I add, beautiful too," he said, hoping he wasn't spreading on the niceties too thick.

She blushed and said, "Thank you. You didn't have to say that.

He had to make his move before another single man on the island did. After all, she was the most beautiful woman there as far as he was concerned. "I meant every word of it, and yes, I did have to say it, because you are."

"You know, the whole illusion of this trip has a way of making people feel and see things that will disappear the moment the trip ends." She pursed her lips, giving him the, "don't play me for a fool" type of look.

"Believe me, it's not the trip. You have been on my mind ever since I met you at the hospital." There, he confessed his true feeling. It felt good to get it out. She probably thought that he was the type of man who would say anything to get next to her. True, most people did come to places like this to do things they would never otherwise do, but not him. His feelings were pure. He just had to get her to believe it.

*****

She wasn't about to confess that she had fantasized about him ever since their impromptu lunch. Who knew what he had on his mind. He probably assumed that he would get lucky by speaking such smooth words. Either with her or some other unsuspecting female on the trip, but rest assured it wouldn't be her.

One thing she couldn't deny, he wore the heck out of the sleeveless t-shirt and shorts. From the looks of the total package, he took great care of his body. The muscles in his legs led up to the length of his body. She fanned herself with her hand at the thought.

"Are you hot? We can go back inside," Wyatt asked.

"Oh no, I'm fine," she lied. "A bug flew pass by face." He looked at her strange and she knew why. There wasn't a bug in sight. Admitting that his presence caused an onset of hot flashes was a bit too forth-coming?

"Are you here with your girlfriends from the hospital?"

She sensed that what he really wanted to know was, was she there with another man, but instead, she turned the tables. She wasn't ready just yet to give him any answers until he answered her question. "Are you here with your friends?" she asked, flexing a clever smile.

"Yes, I am," he responded, to her surprise. "So, are you going to answer my question?" Like a love sick puppy, his eyes pleaded for an answer.

"I'm here with my girls that you met at the hospital. I left them earlier by the pool. Watching people prance around butt naked isn't for me." The both laughed. "Now, Tara, the feisty one is probably out chancing after a man."

They had long left their table to take a stroll, but not venturing out too far from the resort. They conversed until the moon shone over them, casting its spell of something deeper brewing. For the first time since the loss of her family, Joi was enjoying the company of another man. Wyatt seemed, as far as she could tell, the perfect gentleman. The trip for her had prospects of becoming a memorable one. This was the vacation where she'd planned to reclaim her life and learn to love or at least rediscover the woman she used to be.

Chapter Nineteen

"Something just isn't right about this resort," Joi said with a disturbing frown. Yesterday at the pool area, people were darn near naked. Now today, she watched with wide eyes as a couple was behaving inappropriate in public view. "The brochure the three of you handed me, advertised that this resort was a haven for vacationers seeking a Christian atmosphere." Her instincts told her that the three had pulled the wool over her eyes.

"Well, uh…it's better that you found out now than later, I suppose." Becky fidgeted with her blonde curls, while a glint of guilt shaded her tanned face.

"Better to know what?" Joi furthered questioned, now becoming irritated with the three of them. They lied to her and tried placing the blame on Tara when she'd asked about the resort on yesterday.

Tara, being the outspoken one, said, "That we gave you a phony brochure. If we wanted to go to church, we would have stayed at home." Her braids swung around her head like a bobbled head doll when she spoke.

The others agreed with a nod, but Tara shot daggers at them with her eyes.

"Church, church, church, is all you talk about. There is more to life than church." Tara stood her ground. "I'm not saying that there is anything wrong with serving and praising God. But Joi, God wants us to have fun to."

Upset wasn't the word to describe how she felt, but the girls had a valid point. Joi zipped her lips and listened to her friends lecture her about how dull and boring her life had become. Church was the only thing keeping her sane. It made her feel safe and secure. She depended on the teaching and counseling of her pastor to get her through the long, lonely days of living without her family.

"If we had told you the truth, you wouldn't have come," Albre added in Tara's defense.

"So, now, the two of you decide to back me up?" Tara snapped.

Neither of them answered.

"Church is important, Joi. We are not attacking your faith. But ever since—," she stopped, swallowed hard as if something had caught in her throat. "Ever since the death of Michael and the boys, you stopped living," Becky stated.

The anger she felt earlier toward her girls friends had now simmered. "I want to stay mad at the three of you, but I can't. I know you mean well." She stepped over to her friends and hugged them. They were right. She had lost herself in her grief.

"So, does this mean that you forgive us?" Tara asked with a look, itching to get into mischief.

"Yes... this time." Joi reprimanded them with a pointed finger. She changed the subject to something they loved to talk about, men. "Do you all remember the firemen we met at the hospital cafeteria a couple of months ago?"

"Girl, we didn't come on this trip to talk about our jobs and firemen who are thousands of miles cross the sea," Albre retorted, her accent sounded thicker with each word.

"I know that's right," Tara and Becky chimed in.

"No, no, no... that's not why I brought that up."

"Then, why mention them?" Tara asked, checking herself out in the large glass window outside the resort.

"They are here on this island. I've already spoken with Wyatt." Delight laced her lips at the mention of his name. "He is the older, tall, dark and super hunky one that apologized for his friends' behavior that day."

"Oh, yeah...now I remember." Becky's sparkling blue eyes danced in her head at the mention of them.

"This is going to be the vacation to end all vacation," Tara squealed. "I can't wait to meet that smooth talking wild one." She snapped her fingers, trying to recall his name. "Jay. No…Jim, no. Jett, that's it. I can't wait to tame him."

"Okay girls. Control your raging hormones." Heck, who was she fooling? Her hormones were just as out of control. The moment she discovered that Wyatt was in Jamaica, her good sense had gone out to sea. She needed to take her own advice and arrest her speeding heart before it crashes.

Her disappointment had waned after learning that she had been tricked about the type of trip they were on. Now, she understood why people were running around in bathing suits they had no business wearing. Some of their bodies should have been outlawed from public viewing. She had no plans of bearing all in front of complete strangers.

The one who concerned her most after revealing that Wyatt and his friends were at the resort was Tara. She nearly flipped her lid the first time she laid eyes on Jett. Joi had some reservations about him. Wyatt and the others seemed self-controlled. On the other hand, Jett was a little rough around the edges. She did not want to see her friend get hurt by him or any man.

Joi prayed daily that she would find love again, and with Wyatt on the same trip as she, maybe it was a sign. First, she had to stop feeling guilty about wanting affection and attention from the opposite sex. The word, adulterous continued to haunt her each time she tried to move forward and give this love thing another try. Michael was dead and she was still alive. Then, why did she feel as if she was sneaking around behind his back. She had better get herself together before Wyatt thought that she was some sort of nutcase.

"Joi, how did you find out that they were on the island?" Albre asked. Her slanted eyes seemed too widened at the mention of the four gorgeous firefighters.

"When I left the three of you by the pool area to head back to my room, I ran into Wyatt's chest." The thought of her face colliding with his hard rock abs caused her to shiver.

"You like him don't you?" Becky asked with a knowing smile.

"I don't know the man." She tried down playing her attraction to the smoking, hot firemen.

"You were introduced to his chest. I'd say you know him very well," Tara laughed.

"Real funny." She tried keeping a straight face, because her friends could read her well.

"You don't have to admit it, we can see it on your face," Albre said.

"I'm finish with this discussion." Their words hit home and the last thing she wanted was for the three of them to start meddling in her business. "Since the three of you deceived me into thinking that this was a Christian resort, if there's such a one. Let's go take a look around. I need to see what you all have gotten me into."

They headed inside the restaurant area for a bite to eat. People were acting as if they had lost their minds. It was truly heathen territory. Tara seemed to fit right at home amongst the colorful tourist, but, Joi and the others watched in shocked at some of things people were doing and saying.

Joi wanted to lock herself inside her room until it was time to go home. This was not her cup of tea. She didn't consider herself prudish, but she had standards; standards she wasn't lowering on this trip.

Chapter Twenty

"Man, we had a great time checking out Jamaica's hotspots last night," Jett said as he choked down his breakfast.

"We thought you were coming," Paul added, "But you stayed in this room like some old man."

Seth seemed more interested in his food than their conversation.

Wyatt took a sip of his orange juice before setting his friends straight of his whereabouts, "Who said I was in my room?" He shot them a dismissive glance.

"As straight lace as you are, we know you weren't with a woman," Seth added.

Wyatt was in such a good mood after learning that Joi was at the same resort that he ignored his friends' wisecracks. Watching the waves crashing back and forth against each other from their beach front patio, he couldn't wait to tour the island and create some memorable moments with Joi.

"For your information, I wasn't alone." Wyatt's statement had their undivided attention. Each dropped their utensils as they waited like eager school boys for him to elaborate.

"The woman had to be in your dreams. Because we covered most of this island last night and there was no you... or, you with a woman." Paul said, giving Wyatt a doubtful stare.

"I'm a grown man. What do I have to lie about?"

"What's her name?" If Jett had hind legs he would be sitting upon them with his tongue hanging out.

"Joi," Wyatt said, his eyes peeking at them over the rim of his glass of orange juice.

"Joi?" Jett asked, confused. "Isn't that the nurse back at the hospital? The one who you have the hot's for?"

"Yes and yes." Why hide his feelings? Joi was a beautiful, classy lady. A lady he wanted to get to know.

"Man you're crazy. Joi is back at home in Shreveport." Jett shook his head, shooing him with his hand. "Paul you were right, the woman he was with last night was in his dreams.

The three let out a hearty laugh at Wyatt's expense, and then commenced eating.

"She and her girlfriends are here at the resort. We hung out last night." He gave them a serious look.

Then, they stop eating long enough to hear him out.

Before he could say another word, Jett bombarded him with question after question about Tara. Now, he knew that he would have to keep a close eye on him. Jett meant well, but he was rough around the edges when it came to women. His aggressive approach turned most of them off, igniting his short temper.

Once they had finished their breakfast, they went back inside, got dressed and headed out for a day of fun in the sun. Just like at home, the guys were as flirtatious and obnoxious in the Caribbean. Who knew what diseases were floating around out there? He had zero interest in a one night stand. Sadly, he couldn't say the same about the others. They were eating up the attention from the beautiful, exotic women on the island, especially Jett.

As they passed a group of woman possibly in their sixties on the beach, Wyatt felt a slap across his backside. He turned to investigate and noticed a naughty, older woman blowing him kisses. Her companions seemed to have gotten a kick out of it and blew kisses at him as well.

"Nice backside beefcakes!" One of the women yelled as the breeze tossed her grey hair across her wrinkled face.

"Did you guys see that?" Wyatt asked, looking back at the frisky bunch of women who were old enough to be his mother.

"Those were the women Wyatt was with last night," Jett teased, letting out a gut busting laugh. "The change in climate is causing him to hallucinate and making him to believe that he was out with Joi last night."

Their laughter was infectious, causing Wyatt to join in. Then, their smiles were slapped right off their faces when Joi and her friends appeared out of nowhere. The yellow, strapless mini sundress Joi wore showed off her silky toned shoulders, causing her skin to glisten from the sunrays. The highlights in her short wavy hair sparkled around her diamond shaped face.

"Hello ladies," Wyatt said, expressing more excitement than usual.

The women spoke in unison. Wyatt noticed Tara checking Jett out and he doing the same to her. There were definitely sparks between the two. He hoped his hotheaded friend wouldn't go and ruin things. If everything went well, they each could possibly find love in paradise.

Jett pushed passed the three and headed straight to Tara. Wyatt had to give it to his young friend, shy he was not. He went after what he wanted, a lesson he needed to take from Jett's playbook when it came to his own love life.

The others followed Jett's lead and left Wyatt alone. Awkwardly, he and Joi stood as they wiggled their toes in the sand. He broke the silence and asked, "What are your plans for today?" Those were the only words that he could think of to say. What he really wanted to ask was, if she'd spend the next six days with him in Jamaica, but it sounded a bit too forward. He had to take it slow. It was easy to get sucked into the mesmerizing images of the trip. So, his only option was to let things happen naturally.

"The girls and I haven't' decided."

"Is this your first time to the Caribbean?"

"Yes," she said with an inviting smile that warmed his heart. "Is this your first time?"

"Yes. I was hesitant about coming, but seeing you here, I'm glad that I came." He was more than happy. If things went sour with his boys on the trip, he could ditch them and hang out with her. Also, it would give him the time he needed to win her over.

"The girls tricked me into coming." She let out a dry laugh.

"Tricked? How?"

"They led me to believe that this was a Christian resort. I knew something wasn't right when I began seeing half naked men and women running rampant throughout the place, and secular music blasting in the restaurant that turned out to be a nightclub."

He laughed at her as she expressed her surprise about the resort. "My friends did the same to me."

"The nerve of them."

"Nerve is right," he said as they began to walk the length of the beach. "I'm all for fun, but, I'm a one woman type of man."

Without a doubt, he'd scored a point by the way she glanced up at him and smile. Happy that she was a God-fearing woman had him wanting to get to know her even more. Their friends had wandered off in another direction, allowing them to have an uninterrupted conversation. Wyatt couldn't believe how fate kept throwing the two of them together. He just hoped that she was feeling him, because he most definitely was feeling her.

Chapter Twenty-One

Joi placed a large hat on her head as she strutted her sandaled feet down the pavement. She and the girls took in some late night sightseeing of the island, which left her a bit exhausted this morning, but excited to see more of paradise at the same time. They continued down a long ramp leading to the beach area to find the perfect spot to soak up some sun. Each with their tote bags strapped on the shoulders, bask in the beauty of the tropical island.

Happy she had taken a leap of faith and joined her girls on the trip, Joi inhaled a nostril full of Caribbean air. "Had I known that fresh air was what I needed to open my sinuses, I would have taken this trip much sooner."

The three rolled their eyes at her, knowing the struggle it took in getting her there.

"Whatever, Miss Square Pants," Tara joked, tugging on her arm; it was no secret that Joi had been kind of uptight lately when it came to venturing outside of her comfort zone.

The ladies pranced down the sandy beach with anticipation of having an exciting day. Joi discreetly spied the beach for any signs of Wyatt. As much as she loved hanging out with her girls, things had changed after learning that he was there on the island. Who wanted to waste seven days in paradise with three females when there was a strong, strapping male roaming the island.

Delusion must have sat in. Joi couldn't believe the thoughts swirling around in her head. She had to get a hold of herself. She was a God-fearing woman and had no business allowing her mind to stray into the gutter. Tara's way of thinking had begun to rub off on her. She shook off the notion of spending time with the sizzling fireman.

Maybe the change in atmosphere or her years of being alone stirred up such emotions. After all, it had been a while since she'd taken interest in a man. The island had put her in a different state of mind, where she wanted to take steps to starting a new life.

Inwardly, she prayed that her views about his dangerous job as a fireman wouldn't get in the way, and, she hoped that he wasn't pursuing her on this trip for other reasons. Trying to rid her mind of that possibility, Joi focused on the positive.

After their encounter yesterday with Wyatt's friends, Joi sized Jett up to be the controlling type. She hoped that Tara realized what she was getting herself into with him. He seemed more of the rebel type. Joi had a knack for reading people. Wyatt's other friends appeared harmless, but she hadn't gotten a good read on them just yet. She was too busy figuring out Wyatt.

In her mind, Wyatt had the total package when it came to men. He was not only handsome, but charming as well. How he managed to hook up and marry a woman like his trifling ex-wife, baffled Joi; but, people do crazy things with it comes to love.

On yesterday, she and Wyatt discussed many subjects. Their professions had been a hot topic, as well as their love for God and the church, which still shocked her. Here, she alleged him to be the partying type that chased women. For future references, she had to stop assuming the worst about people and just let things happen. Wyatt appeared to be loving, caring and sweet, wrapped into a six-foot-five chocolate package.

When Wyatt's hand accidentally brushed against hers last night, a feeling she had long forgotten surged through her body. What woman could mistreat a gentle soul like him? He was in search of love too, she assumed.

Their evening together brought back so many happy memories of her and Michael. How they would sit for hours and talk and laugh about any and everything, but he wasn't Michael. At one point in their conversation, she almost called Wyatt her deceased husband's name. She better get her act together before they meet again. One thing she knew about men, they didn't appreciate being compared or called by another man's name. An accidental slip of the tongue might run him off.

"This spot is perfect," Joi said, tightening the wrap around her one-piece bathing suit. It had been a while since she last worn one, but compared to most of the women on the beach, she had nothing to be embarrassed about. Approaching her thirty-fourth birthday, she admired how well her figure had held up. As she turned to view her surroundings through her shades, she smiled as lovers strolled passed her hand in-hand and surfers hit the massive waves.

The women spotted empty loungers, tossed their wraps and bags on them and headed out to test the beautiful blue water. They frolicked in the sea like adolescents as the waves pushed against their bodies.

The salt water blinded Joi as a pair of hands touched her on the shoulders. With blurred vision, she opened her eyes to God's most wonderful creation. As her impaired vision returned, there he stood, gorgeous as ever. Her prayers were answered when she learned that the pair of hands belonged to Wyatt. He'd found her amongst the many tourists on the beach.

"Hi, gorgeous." Wyatt greeted. His massive height blocked the sun from her burning eyes.

Like jelly, her insides giggled at the sound of his powerful voice. "Hi…Wyatt." Her breathe caught in her throat. She looked around for her friends and spotted them on dry land with Wyatt's friends. She hadn't realized that they had left her in the water alone with, *Adonis*.

His bare chest glistened against the sunrays and his teeth were whiter than the clouds above. The island had stricken her lonely heart with desire and passion. She wanted to step outside of her comfort zone and touch his chest, to feel if it was real. She needed proof that he wasn't a mirage or that the heat in paradise hadn't affected her senses. Surely, no man's body could be that toned.

Her nerves had gotten the best of her and she pushed away from him. She wasn't going to allow the illusion of the island to cause her to become footloose and fancy free. Her mother did not raise her that way. She had a great time conversing with him yesterday; today, proved to be a different story. The exposure of his toned, flat abs had her struggling to stay focused on his face. This man caused her imagination to run wild as she tried her best not to drool in his presence.

What would Michael think about her having warm and fuzzy feelings for another man? Her heart deflated in her chest. She had to push those forbidden feelings aside. These types of vacation settings were a trap to seduce people into doing things that they would not normally do.

Gently, he grabbed her arm just as she was about to head to shore. "Joi? What wrong?" he asked, which sent her blood whooshing straight to her head. "Did I do something to offend you?"

"No...uh, it's me. I don't want to give you the wrong impression." Once on dry ground, Joi reached for her towel. She wrapped it around her soaked body to hide from his probing eyes.

"I won't lie and say that I'm not attracted to you. You stole my heart the first day that I saw you." He stepped in closer to her, which caused her to shake in terror. No man has ever been allowed to get that close to her since Michael.

"I'm still in love with my husband." There, she said it. Maybe he'd take a hint and stop pursuing her, especially if his intentions weren't pure.

"I'm not asking you to forget your husband or even your boys' memories." His words sounded sincere, but her heart wouldn't allow her to believe them. "I'm asking you to make new ones with me."

Before she could utter another word, Wyatt closed the distance between them, trapping her between two beach loungers. Tenderly, he cradled the back of her head in his strong hands and took her breath away with an explosive kiss.

His bold move caused her body to go stiff. Her eyes fluttered from the hot, steamy kiss he'd just laid on her. Her body temperature rose with desire. A desire that she had thought died two years ago.

*****

Wyatt slowly pulled away from Joi as hard as it was. He had to cool his heels or he'd never let go of the woman before him. "I've wanted to kiss you ever since the day we had coffee together." He made no apologies for his action. Wyatt stared down into her surprised face. She had enjoyed it just as much as he, because she did not resist.

Her face reddened. Wyatt wasn't sure if it was from embarrassment or desire. He hoped the latter. "Where are the others?" she asked, never pulling away from him, which spoke volume that she was into him.

"I guess they headed back to the resort." He didn't care where they were. The only thing that mattered to him was being alone with her. "Joi, give me the chance to prove myself to you. The feelings that I have for you are real. It has nothing to do with the allure of this beautiful island; although, it does help me to express my feeling more freely."

"And why is that?" she asked, pressing her hand against his chest, which caused his insides to cave in. Her weary brown eyes tugged at his heart. He could see the sorrow that she had been carrying.

"I've noticed you long before my buddies and I bumped into you and your girlfriends' months ago. I didn't approach you because of the wedding band on your finger." He brushed his thumb against her soft cheeks.

He had rehearsed in his mind a hundred times how to approach her, but somehow, God took control of the situation and here they stood. With a bad marriage behind him, Wyatt wanted to experience real love. Trina, his ex-wife, took more out of their marriage than she gave, leaving him with a broken heart and trust issues.

"I wear my ring, because I can't accept the fact that my family is gone."

Wyatt grabbed hold to her hand, urging her to take a stroll with him down the beach. His instincts told him that she needed a friend, someone that she could trust. So, he opened his ears and heart as she rehashed the worst day of her life. Guilt riddled him. Here, he was with this amazing woman, trying to find a place in her heart, when she was dealing with something much deeper than he could have ever imagined.

He could not picture in his mind how he would react if he'd lost his entire family as she had. Truthfully, he didn't know what else to say, and thought it best just to be supportive and help her to open her heart to love again. More than anything, he hoped that she would learn to love him.

Chapter Twenty-Two

Wyatt escorted Joi back to the resort and found the others laughing and having a good time near the pool area. *Things couldn't get any better than this,* he thought. A tropical, cool breeze helped to relax his tensed body. The amber, evening sky and romantic ambience of the island put him in an, *everything is alright with the world,* type of mood. His friends were on their best behavior, especially Jett. As far as he could tell, the calmness of the island had tamed the savage beast inside of him.

Things were perfect. The woman who he desired to have in his life was standing beside him. Her hands nestled inside his as they approached the others. He continued to warn himself to take it slow. The bad break-up with his ex-wife had taught him to never rush into a relationship again. No matter how beautiful or gorgeous the woman may be, and Joi definitely was all of the above.

"I see you two found your way back safely," Jett said, giving them a mischievous look as he sat cozied up with Tara.

"If you were that concerned, you would have come looking for us," Wyatt joked as he and Joi joined them.

"You're a big boy. You can take care of yourself and that pretty lady beside you," Jett said, giving Wyatt and Joi a 'once over.'" The others talked and laughed in the background.

With an alluring stare, Tara swatted at Jett to behave. Wyatt could see that she wanted Jett's undivided attention for herself, which was fine with him. The longer she kept him entertained, the less he had to worry about Jett's over top personality ruining their evening.

Everyone appeared to be getting alone great and that made Wyatt happy. If he wasn't so blinded by the beautiful goddess beside him, he'd thought there was a love connection between the others as well. Paul seemed to be into Becky. Tall blondes were his type and Seth and Albre, clearly had something in common, they both spoke Chinese. Tara and Jett had begun their own private conversation, while he and Joi conversed about their likes and dislikes when it came to dating.

As their talk progressed, Wyatt realized that he and Joi enjoyed some of the same things. He began to find himself drawn to her more and more. His attraction had passed her outer beauty. He wanted to know more about the woman inside. Where had she been all his life? He would have still been married if he'd met a woman like her. Joi was grounded. She didn't appear self-absorbed or concerned about name brand labels, as Trina had. If a designer name wasn't attached to what he bought her, she would toss it back at him.

Later, the others called it a night, but he and Joi lingered near the pool area until midnight. Thankfully, they were staying at the same resort. Wyatt believed that it was a sign from above. He considered himself favored by God when he learned that they had booked the same trip.

Wyatt and Joi sat at the edge of the pool, enjoying the view, and like an awkward teenager, trying to impress his date, he asked, "What is your favorite color?" He swirled his bare feet in the water.

"It may sound weird, but orange." She dipped her feet into the water beside his. "What is your favorite color?"

"Blue," he answered, rubbing his feet up against hers.

"Why blue?" Her gorgeous brown eyes sparkled under the subdued lighting. Never had he experienced a woman, exuding sex appeal and innocence at the same time.

"Blue represents tranquility. It's soothing." He intertwined his fingers with hers but felt a slight resistance. Wyatt couldn't help himself. Being near her made him weak which warranted caution. He had fought the demons of temptation in the past, which tested his faith and will power to remain strong until God sent him a mate. The last thing he wanted to do, was fall into temptation's trap on the island, ruining his credibility with Joi.

Although, he'd been trying to walk the straight and narrow, he did carry a secret that might push Joi away. After experiencing the devastating loss of her family, his secret may cause further hurt. She was a decent woman. So for now, he had to take it slow and easy.

Trina's evil and conniving ways almost drove him over the edge years ago, causing him to do the unthinkable. Now, he was a changed man, a better man after overcoming his rocky past.

"Why of all colors, Orange?" he asked.

"It's loud, fun and, spontaneous ..." Her voice trailed off. "Like the girl I used to be." Her voice swelled with sadness. Sadness, he could never imagine or wanted to experience.

Wyatt moved in closer to her, knowing she had a void that he could not fill. Although, he would never try to take the place of her husband, he hoped to be the man who could bring back that free-spirited girl she once was. Without thinking, he stroked the side of her cheek. Consumed with wanting to take her hurt away, his hand eased down to her pointed chin. He held it with the tips of his fingers and drew her lips into his. She flinched as if wanting to resist, but she relaxed and gave in to him.

The last thing he wanted was for her to think that he was trying to take advantage of her vulnerability. So, he pulled back. He wanted to prove himself worthy of her, and taking advantage of the situation wasn't going to win him any brownie points. He wanted their friendship to transform beyond the allure of the island. The pull of Jamaica had a way of playing with a man's emotions; emotions that may not be real, but he knew that his were and wanted what was happening between them to continue when they landed back in Shreveport.

*****

The morning air offered Joi what she needed the most, relief from her clogged sinuses. As she took in the beautiful weather, her girlfriends entered their sea front balcony. Dressed in their summery attire, they took a seat at the table with her. She thought that they were going to sleep in, while she slipped out for a bit of soul-searching. Like roosters, they were up bright in early to start the third day of their vacation.

When Wyatt had walked Joi to her room late last night, the girls were asleep. She tipped toed in before any of them had a chance to awake and ask her questions about her and Wyatt. She had to sort out what was happening between the two of them herself. He seemed too good to be true. He said all the right things a woman wanted to hear, but, she wasn't naïve either. She had watched enough criminal shows to warrant caution. One minute she could be talking to Mr. Right and the next, he'd turned out to be Mr. Wrong.

The girls piled their plates with food that room service had delivered up to their room. Question after question began flying from their mouths.

"Have the two of you slept together, yet?" Tara asked. She cut through the chase to get the answer that she desperately craved. That was the type of person she was.

"Tara!" both Albre and Becky yelled.

"It's not polite to ask such questions," Albre said.

Joi could see straight through Albre, she wanted to know just as bad as Tara.

"So, have you?" Albre inquired in a more subdued voice than Tara.

"Are you all listening to yourselves?" Joi looked back and forth at them. "I didn't come on this trip to get my groove back. I'm not Stella. I do not sleep around," Joi said matter-of-factly.

In a mocking tone, Tara quipped, "Miss. Holy Roller doesn't sleep around."

"Enough, Tara," Becky commanded. "You know Joi is not that type of woman."

"Sorry," she muttered under her breathe and then slumped back in her seat.

"And Wyatt doesn't appear to be that type of man, either." Albre added.

"He's not," Joi said, taking a sip of water. "He's an interesting man who has gone through just as much as I have. I enjoy his company and that's it."

"This vacation seems to be what you needed," Becky said and smiled. "I haven't seen you laugh this much in a while. I know it's because of Wyatt and not us."

"Girl, if you don't snag him, I will," Tara joked while taking in a mouthful of scrambled eggs. "Wyatt is sexy as heck. And don't forget a fireman. I'm surprised he's still single."

"There's more to a man than his outer appearance," Joi quickly added. Though she had to agree with her friend, sexy wasn't the word. Wyatt was smoking hot.

"Like what... Girl? I don't know any woman who wants a man that she can't stand to look at," Tara said. "I go for the outer."

"Now, I see why you always pick the wrong men." They laughed at Joi's comment. Tara cut her eyes at them and continued eating. It was the truth. She loved her friend like a sister, but she had to wonder at times what Tara saw in some of the men she dated.

They continued their early morning breakfast on the balcony, soaking in the warmth and gorgeous Caribbean scenery. Joi wished she and Michael had had the opportunity to visit the tropical island. All the things they had planned to do together, she'd found herself doing them with her girlfriends and another man. Flying on an airplane, vacationing on a romantic island and lying on the sandy beaches were their dream. She was here, but without him.

She shook off the spirit of gloom and doom and continued with their debatable conversations that somehow always led back to the opposite sex and shopping. Joi counted herself blessed. Most people would never experience the joys of having great friends like the ones who sat before her.

Chapter Twenty-Three

Bright and early the next morning, Wyatt headed for the beach to watch the sunrise over the Caribbean Sea. With legs out-stretched, digging his heels into the sand, he bathed in the intoxicating view. Like a sweet, soothing melody, he listened as the waves made their swooshing sound against each other. Images of Joi's angelic face flashed before him as he closed his eyes, indulging in his fantasies.

"If only Joi was here beside me," he groaned, relishing in nature's beauty, alone. His feelings for her were different than they had been for his ex-wife. Now, he knew what real love was. Each time they were together, he found it harder to say goodbye. He wanted to be near her always. His nostrils had memorized the sweet, intoxicating perfume she wore. Even in his dreams he could smell her.

The soothing sounds of the crashing waves helped to calm the raging storm of mixed emotions washing over him. A part of him wanted to go and knock on her door to confess how he truly felt, and the other half of him became timid because of the caliber of woman she was. He could tell when they first met that she wasn't the type of woman to dive head first into a relationship, especially after the nightmare she'd been through. He had to tell himself to take it slow, but the need to be near her fueled his desire.

The morning air kept him cool as he enjoyed the singing of the birds flying overhead. The guys deciding to sleep in late gave him the time he needed to clear his head. The calmness of the morning was the therapy he needed to sort out his feeling about Joi.

A smile inched its way upon his face when he realized that Joi and her friends had seen the same advertisement as he and his friends about the trip to the Caribbean. One thing that Wyatt believed in, and that was fate. In his mind, nothing happened by accident or chance when it came to finding the right woman. A woman created for a man to be with for the rest of his life. Too bad he didn't possess the same spiritual wisdom when he had hooked up with Trina. It could have saved him a lot of heartache, pain and stress. Her leaving him for that doctor was the best thing ever happened to him.

Now, he was free to find the woman that he was destined to be with, and he believed he had found that woman in Joi. She was simple, yet beautiful and amazingly smart. He wiggled his toes in the sand as the cool morning temperatures began to heat up. He had no plans of returning inside to join his friends.

He dusted the sand from his hands and looked toward to the sun as it blasted its scorching rays down on him. Today was turning out to be another sweltering day in the tropics. However, anyplace was better than fighting dangerous fires back home that threatened to claim his life, as well as the people's lives he was trying to save. What he really wanted to do was go find Joi and spark up some flames with her.

A soft, but recognizable voice pulled him back into the present. Quickly, he turned in the voice's direction, hoping his ears weren't playing tricks on him. To his surprise, the half-pint beauty he'd been obsessing over had appeared out of nowhere, like a Genie in a bottle.

"Is it okay if I join you?" she asked, her honey brown skin glistened in the sunlight.

Caught off guard, Wyatt stared up at her for a couple of seconds before speaking. His heart hammered out of control? He'd dated countless women before. Why was he acting like a goofy school boy now? "Su-rr-ee," he slurred.

With his hand acting as a visor to block out the sun, he opened and closed his eyes to make sure that the heat hadn't affected his ability to see straight. Like a nerd, he wanted to stand up and do the happy dance, but, doing that may have scared her off.

Joi wore a strapless, tropical sundress that complimented her petite frame. He observed everything about her. From her manicured toes all the way up to her makeup free face. It made her looked much younger than a woman in her thirties. He'd sworn the gold flecks in her eyes sparkled in the sunlight. *Where have she been all my life,* he thought, clutching hold to his chest.

With the quickness, he snatched the beach towel from underneath him and spread it out for her to sit.

"Thank you," she said, tightening the hem of her dress as she eased down on the towel. "You're out early this morning?"

He had to get a hold of himself before Joi thought that he was some type of weirdo. "I needed some fresh air. The guys were sleeping, so I decided to ease out and take a breather."

"Same here. The girls and I were up early, chatting and eating breakfast." She squint her eyes up at him. "I had to step out for a second to hear myself think. You know what I mean?"

He knew exactly what she meant. Taking this trip with his friends was fun and something he had never done before, but he missed his personal space. He wasn't used to sharing a place with three other people. He normally woke up to peace and quiet, not the radio, television and cellphone blasting at the same time. Thankfully, it was temporary. One more week of this and he'd have to strangle his buddies.

"I most certainly do," he smiled, trying hard not to appear overly excited that she was sitting next to him. The last thing he wanted to do, was make her nervous with his staring, but he couldn't help it. Wyatt wanted to reach out and touch her silky skin to see if it was as soft as it looked. Without a doubt, she exuded true beauty. "What does a woman who has it together need to think about?" He raised his brow, hoping he hadn't crossed the line by asking such a personal question.

"Stuff," she said, drawing circles in the sand with her finger.

"What kind of stuff?" He paused when he'd noticed the way her face scrunched up. He had invaded her personal space. "Sorry, I didn't mean to pry."

Her face relaxed after his apology. "I just have some things that I need to sort out in my head."

"Well, you've come to the right spot. This is a peaceful place to do just that and to become one with God."

A surprised look shone on her face when he mentioned God.

"You talk to God?"

"Yes, throughout the day," he said, wiping the beads of sweat that had formed on his forehead. "Working as a fireman, I need His protection around me."

"Michael used to say the same thing. We prayed together before he left for work each day." Her voice dropped, "I don't ever think I could marry someone with a dangerous profession again."

Ouch!

He understood that she was going through a tough time with losing her family, but his heart sank at her admission. A fireman's job was dangerous, but he hoped that someway, somehow that he could convince her not to close her mind on the prospect of them building a relationship together.

"Life, itself is dangerous, Joi. A person's occupation shouldn't matter when it comes to finding that special someone." He had to try and say something to plead his case.

"I know that, but the stakes are higher when you're facing danger every day on the job. I can't go through the wondering and praying if my husband is going to come home at night."

"But your husband wasn't killed in the line of duty," he stated, realizing too late that he should have kept those words to himself.

A beat passed before a word was spoken between them. Then he really felt like a heel for bringing up how her husband had died. If it were possible, he'd kick himself. This woman had captured his heart and the last thing he wanted to do was sound insensitive.

"I shouldn't have said that. I'm sorry, Joi." Without thinking, he pulled her hand into his as a gesture of his sincerity. He had hurt her feelings, it shone in her eyes and to make matters worse, he was jealous of a dead man who controlled her from the grave.

"No, he wasn't killed in the line of duty. Still, it doesn't lessen the dangers of being a policeman or fireman." A stinging pain pierced through him when she said the word, fireman.

"You have no control over who you fall in love with," he said, still holding on to her hand.

"I turned off that emotion a long time ago. I'm numb when it comes to love."

How was he going to breakthrough this woman's heart? More importantly, how was he going to get her to fall in love with him? Although he didn't want to admit it to himself at first, he had fallen hard for her.

"You are a vibrant young woman. Why would you want to spend the rest of your life alone?" Wyatt turned to face her. If he didn't do anything else on his vacation, he was going to spend every moment trying to win her heart.

"I can't let go of him. And I don't know how to let another man in," she said, choking on her words.

"Turn it over to God. I had to do the same when it came to the hurt my ex-wife put me through. I could not have done it on my own, so I let go and gave it to Him."

They sat in silence, watching the waves dance across the sea as morning turned into noon. It was therapeutic, having someone to open up to about his failed marriage, and he guessed it was what she needed too. When the tears began to trickle down her cheeks, he stretched his arms around her and held her close.

Chapter Twenty-Four

"Tara, if you're not out of that bathroom in three second, you're going to get left behind." Joi yelled outside the door. Albre and Becky stormed out the room, leaving the two of them.

"I'm coming, I'm coming," Tara shouted, "Perfection can't be rushed."

Joi tossed her handbag across the bed and stormed into the bathroom, dragging Tara out by the arm. "The tour bus will be picking us up in five minutes and I'll be darn if I miss it on account of you."

"Ok-ay-ay," Tara sang, grabbing her bag and sunglasses off the dresser.

Joi retrieved her handbag off the bed and she and Tara went in search of the others. Today they had made plans to do some shopping and sightseeing. She wanted to experience as much as she could before returning home in a few days. With only a short time left, having fun soared to the top of her list. Hopefully, Wyatt would be a part of that fun.

Their week in paradise had flown by, and her time with Wyatt had been the best of them all. He was a good listener and had a great desire to know more about her family. She didn't know for sure if he liked her or was he caught up in the hypnotic effects of the island. One thing she knew for sure was that she wanted him, but wouldn't dare act upon her feelings. Although, he'd never admit it, Joi believed his ex-wife still had a hold on him. Who was she kidding, the love she once shared with her deceased husband continued to influence her decisions when it came to moving on with her life.

"Are you satisfied, Miss. 'always have to be on time,'" Tara snapped, interrupting her thoughts. "The bus hasn't arrived."

Outside the resort, Joi and Tara spotted Albre and Becky chatting with several exotic and very attractive men. They looked like two hungry cougars going in for its prey. Neither one had steady boyfriends and with the island loaded with single men who were more than willing and ready to mingle, excited them. She had no plans of being someone's catch of the day. She had a hard enough time warming up to Wyatt. The thought of throwing herself on a group of sexy strangers was out of the question.

When Tara saw the oasis of men surrounding her friends, she brushed pass Joi to join them. Her hands flew up in frustration. What was she going to do with the three of them? She didn't want to come off as a fun sucker, but having a group of men salivating at the mouth to devour her, turned her off. She was an old-fashioned girl with old-fashion values when it came to dating and finding a mate.

"Let's go girls," Joi hollered. They were so enthralled with the male attention they were receiving that they gave her a dismissive wave. "The bus is here. Come on." This time she shouted much louder. They said their goodbyes to the throng of men and mopped on the vehicle.

Tara voiced her annoyance with Joi first. "I love the Caribbean culture. I was getting a personal lesson on the subject before you tore me away with your screaming and hollering."

"Uhuh," Albre and Becky agreed as they took their seats on the tour bus.

"I didn't come here to be harassed by a group of strange men," Joi said, turning in her seat to stare out the window. "I could have stayed at home and got that."

"Speak for yourself," Albre chimed in, "These men are different. They are Caribbean or should I say, 'West Indian.'" Her eyes twinkled with each word she spat.

"Different... how?" Irritated with her friends' men chasing ways, Joi opened her activity brochure and began browsing through its pages.

"They have accents," Albre joked as the others laughed at her silliness.

"We came here to forget about our hectic lives as nurses, let down our hair, and live a little," Becky added.

With her eyes, Tara shot daggers at Joi, which she pretended not to see. Once Tara had time to cool off, she'd eventually snap back to her fun-loving self. For now, with arms folded like a two-year-old, she pouted in her seat.

The tour guide drove them to the birthplace of the legendary King of Reggae, Bob Marley. Tara's mood began to lighten as the tour guide spoke of the island's historical facts. The scenic drive was amazing. It was everything they had expected and more. When they drove by a fortuneteller's home on their excursion, Joi noticed that intrigue peaked on Tara's face. Tara dipped and dabbled into the mystical unknown. Joi had no interest or desire in calling up the dead.

******

"What's going on between you and that nurse?" Jett asked in a sneaky tone.

Wyatt allowed his friends words to stir in his head for a second as he hopped on his jet sky. Ever since his lapse in judgment two years ago, Jett never seemed to let him forget it. Whenever it benefited him, Jett held Wyatt's mistake over his head as leverage and he was growing tired of it. "We're just friends," he paused, trying to keep his aggravation to a minimum. "Something you wouldn't know anything about when it comes to women."

"Friendship means nothing to me, if I can't sleep with them." Jett cranked out a disgusting laugh that got under Wyatt's skin.

"Look you two," Paul commanded, furrowing his brows at them. "We came to Jamaica to enjoy ourselves—"

"That's right," Seth interrupted. "So, don't come here ruining our trip because of whatever the two of you are secretly beefing about."

Ashamed of his past mistake, Wyatt kept Paul and Seth in the dark about it. With turmoil brewing in Jett, he threatened to expose one of the worse nights of his life. True, he was thankful that Jett had bailed him out, but was tired of kissing up to him for his pledge of silence. Jett's, "act of kindness," words Wyatt used loosely, was causing a rift in their friendship. He was becoming a problem and Wyatt hated to think that he'd have to reevaluate their friendship if Jett didn't change from his unbridled ways.

Their instructor walked over to teach them the safety rules for using the Jet Skis. Strapping on their life jackets, they headed out to sea. Riding the calm waves extinguished the fire that Jett had ignited in Wyatt. Just when he began to relax and enjoy himself, Jett drove toward him in high speed. As he neared Wyatt, he laughed and skidded off. Now Wyatt's anger had grown to levels he'd never experienced. Jett's antics had crossed the line.

Whether Jett was having some type of mental breakdown, Wyatt couldn't say. He'd noticed changes with his friend the day after a ten-year-old girl died as he tried to save her. They were called to respond to a house fire, but by the time they arrived, it was too late. The child pounded on the window, screaming for them to save her. His chest tightened by just the thought of that day.

Jett tried his best to go in, but the flames were ferocious. No one could have gone in without putting themselves in harm's way. Days later, according to proper protocol, the chief ordered Jett to see a psychiatrist. He'd noticed changes in his behavior. Like the hothead he was, Jett refused, stating that he was okay.

Wyatt didn't want to admit it until now. Perhaps his friend may possibly be suffering from post-traumatic stress syndrome.

Most men in his line of work down played the symptoms, but it was a fact. Instead of turning his back on Jett, he and the others had to find a way to help him get the help that he needed. Wyatt could never forgive himself if he didn't at least try.

He'd known Jett for years and recognized that the brute on the Jet Ski wasn't him. When he and his friends return home, they have to get Jett into some type of therapy before he self-destructs.

Chapter Twenty-Five

With a headache the size of a Colorado mountain, Joi found a cubby hole outside of the resort to hide. After her tour today with the girls and their bickering back and forth, she needed some me time. She and Tara had been at odds ever since they landed in paradise. The thought had crossed her mind whether she'd made a mistake in taking a vacation with her girlfriends. Coming to the tropics to get buck wild wasn't on her list of things to do.

She enjoyed the sounds of nature as her head rested against the lounge chair. Her mind strayed on her time spent on the island with Wyatt. He had a smile that could cheer up the saddest of hearts, and hers had been sad for a long time. Too bad friendship was all she had to offer him. A girl couldn't be too careful. Men had a way of appearing sincere when they were trying to get their hooks in a woman. The last thing she needed or wanted was to be made a fool of. Jamaica had a way of luring a person into its fantasy. She had to keep her wits about her. The thought of having a romantic tryst sounded great, but she would have to live with the guilt once she arrived back home.

A familiar voice pulled her out of her thoughts, which caused her heart to shudder. She stilled her nerves when he began to speak.

"My, my, my…we meet again," the deep voice said as she slowly opened her eyes. "Now, tell me this isn't fate?"

She recognized that sensual voice anywhere. "Wyatt?" She sat up straight, closing her bathing suit cover up. She wasn't comfortable lying in front of him in her two-piece bikini. And she didn't want to temp him with any impure thoughts.

"Why are you hiding behind the pool area?" he asked, curiosity written across his face.

Standing like a giant beside her lounger, Joi had to keep her mind focused on his face. Wyatt's presence was truly a sight to behold. He had the total package. He was definitely a man that women took notice of. And he certainly had her undivided attention.

"I needed a moment to myself," she said, holding tight to her bathing suit covering. "The girls and their drama were getting on my nerves."

"I here you." A beat passed. "Mind if I join you?"

She had reservations, but allowed him to join her. Her southern hospitality got the best of her. "Sure," she gestured, patting toward the end of her lounger. The weight of his body caused her to slide into him. "Oops!" She shouted as she struggled to keep her balance.

He grabbed her around the waist to keep her from flying off the lounger. Their closeness made her aware of his masculinity like never before. His touch made her body come alive. An awakening she had long forgotten.

"I didn't mean to cause an earthquake," he joked, still holding her close.

She wanted to get out of his embrace, but couldn't find the strength to do so. Rubbing her hands through her hair, she struggled to find her voice. "This seat isn't made for two."

"Oh... I thought it was one size fits all," he said in a ragged whisper.

Is he about to do what I think...? Before another word could utter from her lips, he pulled her face up and her lips met his. Her reasoning and good Christian girl with southern values was tossed out the window. Not only was he tempting, but his kissing skills were on point.

He stopped abruptly. Placing his hands beside him like a kid caught doing something forbidden. "I-I didn't plan to do that. Please except my apology." Joy and pain rested upon his face.

Apology? That was the best kiss she had in a while.

She felt somewhat disappointed when he, without warning ended it. "No need to apologize," she said.

He ran a hand through his short, cropped hair as if in deep thought and blurted, "I'm not sorry, Joi. I like you, I think about you nonstop. And I want to get to know you better." Gently, he brushed his powerful hand against her cheek.

His luscious brown eyes had genuineness in them, but she had to fight whatever feelings she had started to develop for him. "Please, don't say things that you don't mean, Wyatt," she said, taking hold of his arm. "I'm not ready to start over, I just can't."

"You don't want to be loved?" He gave her a questionable look.

"Yes… no." She answered unsure. "One day, I suppose."

"So, you're going to let life pass you by without ever experiencing or giving love another try?" He looked her square in the eyes, running his hands through her short curls and pulled her even closer to him. "If you didn't want to be loved, you would have slapped me the other day at the beach and pool area when I kissed you. Or, you would have run away or cursed me out when I just kissed you."

Their timing wasn't right, although her heart told her differently. "That doesn't mean a thing," she lied. "You're just caught up in the seduction of this place."

"What I feel is real. No island can make me feel a certain way, especially when it comes to my feelings for you."

"Please don't make this any harder."

"I won't press the issue. But, since you're not looking for a relationship, can we at least be friends?"

"Yes, but a friend with no benefits." She wanted to make sure he knew where she stood, in case he had the urge to kiss her again, thinking it would lead to something more.

"Since we're friends now," he said, flashing the most gorgeous smile down at her. "Can I pick you up tomorrow to go zip lining?"

"I'm scared of heights," she said, putting some distance between them on the lounger.

"I won't let anything happen to you. Besides, I need a break from the guys."

"I need one also from the girls."

"So does that mean you're going?" He pleaded with his eyes.

"Okay…I'll go, but you better not let anything happen to me." She nudged him on the arm as they laughed and made plans to meet for their outing on tomorrow. A day away from the girls maybe what she needed, and spending it with the gorgeous man next to her was even better.

*****

Wyatt felt as though he was going to jump out of his skin with excitement. Joi had accepted his invite to go zip lining with him. He would walk on a bed of fire before allowing anything to happen to her. Her warm and engaging smile told him that she was a good woman. The perfect woman for a man like him to settle down, have children and to grow old with, but she only offered him friendship and nothing more.

His ex-wife had really done a number on him as far as trust was concerned. Nevertheless, he was ready to take another shot at love. She had left him for a doctor, stating that he was all the man that Wyatt was not. He may not have a lot of money, but her needs were taken care of; however, according to Trina, his best wasn't good enough.

With a little prayer, Wyatt had intended to win Joi over. Friendship wasn't going to be enough for him, especially with a woman like her.

He stood up from the lounger and then pulled Joi up afterwards. "Thanks for agreeing to spend tomorrow with me," he said, straightening his shirts. "It seems that Jett and I have done nothing but, butt heads since arriving in Jamaica."

"The same with Tara and me. We have never seen eye to eye on things, but this trip is turning more into a nightmare than pleasure," she snorted, stretching her neck to look up at him. "She and the girls are leaving tomorrow morning, heading to Ocho Rios, but I decided to stay behind."

This is my lucky day. That was good news for Wyatt. It gave them more time to be together. Since things weren't going as planned with the boys, he could spend the remainder of his stay with her. "If you don't mind me asking, why aren't you going?"

"I'm not much of a partier. I guess they are sick of me blocking their fun with the male natives," she forced a weak smile. "They said that I'm old-fashioned, and the crime shows that I watch, have made me paranoid. Everybody isn't who they profess to be."

"Yeah, you're right. You can't be too careful." He scratched his head. "The fellas tell me that I'm too old school for them." Her face had a look of surprise. "Regardless of what women think, every man isn't into sleeping around."

Wyatt loved the idea of being in a committed relationship. His ex-wife led him to believe that she wanted the same thing. Later, to learn that she had high hopes of him running the fire station where he worked. When he didn't meet her expectation, she left, ending their five year union.

"Since the girls are leaving, it will give me enough time to learn more of Jamaica's rich history. They only care about half-naked men streaking up and down the island anyway."

They both laugh.

"Well, beautiful lady, I better let you go before your friends put out a missing person report on you," he joked, trying hard not to scoop her up into his arms to kiss those tempting, plumped lips of hers.

Her cheeks reddened at his sentiments. He meant every word. Her natural beauty shone through her pint-sized frame. "Yes, I better head back. Though, I doubt that they miss me."

He wanted to tell her that he already missed her, although she hadn't left. A goodbye kiss was out of the question, he didn't want to risk what was blossoming between them. Something was happening— something much more precious than vacationing in the Caribbean. Whether Joi wanted to admit it or not, he discerned that she had feelings for him just as he had for her.

Chapter Twenty-Six

"We'll see you later tonight, Old Maid," Tara quipped as the three hugged and kissed Joi goodbye. "Are you sure about staying here alone?"

"For crying-out-loud," Joi stressed with her hand propped on her hip. "Yes, I'm sure. Trust me. I will not be sitting around in this room twiddling my fingers waiting for you all to return. Now go." She pushed them out the door. She hadn't told them about her going zip lining with Wyatt. Suspicion would have ruled their naughty little minds, activating their amateurish detective skills. She didn't want them to read more into her and Wyatt's friendship than they already had.

Locking the door after the girls had left for a day in Ocho Rios, Joi made ready for her day with the sexy fireman. She said it once, she'd say it again, "With Wyatt's looks and tone built, he could have easily graced one of those pin-up calendars for firemen." He was just that gorgeous.

Sincerity peered through those seductive eyes of his, but a girl could not be too careful when it came to the affairs of the heart. She gave herself a 'once over' in the full-length mirror, and then sauntered out the door for what she hoped to be a magical filled day.

*****

Peering out the window as he sat in the lobby of the resort, Wyatt meditated on how blessed he was. Excited wasn't the word to express his feelings. Today had arrived. He and Joi were really going to go zip-lining.

He reached in his shirt pocket and pulled out his cellphone. Wyatt punched in Joi's cellphone number to let her know that he was waiting for her downstairs. As the phone rang, he felt a tap on his shoulder, causing him to abruptly disconnect the call.

"Hey, You," Joi greeted with a smile that could brighten any man's day.

With the reflexes of a grasshopper, he leaped from his seat, giving her a warm embrace. The khaki shorts she wore, showed off her shapely legs. Her *Asics* tennis shoes told him that she came prepared for their hike through the jungle. The white t-shirt she wore that read, "I'm a survivor" brought a smile to his face. A woman after his own heart; indeed she had been a survivor.

"Good morning." He could feel his eyes dancing around in their sockets when he stared down at her. Even dressed down, she looked scrumptious. "I like a woman who's on time."

"You said to meet you downstairs at 8:30 am to catch the shuttle bus," she said, adjusting her Fanny Pac around her slender waist.

"Women are known to be late." He knew before the words left his mouth that he'd said the wrong thing.

She coughed and then gave him a sidelong glance, letting him know that his choice of words did not set too well with her.

"Allow me to rephrase that statement. Some women are known to be late." He wiped his brow. He had managed to dodge the bullet this time. Wyatt made a mental note to choose his words carefully the next time. He wanted to win her heart, not run her off before he had a chance to do so.

"Yes, get that straight. I don't want to be lumped into a category with every woman." She folded her arms, giving him a halfcocked looked.

"I like that." he smiled. "A woman who isn't afraid to standup for herself." She was small in height but stood tall in the confidence department.

"Don't let my size fool you. I'm no push over." When she craned her neck up at him after her sassy remark, Wyatt swore that he was staring in the face of an angel. Beautiful, yet simple, the type of woman he desired to make his.

Two hours later, they stood in the middle of the rain forest. A certified canopy specialist led them and the others on a hike through trees as high as the heavens. Words could not describe the oneness he felt with nature. The look on Joi's face said that she had felt the same. Every step of their walk, she became more and more captivated at nature's wonder.

"Wyatt, this place is heavenly," she said, taking in every inch of her surroundings.

He had hit a home run, inviting her to experience the Caribbean jungle with him. "Never in a million years would I have considered hiking in the Jamaican Jungle exhilarating." The awe in her eyes made him want to love her with every inch of his being. Her attraction toward the simple things in life told him she was the one. She may not be his as of yet, but his spiritual heart told him that she would be.

He that finds a wife finds a good thing, he mumbled to himself. And he most definitely has found his good thing.

They continued on their path and eventually made their way upon the deck to zip line through the foliage they had just journeyed through. The canopy specialist announced that they would experience nature from an entirely different view. Moments after the instructor explained to them the safety rules, Joi held on to Wyatt's arm for dear life.

"It's okay." He wrapped his arms around her shoulders. "I promise that I won't let anything happen to you." He pulled her back, cupped her face into his hands, looked square into her terrified eyes, and said, "Cross my heart. I'll be right behind you."

A tall, dark-skinned, lanky native snapped her in and sent her zipping through the jungle. Her screaming stopped midways down her cruising. As she began to look down at the trees, she tossed her head back in laughter.

Now it was his turn.

With a new appreciation for gravity, Wyatt watched as Joi breathed a sigh of relief to have her feet planted safely on the ground. He wanted to go again, and talked her into going for a second round.

Their jungle excursion had come to a close, and Wyatt had to think of something and fast to keep their day from ending.

"Once in town, let's catch a cab and grab a bite to eat?" His chest tightened, hoping that she wouldn't say no. Sucking in his breath, he waited for her answer.

"Sounds great, I'm famished." She rubbed her belly.

Happy for the time he'd spent with her made the bumpy ride back to the resort more bearable. The bus was congested, which made it hard to hear, let alone talk. So, he and his zip lining buddy took in the scenery on the way back in town.

Later, they each retreated to their own domicile, freshened up and headed for a late lunch. The cab driver stopped in front of a popular tourist attraction, Margaretville. "Wow, we have to take pictures of this place before leaving," Wyatt said, paying the cab driver before exiting the vehicle.

"The others are missing out." She took hold of Wyatt's extended hand and exited the cab. "This place is called, "The Hip Strip." I read it in the brochure."

He loved her child like enthusiasm when it came to experiencing the Caribbean's attraction and history. There wasn't a snooty bone in her body as it'd been with Trina. Instead of embracing new things, she thumbed her nose up at it. "I heard the food is to die for." They rushed inside to indulge in the Jamaica's cuisine.

"As hungry as I am, I could eat everything on the menu," she snorted, glancing wild eyed throughout the place.

"Unless you're planning on washing dishes for our supper, I think you better take it slow and easy on the food." He squeezed her hands in a friendly gesture. "I didn't bring enough money to pay for every item on the menu."

They laughed.

"Oh, don't worry. I'll spot you a couple of dollars."

"Beautiful and has her own money. I like that," he teased as they found a nice cozy table in the corner of the restaurant.

After they finished their meals, the two decided to stroll down Gloucester Avenue. The sun began to beat down on them, but they continued in their sightseeing. Wyatt was glad he'd left his buddies to hang out with Joi. Like a hungry pack of blood thirsty wolves, they were on a mission to seek and conquer any woman on the island that gave them attention. There was more to explore in Jamaica than that.

Wherever the boys were, he hoped that Jett was behaving. Keeping tabs on him and his explosive behavior made for a full-time job. He had grown tired of being responsible for him. If only Wyatt hadn't made that stupid mistake, then he wouldn't feel that he owed him. Wyatt tried blotting that dreadful night out, but Jett would never allow him to forget it.

"Joi, since your friends are not coming back until in the morning..." he stopped.

She raised her freshly arched brows at his unfinished statement.

"Would you come and join me on a buggy ride later tonight?" Why was he freaking out? He'd asked women out before. "I don't want to hang out with the guys. Their lifestyle is a little too fast pace for me."

"I'd love to, Wyatt. Today was the best."

"Thank you," he smiled.

"For what?" she asked. Her eyes dancing in surprise as they walked back to Margaretville.

"For not shooting me down," he said, waving for a cab.

"You're good company. Besides, it's refreshing to know that I don't have to worry about you taking advantage of me."

"I do like you Joi, but I would never do any such thing. My mom would slap the taste out of my mouth if she knew that I even came close to mistreating a woman."

The cab pulled up and took them back to the resort. When Wyatt made it to his room, there was no sign of his roommates.

"Good," he whispered under his breath as he quickly freshened up and dashed out before they returned.

He wasn't in the mood for explaining where he'd been to a bunch of knuckle heads. They would never believe that he and Joi were just hanging out as friends. He was happy that they were getting to know each other. Maybe, she would eventually see that he was a good man and give him the chance to love her.

Chapter Twenty-Seven

In the worse Jamaican accent she'd ever heard, Wyatt said, "Hi, pre-tee ladie, don't you look beau-tee-ful this evening." Walking toward her wearing a huge grin on his face, he handed her a bouquet of flowers.

"Oh, Wyatt, you shouldn't have." She held them in her arms as if she was Miss America, accepting her crown. Dipping her nose into the array of flowers, she inhaled their intoxicating fragrance. "Thank you. They are lovely."

"Not as lovely as you." Under his intense stare, she fidgeted with the plastic surrounding the bouquet.

Feeling the heat rushing to her cheeks, she struggled to find her voice. If she ever decided to married or date again, he would be the type of man she chose. "Uh... thanks. You didn't have to say that."

"But I wanted too."

Although he had promised to keep his hands to himself, he reneged on his word. Wyatt pulled her into his embrace. "I want to kiss you, Joi. It's all I've been thinking about since we parted earlier."

She closed her eyes when his powerful hand stroked against her cheek. If memory served her right, they were friends. They had not crossed over to lovers, but she felt a connection with him, a connection that scared her to death.

"Wh-aa-at," she stuttered. Oh *Lord! What am I getting myself into?*

Ready or not, Wyatt bent down and joined his lips to hers. She wanted to faint right then and there. When he walked her back to her room earlier today, she wanted to revoke their friendship agreement just to feel his lips against hers one last time. She was disappointed when he did not try to make a move on her.

Like a flint, Wyatt lit her fire each time he came near her, but she wasn't the right woman for him. He needed someone that could give him her whole heart, because she was unable to give him hers. Michael's spirit seemed to consume her entire being. Yes, he was dead, but her heart continued to ache for him. The way he touched her, even his smell still possessed her.

"You can slap me now." Through labored breathing, he struggled to speak when their lips parted. "It was worth it."

When he lifted her face to his, she was sure he could see the uncertainty in her eyes.

"We better get going," was all she could think to say. Her loyalty lied with a dead man. Michael was the first and last man that ever touched her. How could she forget what they had? Now, Wyatt had entered her life, causing confusion and doubt.

He released her. "I want you to be mine, Joi." He stopped, took a deep gulp. "I will do everything within my power to prove that I am the right man for you."

"I love my husband."

With the tip of his finger he rubbed her chin, and said, "I know you do, but it doesn't take away the fact that I want to be with you." A galloping noise caused them to turn their attention towards the resort's large glass window. The driver for their buggy ride had parked out front. How was she going to concentrate on their ride around Jamaica with the confession he'd just laid on her?

"That's our buggy," she said; trying to act calm, but deep down inside she was downright terrified.

"So, it is." He looped her arm through his and escorted her out the double glass doors.

*****

The weather had proven to be perfect for a ride under the stars. If only he could convince Joi that they were good for each other, the night would be even better, but, he didn't want to appear insensitive.

Her husband was dead. He is alive and breathing, he screamed inside.

"The island is beautiful. Thanks for the invite," she said without bothering to look at him.

"Is something wrong? You've been quiet throughout the entire ride." He knew his straightforwardness back at the resort's lobby put her on edge. Heck, he was tired of playing it safe. Where had it gotten him, nowhere? Back at home, his take it slow attitude always gave Jett the room he needed to move in on his territory, but not this time. "I didn't mean to make you nervous or put you in a weird position, but I meant every word I said."

"I know you did, Wyatt. That's why I don't want to lead you on." Her voice barely above a whisper as the noise from the buggy ride threatened to drown her out. "But—"

"But what?" He interrupted. "Joi, you can't live the rest of your life in the past. You're a young, vibrant woman. You have a lot of living ahead of you." Frustrated, he sat back against his seat like a brooding child.

"I don't expect you to understand." With her hands folded in her lap, she exhaled an exasperated moan. "True, you lost your wife, but she is still alive. My family is dead." She burst into tears, causing him to feel horrible.

"Calm down. I'm sorry. I didn't mean to make you cry." Pulling her tiny body into him, he rested his chin against the side of her head. "It's going to be alright, baby." He did his best to console her with no success. He figured she just needed a good, hard cry.

Later, she pulled herself together and apologized for her temporary breakdown. "I feel like a fool," she expressed through her red, puffy eyes.

"You're not a fool, Joi. You won't allow yourself to get pass the grieving stage." He wiped her tears away with the side of his thumb. "You really need to talk to a grief counselor."

"My mother made me an appointment to see one when the accident first happened. I was still in the denial stage and thought that I could handle it better on my own."

"Well, I'm no expert, but your way hasn't worked." A bump in the road made them pop up in their seats, causing spontaneous laughter between them, which lightened the mood. "If you ever care to continue this conversation, I'm here."

"Thank you. I didn't mean to ruin our scenic ride."

"Just to be close to you made the ride enjoyable for me." With that being said, he ran his hands through her short curls and kissed her. Without making any apologies for his actions, he expressed his love for her. She did not resist and he didn't stop. She wanted him. He knew that with every fiber in his body. A woman as reserved as Joi would never allow a man to touch her, let alone kiss her, if she was not into him.

Chapter Twenty-Eight

For the second time today, Wyatt had walked Joi safely to her door. The passionate kiss he'd laid on her during their buggy ride left no doubt about his feelings for her. She wanted to fall in love again and have more kids before her biological clock ran out, but how was she supposed to move on? Joi believed that she would be abandoning the kids she'd lost.

With mixed emotions swirling in her head and a man who was more than willing to love her with no strings attached, frightened her. "I told you I could have seen myself up to my room." She turned the key in the lock, cracking the door halfway open, not wanting him to get the wrong impression.

"I'll feel better knowing that you were safe inside, since your friends haven't returned from Ocho Rios." He leaned against the wall with his hands in his pockets, looking delicious as ever.

"That's sweet of you." Knowing she had no right to expect it, but Joi hoped that Wyatt would kiss her good night. He was definitely in the right line of work. Each kiss they shared had been sizzling, red hot and she wanted to continue to burn in his flames.

"I want to see more of you when this trip is over. My head is clear. I'm not caught up in the whole Jamaica aura." He ran the tip of his fingers seductively down her sleeveless arm, which ignited unspeakable flames within her.

"Do you have any feelings for me, Joi?" he asked, moving his hand to stroke each of her cheeks.

His straight-to-the-point questions made her uneasy. "I don't know." She dropped her head. He was slowly drawing her in with his goodness. *Maybe he is too good for me*, she thought.

"I'm not going to hold you hostage in the hallway. But please, seriously give some thought to my questions. Okay?" With his thumb, he stroked the corners of her mouth, and then kissed her good night, which she desperately hoped for but wouldn't dare admit.

"Mmm, mmm," she moaned as he worked his magic with his mouth. Right then and there, she knew that she was in trouble. This sultry, sexy fireman was slowly burning his way into her heart. When their lips parted, her eyes stayed shut, basking in the sensation his flaming, hot kiss had left on her.

Wyatt broke the silence. "I better get going." But, his eyes said differently. He wasn't ready for the night to end, and neither was she. "Joi, I'd like to talk more about you and your loss. It pains me to leave you like this, knowing that you're hurting."

"What difference will it make?" She opened the door wider, gesturing for him to come inside. Although, she did not know any of the tourists staying at the resort, she did not want them overhearing their conversation as they stood in the hallway.

"Healing begins by talking and accepting what has happened" He made himself comfortable in a chair that one of the girls failed to put back at the dining table.

"You know how many people have tried to help me?" she snorted, feeling pity for herself. "Even my girlfriends have, by inviting me on this trip. Nothing has worked." She walked over to the refrigerator and took out two bottles of water and handed him one with a napkin. She then, took a seat on the sofa away from him. "Unless you have some kind of magic pill to cure me, then talking about it won't help."

"Don't say that. We're friends now, and friends would do anything to help each other."

"Friends, uh?" She took a sip of her drink to wet her parched mouth. "Why do you care what happens to me," she asked, suspicion rising in her.

"I'm physically and spiritually drawn to you." He stood from his seat, leaving his drink behind to sit next to her on the sofa.

Her body stiffened as he neared. Michael had told her the very same thing when they met in college. "I'm not ready to love again. What don't you understand?" This time, she tried to sound more convincing.

"I hear what your lips are saying, but you heart says differently."

"And just what does my heart say?"

"You want the type of love and relationship you once had with your husband. But you don't know how to let go of the past to start anew." He scooted to the edge of the sofa to face her directly, which caused her breathing to increase. "Joi, I want to be that man. A woman like you doesn't come my way very often. After my bitter divorce, I lost trust in women. Then I met you, and I let down my guard. I see something special in you."

"Me?" she questioned, pointing at herself.

"Yes, beautiful lady. You." He lifted her hand to his soft, sensual lips and kissed it.

Why can't you be Michael saying these things to me? She removed her hand from his and placed it back into her lap.

"Tell me the entire story about your family's accident, Joi. I know you didn't share everything with me back home or on the beach."

When she opened her mouth, the story of her husband and her sons' fatal crash gushed from her lips like water spewing out of a fire hose. She had his undivided attention as he listened to her story. He messaged her hand each time he thought that she was going to fall apart. No doubt, she was bitter to say the least.

"How awful," he exclaimed after hearing her story. "Have you tried reaching out to the young lady responsible for the crash? I'm sure she's just as torn up about the incident."

"For what?" She looked up at him as if he had cursed her out. "Rebekah is still alive and able to live her life. I believe that anyone who text or drive drunk, deserves the toughest penalty the law allows," she said matter-of-factly.

"Joi!" Shocked filled his face. "Are you serious?"

What's with the uneasy look on his face? As soon as I mentioned drunk driving, his entire expression changed.

Anyway, she brushed it off, believing her anger had her seeing things. "That girl took everything away from me." She jumped from the sofa, hating she had ever invited him in.

"This explains everything—"

"Explains what!" she shouted, cutting him off. Unable to control her anger, she wept. Out of all the people she'd told her story to, she thought at least he would understand her bitterness. With his ex-wife's deception, surely he remembered what it was like to have everything taken away from him in a blink of an eye. "Because of that, girl, I have nothing." Leaning against the dining room counter top, she balled her eyes out.

He came up behind her, spun her around and consoled her. With her head buried in his chest, he said, "Forgiveness heals the hurt." He held the sides of her face into his strong hands, lifting it toward his. "You will never get pass what happened, until you go to the young lady and let her know that you have forgiven her. She has reached out to you on several occasions. Don't you think that she might have some guilt about the accident? Going to her will free you as well as her."

"I can't." She muffled in his shirt. "I'm still angry with her."

"You are a Christian, Joi. You are supposed to be bigger than that."

"I'm also human."

*****

"Man, where have you been?" Jett questioned when Wyatt walked in their room.

"I had to get away for a while," he lied. Truth was, his friends harassing the native women were getting on his last nerve and he wanted no part of it. Besides, he had his sights on one American beauty that no island woman could compare to.

"Well, you missed the best pool party ever. Women were all over us," Seth said, giving Jett and Paul and high-five.

"If we had known that you were going to hide away like an old hermit, we would have left you at home," Paul added as he toweled dried his hair. "Have you had any fun since landing in Jamaica?"

If only they knew how much fun he had. The trip had proved to be everything he had hoped it would be and more. Next thing on his agenda was to help Joi believe that she deserved to be happy. She would make him the perfect mate. If ditching his friends meant increasing his chances at another shot at love, then it would be well worth it.

Wyatt marveled at the fact that neither of his friends had ever experienced true love. He had no plans of allowing Joi to slip through his fingers. No matter what it took, he was determined to win her love. The hardest part was getting her to see that her deceased husband and kids wouldn't want her to live the rest of her life mourning them.

"Don't assume that I was sitting idly at the resort." A mischievous grin eased onto his face.

"Then, who were you with?" Jett popped him across the back with his towel.

Paul and Seth looked on, waiting in suspense on his answer.

"That's none of your business." With that being said, Wyatt grabbed his shaving kit off the dresser and disappeared into the bathroom.

Jett yelled behind him. "Well, be that way. Keep your invisible women to yourself."

Chapter Twenty-Nine

"Is this what you've been doing since we left?" Tara interrogated Joi after finding her lying in bed when she and the girls returned from their trip the next morning.

"No, I had a long day yesterday and got in pretty late last night," she said, sitting up.

Her heart-to-heart talk with Wyatt had lasted until the wee hours of the morning and she was worn out. She did seem to feel better, but his advice about going to see Rebekah, the teen who killed her family was out of the question.

"Girl, Ocho Rios lived up to its name." Tara showed off her dance moves, prancing around her bed.

"Where are Becky and Albre?" She raised her head, looking around the room.

"Sleep. They are just as bad as you," she grunted. "They can't hang with the big dawgs. They were ready to head back to the resort last night before midnight."

"See, I knew better, Joi laughed. "I don't know where you get your energy from. Nobody can keep up with you."

She had lain in the bed long enough. It was time that she and the others pack up to head back home. The trip taught her a lot about herself and helped her to do some major soul searching, but a relationship with Wyatt was out of the question. His job was a major concern of hers. In less than twenty-four hours, the spell she'd been under would be broken. Who was she kidding; she and Wyatt did not stand a chance of being together once they arrive back to Shreveport?

"What did you do yesterday, Missy?" Tara questioned.

"Wyatt and I hung out the entire day," Joi said, grabbing a towel out the towel closet and her bath caddie.

Tara screamed from the top of her lungs. "I knew your little sneaky behind had a reason for staying behind." She followed Joi into the bathroom. "So, what did the two of you do?"

"Hold on one minute," she said, placing the caddie next to the shower. "I don't do one nightstands, if that what you're implying."

If any of the girls knew her, it was Tara. Friends since high school, she knew better than anyone that she was not that type of person. Having casual sex wasn't in her DNA. Joi kicked Tara out of the bathroom, locking the door behind her.

Yelling through the door, she said, "I hoped the two of you did more than just talk."

*****

Later that night, the girls decided to go out in the town. It was their last night in the Caribbean and they wanted to make it a memorable one. The four were dressed to impress, as they strolled into a popular Jamaican nightclub. Once inside, they found a table in the center of the room and made themselves comfortable.

"This place is jumping," Tara said, bobbing her head to the sounds of Reggae music blasting from the speakers as natives and tourist showed off their best moves.

"It most certainly is," Albre said.

"Joi, are you okay?" Becky asked. "You're not going to Hell just because you are in a nightclub."

They laughed.

"I've never been better." She joined in on the fun. It was their last night on the island and she had no plans of ruining things. "Stop worrying about me and let's go and enjoy ourselves."

"Now that's the Joi, I remember," Tara said, snapping her fingers.

For the first time since the loss of her family, she felt alive. Surprisingly, she was having a great time. Several gentlemen came to their table and asked them to dance. She noticed Tara, and the others cutting their eyes in her direction. Not wanting to spoil the mood of the night, she took hold of one of the gentlemen's hand and danced her way, centered stage to the dance floor.

*****

"Wyatt, isn't that your girl out there on the dance floor with some Jamaican rough-neck?" Jett so eagerly pointed out. "If you need me to, I will gladly go punch his lights out."

"Are you crazy?" Wyatt pressed a hand on Jett's chest, holding him in place.

"Do you stir up trouble everywhere you go?" Paul demanded. "Chill, Bro."

"Yeah, chill," Seth echoed. "A woman is not a man's property. You need to get that through that thick skull of yours."

"If she wants to be with me, then she belongs to me," Jett so arrogantly said, knocking Wyatt's hand away from his chest.

"Man, don't come here with all that," Wyatt advised. "This is our last night in Jamaica. Try having a good time without getting fired up.

"Whatever." Jett walked off, leaving the three of them standing in the middle of the crowded nightclub.

Joi did look amazing out there on the dance floor, and she seemed to be really enjoying herself with her dance partner. How he wished it was him out there dancing the night away with her. Paul and Seth left him to search for a vacant table. As for Jett, Wyatt could have cared less where he ran off to.

Unable to take his eyes off Joi, desire consumed him. He wanted her and had failed at convincing her to give him a chance. Jealousy lit within him. He wanted to storm over to where they were dancing and barge in, but, he wasn't that type of man.

"Is that all you're going to do tonight? Spy on Joi dancing with her, Jamaica Lover?" Jett teased, trying to push Wyatt's buttons.

"You're back, uh?" he asked, never taking his eyes off Joi. From the look on her face, she didn't seem to have a care in the world. Just last night she was balling her eyes out, and now, she appeared to be enjoying herself −without him.

"What is it with you and that nurse? Can't you see that she doesn't want you?" A smirk lined Jett's trouble making face.

"That's enough." Anger began to brew inside Wyatt. "What's with you?"

"You owe me, remember," he threatened through clenched teeth.

"If I had known that you were going to hold my mistake over my head, I would have just gone to jail." Jett had become a thorn in Wyatt's side. "Besides, you took the wrap for me. Remember, I was out cold. You made the decision to protect me, I didn't ask for your help."

"I lost an opportunity to be promoted by covering for your behind. Had I known that helping you would destroy me, I would have left you that night to defend for yourself." The venom oozed from Jett's mouth with everyone word he spoke.

"If that's the reason for your foul moods, then, I'll go and turn myself in," he said, "But I'll be darn, if I will allow you to continue to hold this over my head."

"If you do that, then we'll both be kicked off of the fire department." Jett began to change his tune. "Forget it, let's go and find the others.

Wyatt grabbed Jett by the arm and said, "For the record, don't ever try strong-arming me again."

They found a vacant table not too far from the girls. Wyatt watched as the gentleman Joi was dancing with escorted her back to her seat. He froze when the guy with dreads kissed the back of her hand. The 'green-eyed' monster rose inside of him. Like lightening, he shot from his seat, leaving his friends to head to Joi's table.

He cleared his throat to get her attention "I see you and your girls had the same idea as me and the guys."

"Wyatt...hi." Her face told him that she was surprised to see him there. "Have a seat. The girls are out on the dance floor."

"You seem to be in a better mood?" His eyes combed her from head to toe. She was sexier than he'd last remembered. The mini-shirt fitted the contours of her petite frame. Her stilettoes complimented her shapely legs. He began to envy her deceased husband. He had the pleasure to be with a woman as graceful as she.

"I am," she said, giving him the most gorgeous smile.

"I'd like to think that I had something to do with that?" He sat next to her, fishing for answers that he already knew.

"You did." She touched his face, which brought a smile upon his. Maybe he didn't know the answers.

"Let's dance?" She stood, tugging at his arms.

"Sure." What else was he going to say? If she had asked him to swim across the Caribbean Sea with her, he would. He just wanted to be in her presence.

He came to the nightclub to hang-out with his boys before leaving for home tomorrow. But he knew they would understand him ditching them to be with the woman who had been taking up the idle space in his head. He'd missed out on exploring most of the attractions on the island. Maybe, just maybe, he and Joi could return and explore the island together without the interruption of friends.

With a little help from above, anything is possible.

Chapter Thirty

Joi did a clean sweep throughout their room at the resort. The last thing she wanted to do was leave any valuables behind. It was time to pack up and head back home to her hectic life as an emergency room nurse. Truly, the last seven days for her had been a dream, but now it was time to wake up and get back to reality.

Tara and the girls were smart. They packed last night before going out on the town. Now, she wished had done the same. She didn't realize how much stuff she'd purchased. Her suitcase was stuffed as she tried her best to close it. Giving up, she grabbed one of Becky's empty bags and placed her things inside it.

The girls were downstairs in the dining room, eating breakfast before heading to the airport in two hours. She left the room to join them, because her stomach had a war erupting inside her from hunger. As she headed where they were seated, she wondered if Wyatt and his friends had left the island. Last night had been a blast, but something troubled her about Wyatt and Jett's relationship. The two seemed to be at odds with each other quite a bit. Well, their friendship was not for her to judge.

"I hope ya'll left me something to eat," Joi teased, noticing the stack of food packed on their plates.

"Yes, Smarty Pants, we left enough for you," Tara said, tossing her braids off her shoulders.

"Have you finished packing?" Albre asked.

"Yes, I am. I didn't realize how much stuff I bought." Joi grabbed a pitcher filled with orange juice and poured herself a glass. Thankfully, the girls knew what she liked to eat and had her plate already prepared for her.

Becky kept watching Joi as if she had something on her mind.

Joi tore into her breakfast, trying her best to avoid Becky's probing eyes. Whatever was bothering her, she wished she'd just ask, because the constant staring was getting on her nerves.

"Is there something wrong, Becky?" Joi inquired, tired of her friend's piercing blue eyes cutting into her like razors.

"Yes, there is something wrong. Why are you keeping you and Wyatt's relationship a secret?"

"What?" Joi gasped. "There is no relationship."

"Well, from the look of things last night, something is going on," Becky snapped.

"We were wondering when you were going to come clean with us." Albre added her two cents as Tara, the instigator behind the entire conversation sat back and watched. Joi was no fool. Tara had them doing her dirty work.

"Just so the three of you will know, there is nothing going on between Wyatt and I." Joi tried her best to get her point over to them.

"Jett said the both of you have been sneaking around the entire time on this trip," Tara commented.

"He what?" Joi shouted, trying her best to contain her anger. She'd lost her appetite and pushed her plate aside. "I can't believe that he would make up of such a lie."

"What do you expect us to believe with your disappearing acts? Then, when we left to visit Ocho Rios you stayed behind," Tara added.

"Wyatt and I are friends and nothing more," Joi corrected. "I expected better from the three of you. I'm not that type of person."

"Well, if you weren't prancing around being so secretive, our overactive imaginations would've never started to run wild," Becky responded.

"I guess you're right," Joi said.

"No, I know we are right," Tara barked.

So, that little weasel, Jett had been going around spreading lies about her and Wyatt. Her first mind told her that he was trouble. Wyatt better watch his back. With a friend like Jett, he was liable to end up in a lot of trouble hanging around him. One thing Joi hated and that was to be lied on.

She and Wyatt had a great time in Jamaica. He expressed his feeling for her, but he could've just been caught up in the moment. The island seemed to have that effect on them. When things get back to normal once they arrive home, who knows, none of their paths may ever cross again.

*****

"Earth to Wyatt." Paul snapped his fingers, drawing Wyatt back from his secret thoughts of the woman he'd spent several glorious days with in the Caribbean. His friends had no clue how lovesick he was. He wanted to see her before heading back home, but as luck would have it, she and her friends had already left the island early that morning.

The airplane couldn't get him back to Shreveport fast enough. If he didn't learn anything else in Jamaica, he learned not to sit back and allow love to pass him by. It may take months, even years, but he was determine to make Joi his.

"I'm awake," Wyatt exclaimed, rubbing his eyes.

"Man, you look as if you've lost your last friend in the world?"

More like best girl in the world.

"No, Just thinking about what I have to do when I get back home," Wyatt said.

"I hear you, man." Paul eased back into his aisle seat on the plane.

Jett and Seth were two seats behind them. Wyatt craned his neck and found Jett up to his old tricks. He had his sights on the flight attendants. Blinded by his charmed as most women were, they catered to him. Wyatt tuned back in his seat, shaking his head.

Never again would Wyatt travel across the seas with Jett. His over-the-top attitude had proven to be too much for him to deal with. He needed help. Wyatt's part-time job as a paramedic had taught him how to watch for signs of those suffering from post-traumatic stress syndrome. Jett's self-destructive behavior fits the category. If he didn't love him like a brother, he would leave him to his own devices. Love suffers long and he knew that dealing with Jett, there were going to be some long days ahead when trying to convince him to get help.

"I see you and Becky hit it off." Wyatt broke the silence to get his mind off Jett.

"Yeah...so have you and Joi," Paul added. "What's going on between the two of you?"

"Not as much as I would like," Wyatt grunted at the sound of his words. Convincing Joi to give him a chance had proven to be the hardest thing he'd ever done. His heart did break for her and what she had endured, but her choice to remain faithful to a dead man made no sense to him. She was in the prime of her life and letting it pass by because of her loyalty to her deceased husband. Just the thought of it drove him crazy.

"What do you mean by that?" Paul sat up in his seat to face Wyatt.

"Just between us, I care a lot about her."

"But?"

"She's in love with her husband."

"I thought her husband was dead?"

"He is."

"Whew. Man, you had me worried there for a second." Paul breathed a sigh of relief. "You're not the type to go into another man's territory."

"I'm in love with her." There, Wyatt finally told one of his friends, his true feeling about Joi.

"Woe-ee-ee, hold on using the "L" word."

"I don't expect you to understand. When fate sends the right person your way, then you'll know what I'm talking about."

"I just don't want you to rush into things too fast. Remember what happened with your first married." Paul gave him a scolding eye.

"Trust me, I've learned my lesson. There is no comparison when it comes to Joi and Trina."

"You have my blessings, man," Paul said, shaking Wyatt's hand.

"Thanks, that means a lot." Of all his friends, Paul was the most leveled headed one next to Seth. If ever he needed a miracle or a blessing, it was now. He had exhausted every plan on how to win Joi's heart. How could he compete with a dead man?

Chapter Thirty-One

Two weeks had passed since arriving from the Caribbean and Wyatt hasn't heard or seen Joi. He occasionally stopped by the cafeteria, hoping to run into her, but like a ghost, she was nowhere to be found. He didn't want to appear as a stalker, so he stopped combing the hallways of the hospital looking for her.

Today, he ate his lunch with the other firemen at the station. A home cooked meal was just what he needed. Jamaica's dining was everything he thought and hoped it would be, but he had to start back exercising and eating healthier to be fit to help put out fires and save lives.

"Welcome back, Mr. Payne," one of the rookie firemen slapped him on the shoulder as he sat next to him at the table.

"Thanks," he said, looking up from his plate.

"Have you considered applying for the chief position again?" The young man asked. "Word has it that Chief Roy has accepted a position in Dallas, Texas, his hometown."

"I have mix feelings about it." A flashback of the night he made the worst mistake of his life came crashing into his mind. He wanted the position, but feared that Jett might come forward about what happened that night and ruin his chances to apply for it.

"I hope you do, Sir." A sincere look shone on the young man's face. "I have a lot of respect for you and your values. You will lead this department in the right direction."

"Well, thanks for the vote of confidence." The rookie fireman's kind words touched Wyatt. Everyone make mistakes and he decided at that moment to give it a shot. If that night in question comes up in the media, than he'd just have to face it head on.

His record over the years was exemplary. He'd gone beyond the call of duty. So, why shouldn't he go after the position? Jett had to be insane to believe that his taking the blame for Wyatt had cost him that same position when he was never qualified for it, but, somewhere in his egotistical mind he thought he was deserving of it. Deciding to let the chips fall where they may, Wyatt tossed Jett and his erratic behavior out of his mind. He was tired of kissing up to his, *friend*, a word he began to use loosely when describing Jett.

Throughout the day, thoughts of Joi ran through his mind; the only thing that kept him sane was work. He did any and everything to distract himself from daydreaming about her, but nothing seemed to work, which drove him crazy. *Where is she?* He combed a hand through his freshly cut hair. Hating to admit it to himself, he was in love with everything about her.

He could spend the rest of his life with a woman like her, but her grief kept her from seeing him for who he was. From her dimpled smile to the sadness in her eyes had touched his soul. He wanted her and would stop at nothing to convince her to take a chance on him.

The alarm screamed throughout the station, alerting him that it was back to business. He ran and grabbed his gear, said a small prayer as usual when heading out to fight a fire, big or small. He understood Joi's concerns about the dangers that came with his job. She would not be human if she didn't, but to allow it to get in the way of experiencing real love, left him confused.

*****

Joi checked in on her last patient before her shift ended. She left the room, communicated with the incoming nurse about which medications she'd given, retrieved her personal belongings and headed out to the parking lot. Before she could unlock her door with the remote control, a male voice startled her.

"You are a hard woman to track down," Wyatt said, carrying a dozen of red roses in his hand.

Clutching her chest, she turned to face him. "If I had a Taser, you would have been flopping on the payment like a fish. You scared me." She lightly punched him on the arm.

"I've missed you." He shuffled his feet, his nervousness could be felt. "Oh…here, these are for you." He handed her the flowers.

"Thank you. You didn't have to do that, Wyatt." She inhaled the freshly cut bouquet. "I'm surprise security didn't get you for loitering," she joked.

"Remember, I'm a regular here. They know my face." He flashed a harmless smile. "I've been stopping by during lunch hours, hoping that I would run into you."

"Since arriving back from the trip, I've been working double shifts. We are short on nurses in the ER." She shifted the flowers in her arms.

"For a minute there, I thought that you were trying to avoid me." He moved in closer to her and stroked her cheeks. "Have you eaten dinner yet? If not, I would love to take you out."

"No, I haven't."

"We can go to Giuseppe's. I'll follow you there."

"Sounds great."

He watched as she got into her car, and then went to his.

Twenty minutes later, the server placed their Chicken Parmigina and sides of vegetables with garlic and lemon in front of them. "I love dining here," Joi said, inhaling the Italian aroma wafting through the air. "My dinner plans tonight would have been a microwave dinner, diet coke and going to bed early."

"I'm glad that I rescued you then." His rich brown eyes seemed to twinkle under the lighting. "Do you mind if we pray?" he suggested, reaching across the table for her hands.

How refreshing, a man who is not afraid to say his grace in public. Michael had the same qualities. Whenever she and her family ate at home or public, not a drop of food would go into their mouths without him saying grace.

"Amen." They said in unison.

"Mmm mmm, this Chicken Parmigina is the best." She closed her eyes as the flavor took over her taste buds. "The chief put his foot in this meal. It's delicious."

"Yes, it is good," he mumbled. His mouth stuffed.

They engaged in a round of small talk as they ate. But, it concerned Joi to learn that he'd been coming to the hospital for two weeks looking for her. She liked Wyatt's company and the last thing she wanted to do was lead him on. She prayed that he wasn't the type of man who resulted to stalking or intimidation to get what he wanted. Although, he appeared to be sane, a girl could never be too careful. She made a mental note to start back carrying her Taser and pepper spray in her purse.

Wyatt ordered dessert, chocolate Rustico which they shared. She was stuffed and couldn't eat another bite. "Wyatt thanks for the lovely dinner," she moaned, rubbing her overstuffed belly. "Everything was delicious."

Before he could respond, a tall, gorgeous woman approached their table. "Wyatt? I thought that was you." She gave Joi a dismissive wave.

Oh, no she didn't.

"Trina?" Her presences caught him off-guard.

"Am I that easy to forget?" With her hand propped on one hip, she must have thought that she was *Queen Sheba*. She stood at their table as if she owned the place. "You can afford a place like this now?"

Her words caused Joi's insides to boil. *Who does this woman think she is?* Wyatt had told her that his ex-wife had no couth about her. Now, she had an up close view of the woman who broke his heart. Joi did her best to set still, but the very presence of this woman rubbed her the wrong way.

"Joi... this is Trina, my ex-wife," he said. She could tell from his body language that he was trying to suppress his anger.

"Hello," Joi greeted as pleasant as possible, hoping the woman would turn and leave their table. They were having a great dinner until she came and spoiled the mood.

"Yeah, yeah," Trina responded with an airy wave.

Joi turned her attention back to Wyatt. With her eyes, she expressed her displeasure, hoping he'd get rid of her and fast. If he didn't, Giuseppe's was going to turn into a boxing ring.

"Do you want something?" Wyatt finally asked. "If not, you're interrupting my dinner date." He turned and smiled at Joi, squeezing her hand from across the table.

"You can afford dates now," she laughed, lowering her hands to show off the diamonds adorning her fingers. "The last that I remembered you were always pinching pennies."

"Look, go find your doctor friend and leave us alone."

"On that note, chow," she said, snatching her head in the air and flying off on the broomstick she rode in on.

Joi looked at him. Embarrassment wasn't the word to describe the reaction he had on his face. "So, that's the infamous Trina, uh?" She had to take a drink of her soda to wash down the unspoken insults she'd been served just seconds ago.

"I'm sorry you had to endure that," he said with annoyance in his voice. "I guess Trina still loves taunting me."

Wyatt paid for their meals. Although he tried to pretend that Trina's words didn't sting, she knew better. Hurt and shame was written on his face. Joi excused herself from the table and headed towards the ladies room. Out of the corner of her eye, she noticed Wyatt's ex-wife sliding a credit card into the bill-folder, and then handing it to their waitress. The man whom she was dining with appeared to be apologizing, about what, she couldn't make out.

I've seen that guy before. She tried to recall where, but nothing came to mind. Trina didn't look too happy as he patted his pockets, for perhaps his wallet.

Chapter Thirty-Two

Joi let herself in her parents' home with her spare key. She yelled to alert them of her arrival. "Mom, Dad, I'm here." She dropped her purse down in her father's favorite recliner. No one answered. Leaving the living room, she headed toward the kitchen, still no signs of her parents. The muffled sounds coming from the backyard patio lead her in that direction. She pushed opened the storm door and found her parents' in deep conversation.

Starling the elderly couple, they jumped at the sight of her.

"It's about time you paid the people that brought you into the world a visit." With cheer in her voice, her mom rushed to her feet and gave Joi a huge hug and kiss. Her father followed suit.

"Hi Mom. Dad," she greeted, leaving her mother's embrace to fall into her father's, big strong arms.

"Baby Girl. You looked different." He held on to her hand, guiding her to a seat at the patio table.

"I would have visited sooner, but the hospital scheduled me to work double shifts since arriving back from my trip." Her mother rushed to pour her a glass of homemade lemonade, Joi's favorite. "Working the grueling hours left only enough time for me to sleep."

"We know, Baby." Her mom rubbed the back of her hand against Joi's cheek. "A trip to the Caribbean was just what you needed. You came back two-shades darker," her mother smiled.

"I did, Momma." She paused, shyly covering her face with her hands as she did when telling her parents about her childhood crushes. "I spent most of my time with a man."

Her father's head snapped up at the mention of a man. With flared nostrils, she knew her father did not like the thought of his only daughter parading around an island with some strange man.

"A man?" her mother questioned but her father's body remained tensed. "You didn't go over there trying to act like that girl in the movie, Stella. Did you?"

"Momma! She yelled out in shock and embarrassment. Her mouth flew wide opened. "No oo oo. The two of you did not raise me that way. Besides, what do you know about, Stella?"

Her mother never answered, just smiled.

Joi's father wiped the sweat that had formed on his forehead after hearing the news that she had been with a man far away from home. "Whew. I'm glad to hear that you didn't go over there forgetting your Christian values."

Joi pushed up from her seat and sat on her father's lap as she'd done a hundred times as a child. She placed a tender kiss against the side of his face. "Daddy, I would never do anything to displease God or you guys."

"That's good to hear, Baby Girl." He gave her a quick kiss on the forehead, and then grunted. "Your old man isn't as young as he used to be. You better get back in your seat before these old legs give out from under you."

They laughed.

"Okay daddy," she hopped from his lap back into her chair.

"Back to this man," her mother commanded. "Is he someone you met in Jamaica?"

"No. I met him here at the hospital. He's a fireman."

"Shut your mouth." She put on her matchmaking smile, Joi knew that look well. "A fireman…huh? So, how did the two of you end up going on the same trip together?" Joi recognized that her mother's entrapment skills were on high alert, so, she was careful before answering any of her questions. Her mom thought she was slick, but Joi wasn't falling into her trap.

Her father sat at attention, drumming his fingers on the table waiting for her answer.

"It was the weirdest thing," she snorted, but her father kept a stoned face. "He and his friends booked the same trip as me and the girls."

"Sounds like a sign to me," her mom said, folding her hands down on the table.

"Now, Ester, don't go rushing her into a relationship. Besides, we haven't met this... what you say his name is?" her father asked.

"Wyatt. Wyatt Payne." At the mention of his name, a smile slid its way to her face.

"That's a fine name. How does he look?" She covered the side of her mouth with her hand to keep her husband from hearing, but wasn't successful in doing so.

"That's my cue to leave." He stood with his glass of lemonade. "I'll give you ladies some privacy, because I don't care to hear about how fine some man is."

"Bye, Daddy. I'll come inside to see you before, leaving."

"Okay, Darling." He patted the top of her head and bolted toward the house.

Joi filled her mother in on what happened in Jamaica and how Wyatt took her out to dinner last night. Her insides bubbled over with excitement. However, the cloud of uncertainty still loomed over her, whether Wyatt was the man for her.

Her mother never batted an eye as she took in every detail of Joi's adventure in paradise. Her mother believed her and Wyatt's trip was a sign from above, but she shrugged it off as a coincidence. The look on her mother's face told Joi that she was happy for her.

"It feels good to see you laughing and back to your old self." her mother said with a hint of concern in her voice. And then she lowered the boom. "Baby, Rebekah called again, needing to speak with you. Please go and see her. She sounds strange. I'm worried about her."

"Worried!" She's alive. Why are you worried about her?" Resentment rose in her voice as her posture went limp. Her mother managed to ruin a perfect conversation by bringing up her family's killer. Why should she go and talk with the girl that slaughtered her family? She had no plans of ever reaching out to Rebekah, and wished her mother would stop trying to force her to do so; no one put a gun to her head and forced her to text and drive. She made that decision on her own.

"Joi, I've forgiven her."

To hear those words uttered from her mother lips, angered Joi.

"Do you think God is pleased with your unforgiving heart?"

"Mama, I don't want to talk about this. I've made my decision," she said, clasping her hands together. A habit she developed when her mother began to preach at her. She might have moved on, but Joi hadn't. Rebekah made the stupid choice of texting that day. Now, she had to pay a costly price. "Please...let's drop this subject."

"I'm going to pray for you because this isn't the daughter I raised. You're speaking through hurt and pain." Her mother shifted in her seat, pleading her case. "Don't you think she's suffering too?"

"If anyone has suffered, it's me. All she received was a slap on the hand, because her parents have money. She never spent a day in jail."

Joi tried to forgive and move on, but each time she thought about how Rebekah's parents tried making her dead husband and kids out to be the enemy, made it impossible. She sat in court, waiting on a guilty verdict of manslaughter, but heard five years of probation, instead. If ever she had witness injustice, it was then.

Chapter Thirty-Three

"There has to be a man behind that smile and glow you have been wearing ever since we left Jamaica?" Tara inquired as she shadowed Joi in and out of her patients' room.

Like sisters, Tara thought she was privy to Joi's personal business. Since arriving back home, Tara has grilled her relentless about she and Wyatt. Truth-be-told, she didn't understand it either. Many women would love to be in her position. Wyatt was a good man, as far as good men goes. Then, why was she fighting against his affection?

Her thoughts strayed back to the dinner at the restaurant, after meeting Wyatt's obnoxious ex-wife. Wyatt had told her that the man Trina left him for was a doctor, but after witnessing her paying for their meals, she wasn't so sure. From the look on her face, she didn't seem too happy. Trina might be in for a big surprise, if the guy was not who he portrayed himself to be. Joi had watched enough investigation shows that taught her how to sniff out a rat, and that so-called doctor dining with Trina the other night fit the description.

"Why do you and the girls keep pestering me about Wyatt? We are just friends" She placed her last patient's chart in its slot. "Besides...I like his company, he's a good listener."

"Whatever. That quirky smile on your face says otherwise." Tara flashed a knowing look in her direction.

"Read into it what you will. We are just friends. And make sure you relay that message to Albre and Becky."

"Okay, if that's what you're sticking to," Tara grunted.

She and Wyatt were just good friends. This was the twenty-first century. Men and women hung out all the time with no romantic ties. Wyatt has been a perfect gentleman. He'd told her on several occasions that he had hoped their relationship evolved into something more, but as usual, she'd change the subject. She'd just begun to live again. Falling in love at this point only complicated things.

The nurses' lounge couch offered relief for her aching back. She and Tara clocked out at the same time and desperately needed to rest a moment before heading home. "You're all up in my business, what's going on with you and Jett?" She ran a tired hand through her unruly curls.

"That man has some serious issues," Tara said, rolling her eyes in her head. "He's cute and all, but the fire department needs to make him see a shrink."

Through her yearn, she asked, "What happened?"

"He's possessive and controlling. And the funny part is... I'm not his woman."

"Possessive, how?" Alarmed, Joi scooted to the edge of the couch. Her gut instincts told her that Jett was trouble.

"You know, controlling as if I had to get his permission to breath. I had to inform him that he was not my man, and that we are just kicking it as friends."

"What did he say when you told him that?" She hung on to every word, being careful not to miss anything. Her heart pounded as Tara continued filling her in about her nightmare with Jett.

"He grabbed hold to some other woman's arm at the club in Jamaica and left me standing in the middle of the floor in disbelief." She swept a hand full of her micro-braids to the back of her head. "That man is full of himself. He's fine, but he's not that fine that I'll allow him to disrespect me."

"He doesn't seem like the type of person, Wyatt would associate himself with." She shook her head. "But, they say opposites attract. Look at us"

They laughed in agreement.

"Yeah, but I don't walk around like I'm God's gift to the world," Tara said, reclining on the couch.

*****

"Thanks for meeting me for lunch on short notice," Wyatt said, pulling out her chair. "I just had to see your beautiful face."

"You are something else. There are tons of attractive women strolling through the hospital. And you need to see me?" Joi joked.

With raised hands in his defense, he said, "It's the truth. I enjoy your company. You try working around men every single day. Seeing a beautiful woman is a welcoming sight."

"Is that right?"

He changed the subject. "So, how has your day been?"

"Great. And yours?" She had that giddy, innocent school girl glow about her, which he adored.

Apparently, Joi hadn't realized the hold she had on him. Thoughts of her entered his mind every single day. Four months had passed since their trip to the Caribbean's and she still doesn't see him as a possible love interest. Impulse told him to jump across the table and take her into his arms, making her see how much he loved her. In doing so, it may jeopardize their friendship. His only hope for now was to wait on a higher power to intervene.

"Better, now that I'm here with you."

"Wyatt? Stop with the compliments, you know it makes me uncomfortable," she said, blushing.

"Okay. Okay."

"Can I ask you a question?" Methodically, she stirred her sweet tea.

"Sure, shoot," he said with raised brows. What type of question she needed to ask him? He had been an opened book ever since they'd met.

"Why do you hang out with a man like Jett?"

"I guess for the same reasons that you are friends with Tara."

Why is she asking me about Jett? If he's tried flirting with her, I will kill him.

Jett was known for putting the moves on women he was interested in. He liked Joi and had no plans of losing her to him.

With Jett threatening him every other day about the bad choice he'd made the night Trina left him, he questioned their friendship. He wanted to confess what he'd done, to Joi, but pride and shame kept him from doing so.

"Tara isn't a roughneck, unlike Jett."

"He hasn't done anything to her... has he?" Wyatt heart pumped with fear as he imagined what Jett might've done to Joi's friend.

"She said that he's possessive and has major anger issues."

"Yes, that sounds about right." He paused, trying his best not to make excuses for Jett's behavior. "Jett grew up in foster care. He never knew his father, and his mother turned him over to the State when he was just nine-years old."

"Wow," she gasped. "That's awful."

"He's searching for love, but don't know how to go by getting it. The women he dates, eventually leave him because of his controlling behavior."

"That explains his attitude in Jamaica with Tara. He needs to seek help for that short temper of his, because women today aren't putting up with that, and my friend Tara is one of those women. He was lucky that he did not see her bad side."

"Is that right?" He smiled. Deep down inside, Wyatt knew that there were issues that went much deeper than Jett wanted to admit.

"Right as rain," she responded with a shake of her head.

"Enough about them. What are you doing this weekend? The fire station gave me two free tickets to the Jazz Fest."

"My weekend has just cleared. I love me some jazz."

"Sounds like a date," he smiled.

"A date?" She cut her eyes at him.

"Yes, a date. Loosen up, will you." He patted her hand to simmer her down.

Wyatt was happy that she did not refuse. Who knows, maybe the Jazz Fest would open her eyes to see him as a possible catch. Most times, women would fall all over him when they saw him in his uniform. But, this woman couldn't care less about him being a fireman.

Lord, please remove the scales from her eyes, so that she can see that my feelings for her are genuine.

Chapter Thirty-Four

Like a whirlwind, Wyatt tore through the fire department door. He had had it up to his neck with Jett. Behaving in an aggressive manner with Joi's friend did not set well with him. He has tolerated his bad boy ways long enough. Now it was time to set him straight.

He combed every inch of the station. Jett was nowhere in sight. Wyatt asked his co-workers of Jett's whereabouts, but none had seen him. Tired of his searching, he headed to the kitchen and poured himself a cup a coffee. The caffeine had been what he needed to take the edge off.

"Man, I'd hate to be the one who ticked you off," Paul said, sliding in the seat in front of Wyatt, coffee in hand.

"It's Jett again." Wyatt shook his head.

"Oh God… what has he done now?"

"He acted his usual brazen self with one of Joi's friends." He took a sip of coffee. "You remember, Tara?"

"Well, what exactly did he do, because she is a character herself?"

"He tried using his scare tactics on Tara to control her."

"That is serious."

"You're telling me." He blew out a frustrated breath. "I think it's time we sit our brother down for a heart to heart talk."

"Sounds like a plan to me," Paul said, shaking his head in agreement. "So when do you want to take action?"

"Today, before leaving work. You and Seth find Jett and bring him back here… say, around five o'clock." Wyatt knew if they couldn't reach their young friend after today, he would find himself in some serious trouble. The last thing he wanted was for Jett to lose his job, especially if a woman decided to file harassment charges against him.

"I'll see you man, I'm scheduled to wash the fire truck today." He stood from his seat, slapping Wyatt across the shoulders as he headed out the room.

"Okay." Wyatt then grabbed the daily newspaper and tried reading it to get his mind off of the confrontation he would have with Jett later. It was long overdue, but it had to be done. The last thing he wanted was for a woman to get hurt by his young friend's unstable behavior, or him being the one to get hurt because some woman wasn't going to put up with his controlling conduct. Either way, somebody was going to get hurt if he and the others didn't say something about his behavior.

If Jett decided to call him out on the night he covered up his mistake, then he would have to deal with it, but allowing Jett to hurt himself or others had to be stopped. He prayed for guidance and hoped this intervention pricked Jett's heart. Cracking through that hardhead of his wasn't going to be easy, but he was determined to try.

What good was it to go to church, hear an uplifting word, but then watch his brother fall by the wayside? It was time for Wyatt to put to use what he'd learned about being his brother's keeper.

Later that evening, Paul and Seth entered the break room to find Wyatt and Jett sitting at the table. Just their luck, the incoming shift had a meeting before starting their workday, giving them the privacy they needed.

"I'm glad you guys came," Wyatt said with reservation as he glanced around the table. Each had been informed of what their meeting was about, except Jett.

The tension in the room thickened. Their body language was stiff.

"What is going on here?" Jett asked as the creases formed between his eyes when Paul and Seth entered the room.

His breathing increased. Wyatt didn't know how the meeting was going to turn out. But he felt safer about them deciding to meet at the fire station. If Jett went on one of his crazy tirades, then there were others to help to get him under control.

He loved Jett like a younger brother. His well-being concerned him.

Paul looked at Seth, and Seth shifted his attention to Wyatt to start the conversation.

"What happened on the trip in Jamaica?" Wyatt asked, feeling that he should have posed the question another way, instead of being so direct.

"Jamaica? He paused. "Why are you asking me about something that happened four months ago?" The thumping of Jett fingers on the table made Wyatt trod with caution.

"I heard that you got out of line with Tara."

"I can have any woman I want. Why would I go crazy over the likes of her?" By then, Jett's postured had turned defensive.

"That's the problem," Wyatt said as calm as possible. It did not take much to set Jett off if he felt threatened, so he tried to rephrase his words. "We get it. You attract women wherever we go. But they are not your property."

Jett became infuriated. But, before he could unleash it, Paul jumped in to lightened things up a bit. "Hear us out, Jett. We are only bringing this to you because we love you. You're like family to us."

With a nod, Seth agreed, but kept quiet.

"Do us and yourself a favor and get some help for your anger problem," Paul advised.

"There are men sitting behind bars because they made stupid decisions," Wyatt uttered. "If you don't get help or take some sort of anger management courses, you could end up there."

Jett did not say a word. To their surprise, he listened.

"You have to get past the fact that your mother handed you over to the foster care system. Look at what you have accomplished without your parents. God has blessed you with spiritual brothers who care about you. The Bible teaches us to carry each other's burdens, and the three of us are going to help you carry yours." The lump in Wyatt's throat made it hard for him to continue. His emotions overtook him.

Seeing that Wyatt couldn't go on, Seth took over the conversation. "We care about what happens to you. Your parents have missed out on knowing the man that you have become. Our moms and dads have treated you as if you were their own child. Stop beating yourself up about the past."

"Yeah," Paul added. "Controlling someone is not the answer. Women leave you because they are afraid of your erratic behavior."

Jett listened to what they had to say, and for the first time he sat speechless. If Wyatt knew that their intervention would've had this powerful impact, he and the others would have done it months earlier.

Their conversation led to the ten-year-old young girl who'd lost her life in the burning house. Jett broke down in a way that neither of them had expected. He blamed himself for her death, when in reality there was nothing any of them could have done.

Jett decided to take medical leave to get the help he needed.

Seth stood from his seat, rounding the table where Wyatt and Jett sat and gave them both a brotherly hug. Paul followed suit. The heaviness in Wyatt's heart lifted when Jett realized that he needed professional help.

Chapter Thirty-Five

Before Joi and Wyatt went to the Jazz Fest, she made an unannounced stopped by her parent's home to drop off a box filled with romance novels for her mother's book club. Ester and six of her girlfriends started the group when they retired as nurses from Blessed Memorial Hospital. After working in the stressful profession where there was always drama and action, they demanded the same in the books that they read. If the books weren't filled with hot, steamy romance, drama and action, it was cut from their reading list. The ladies have had the opportunity of meeting several national bestselling authors. They called themselves, The Blue-Haired Angels Book Club.

Right on time, Joi thought as a line of cars filled her parents' driveway. Her mother's book club was punctual as always. Wyatt maneuvered his truck in a tight space in front of their home. He rounded the truck to open Joi's door. Then, he grabbed the box of books she had packed for the group. As they headed toward the porch, Joi could hear her mother and friends cackling away. No doubt they were reading something hot and steamy.

Her father's vehicle was nowhere in sight, which meant he had hightailed it out of there. The last thing he wanted was to be trapped inside the house with his wife and her loved starved reading buddies. Listening to them screaming and shouting over some sweaty hero wasn't his idea of fun. So, whenever her mother's group met once a month, he made plans to go fishing.

She let herself and Wyatt in. Instead of calling out to her mother, she and Wyatt followed the sounds of laughter and squealing. A good looking man had no chance among the man hungry cougars in her mother's book club. Too bad for Wyatt, he had no clue what he was walking into.

"Hi everyone," Joi greeted as the women in the room eyes passed her and landed on Wyatt. She could see the saliva dripping from their hungry mouths, ready to tear into him. She had to admit it. He was a good looking man. A woman had to be blind not to notice him.

"Hey, Baby. I didn't hear you come in." Her mother seemed surprised to see her. Maybe Joi should have notified her that she was stopping by. Her mother quickly dropped the book in her hand. Joi was certain that it had some half-naked man on the cover. Now, she understood exactly where her mother found her information about keeping her marriage spicy. Her good ole' Christian mother was reading more than inspirational romance. That was a, *Brazen Romance Novel*, she had in her hand.

"Forgive me for my rudeness," Joi said as Wyatt stood next to her after placing the box on the kitchen counter. "Everyone this is Wyatt Payne, he volunteered to help me haul the box of books over here. And Wyatt, this is my mother, Ester Peterson and her lovely book club, The Blue Haired Angels." Joi pointed around the table, introducing them one by one.

"Lord, have mercy," her mother said, rising from her seat. Joi had never known her mother to be one for a loss of words, but, it didn't take long for her to find her voice. "Wyatt, the fireman you've been talking about?"

"Oooooooo," sounded from around the table.

Wyatt turned in her direction and smiled, which made her uncomfortable.

"How are you, Son? So, I finally get the chance to meet my baby's new man."

"Mama!" Joi yelled to keep from throwing a temper tantrum as she did as a child when her mother said things she shouldn't have.

The rest of the women placed their novels on the table and started making googly eyes at Wyatt. "Now, he's the type of man that should be in one of these romance novels," Mrs. Betsy committed, almost falling out of her chair. "I can see it now," she gestured with an airy wave. "Tall, sexy fireman rescue me, the damsel is in distress from a burning building."

"Uh-huh," the ladies pretended to faint.

Mrs. Sanchez's crossed-eyes were aimed toward the refrigerator, but from the huge smile on her face, Joi assumed she was gawking at Wyatt.

"Joi, if you don't want this man, I'll take him off your hands!" Mrs. Julia screamed, clapping her large hands together.

The ladies' cackling filled the room. Joi could see that Wyatt had no idea how to respond to the attention. She should have warned him beforehand. The ladies were hilarious in their own way. Joi guessed the heroes in their romance novels were the closest they would ever come to a young, strong handsome man. And in walked Wyatt, every woman's fantasy.

When her eyes met her mother's, Ester mouthed, "You better snatch that man up."

Mrs. Julia overheard her mother and said for everyone to hear, "Shoots, if she doesn't, I'll take him off her hands. The only thing my husband does is eat, fart and sleep. My bedroom is so dull you can hear the crickets scratch their legs together."

"Julia, shut your mouth," Joi mother responded. "We don't need to hear what you and Percy do in private."

"Well, if my husband had the energy yours have, Ester, I wouldn't have anything to complain about."

"That's because I know how to keep my man interested,"

"Mama, we have company. Please stop!" Joi shouted, burying her face into her hands to hide her shame.

Wyatt stood in the doorway, killing himself laughing. He was getting a kick out of her mother and friends' shenanigans. What child wanted to hear their parents' discussing their love life? She sure as heck didn't.

"Girl, be quiet." Her mother gave her a dismissive wave. "Maybe if you were more in touch with your sexuality, you might have a man by now."

"Oh-my-goodness!" Joi yelled out in horror "Wyatt, it's time go." Humiliated wasn't the word to describe how she was feeling. Joi was downright livid at her mother and friends. Was sex the topic of every one of their meetings? They were grandmothers for crying-out-loud.

"I'm enjoying myself," he said as he made himself comfortable propped against the kitchen counter. "Besides, the festival doesn't start for another two hours."

She balled her fist up at him, and in return, he puckered his lips, sending her an air kiss. Oh, he was enjoying himself at her expense. She would never live this day down.

"Why are you trying to rush this man off, Joi? We just met Way-tt-tt," Mrs. Betsy sang, batting her lashes as if something had been caught in her bulging eyes.

Joi's blood pressure had soared to a new level—scorching hot. If she had known that her mother and friends were going to shame her, she would have waited until tomorrow to drop off the books. She and her mother were going to have a long discussion after this fiasco.

"Wyatt, are things serious between you and my daughter?" Her mother asked as her friends at the table hung onto her every word.

Why did she have to go there? Their relationship was never going past the neutral zone. She prayed that Wyatt wouldn't get her mother's hopes up. Joi had made it plain and clear where they stood.

"Mrs. Peterson, Joi and I are just friends."

Whew! Thanks Wyatt for not giving my mother any false hope.

"Aw-ww...that's too bad. You two would make a fine couple."

Wyatt looked down at her and whispered where only she could hear. "I think so too."

Joi kept a stone face, careful not to give her mother or him any reason to go fishing for something that wasn't there. Her mother would not let up. Nothing was going to happen between her and Wyatt. So, she might as well stop trying to play cupid.

"What a shame," one of the other book club members groaned from her seat.

"We have to go, Mom, before we get stuck in traffic." She grabbed Wyatt by the hand and bolted toward the door.

"Okay, you kids have fun now," her mom said. "It was nice meeting you Wyatt, and thanks for helping Joi bring the books over."

"You're welcome, Mrs. Peterson," Wyatt said, waving over his shoulder as Joi dragged him by the arm. "It was nice meeting all of you."

Mrs. Julia hollered behind them, "Wyatt, if Joi won't make a commitment to you, I will." A burst of laughter was heard as they headed out the door. Needless to say; Wyatt was eating up the female attention.

"Joi your mom and her friends are hilarious," Wyatt said, laughing as they entered his truck.

"No, they were embarrassing." Shaking her head in shame, she laid it against the headrest.

"You should be thankful to have such a youthful mother. She's vibrant and full of life, so are her friends."

"I suppose you're right, but sometimes she can be a bit too much to handle. She speaks what she feels."

As they headed to the Jazz Fest, Joi was glad that Wyatt had kept his true feelings for her to himself. If not, her mother would have pestered her nonstop about her giving Wyatt a chance. Her mother was a die-hard romantic. She wanted everyone to experience the type love she had. Joi desired that kind of love too and thought she'd found it, until Michael was killed, leaving her alone.

Chapter Thirty-Six

Throngs of people were scattered throughout the downtown Shreveport Riverfront area. The Jazz Fest brought people from all ages, races and cities together. The mixtures of southern cuisines wafting in the air made her mouth water. Joi and Wyatt pushed through the crowd, hand in hand, trying to find the perfect spot to watch the concert.

They found a nice shaded area near the stage. Wyatt took the blanket she'd been carrying and spread it out across the grass. He had been such a gentleman throughout the months of their friendship, and now, she began to see him in a whole new light as someone she could share a future with.

She'd noticed earlier when they pressed their way through the crowd, how women were checking him out. Never had a pair of casual polo, khaki shorts looked as good on a man as they did on him. Her roaming eyes trailed up and down his perfectly fit body. Just when her eyes was about to explore more of him, a female voice stopped her search.

"Hi there good looking," a young, twenty-something, thin-as-a rail female said as if she didn't see Joi standing next to Wyatt.

Really? Joi hadn't dated in years and forgotten how bold some women were. But Wyatt ignored the woman's attempt to come on to him, and then she walked off.

Instead, he took her hand and helped her down onto the blanket. Something deep inside of her was growing—jealousy. Why was she feeling this way? They were just friends, the lie she continued to tell herself. For the first time since they'd been seeing each other, the green-eyed monster had taken over her when the young lady came on to Wyatt. She told herself that she was just being a protective friend. When in reality she was falling in love.

"I heard there is a great line up of jazz artists performing today," he said, now sitting beside Joi, waiting for the concert to start. In the meantime, they made small talk.

"Thank you for coming. If you had not accepted, then the guys would have twisted my arm to hang out with them." Balancing his hands as if weights were in them, he laughed, "A beautiful lady or the guys. I prefer to be with a beautiful lady any day."

His words were causing her to have forbidden thoughts. Months earlier, he could have said the same thing and it would have had no effect. Now, hearing him say those things caused her to feel warm and tingly inside. "I'm glad that you thought of me. Those tickets were going for seventy dollars each."

He belted out a hearty laugh. "Well, I'm glad I saved you seventy dollars. So, looks like you owe me."

The beaming sun caused his smooth, brown eyes to blaze right through her. She had to get a hold of herself. The thought of taking hold of his perfect, manly face and splattering kisses all over it, consumed her. She shook her head, trying to get her wandering mind off of what she wanted to do to him. She had no business thinking such things.

"Owe you... how?" She smiled up at him.

He placed his forefinger against his chin as if in deep thought and said, "Dinner, later tonight."

"I should be able to afford dinner." She tried hiding her excitement but her uncontrollable smile kept giving her away.

The band walked on the stage and the Jazz Fest got under way. She and Wyatt stood dancing along with the others who attended the festival. When a slow, romantic song began to play, they stood awkwardly in the grass. She hoped that he would put his arms around her waist like the other couples, but, she had told him on several occasions that they were just friends. At that moment she wanted more.

*****

Wyatt wanted to take hold of Joi and make out with her, right there on the blanket. The slow, seductive music bellowing from the stage made him wish that she was his. *I can't understand why she doesn't want me?* He believed that he was a good catch, but he did not want just any woman, he wanted her.

Instead of standing there looking stupid and out of place, he grabbed her hand and they sat back down on the blanket. They watched as other couples swayed to the beautiful sounds of jazz.

"Joi, why don't you find me attractive?" There, he asked the question that had been on his heart for months.

"Wh-aa-tt?" she stuttered. He could tell his forwardness caught her off guard.

She turned her head, looking out toward the Red River, but he directed her attention back on him. "Look at me, Joi. What's wrong with me?"

"There is nothing wrong with you."

"Then, why don't you want me?"

"It's complicated," she said, playing with the frayed hem on the blanket.

The music seemed to have faded in the background. He had to get his feelings off his chest no matter how uncomfortable it made her. He had made progress with Jett earlier this week. Now he had to speak his peace to the woman he'd grown to love.

"Enlighten me, because I want to know."

"I'm still in love with Michael, you know that. I think about him daily, even when I'm with … you."

His heart collapsed to the bottom of his stomach, knowing that she thought about another man when with him. *Was she thinking of him the times I've kissed her?* Her words were worse than a slap in the face. How was he going to compete with a dead man?

"And your job doesn't help matters either."

A pool of water filled her eyes and he'd hoped that she wasn't going to cry.

"I can't spend my nights wondering if the man I love will be coming home or not."

Her feelings for him were evident by the way her eyes grew after saying the "L" word. She did love him. The next step was getting her to love him with her whole heart. Although he understood the love she had for her decease husband; surely, she had room in her heart for him. Her slip of the tongue told him so.

"You can't take it back now. I heard it with my own ears." He jumped from the blanket, dancing with joy.

She tried to stop him. "Sit down, you're embarrassing me." Covering her lovely face with her hands, he removed them and leaned in to kiss her.

"We will discuss the changes in our relationship tonight at dinner."

"Wyatt… now wait a minute. Don't go putting words in my mouth." She held up a hand in attempt to stop him, but he continued.

"You stuck your foot in your mouth about your feelings for me." He laughed. "You love me and that's that."

She turned her attention back toward the stage, trying to ignore him. Wyatt couldn't have been happier, until the sight of one female he'd rather forget, blocked their view of the stage.

"Well, well, well. You again," the female sang through her nostrils, before she could utter another word, her male companion showed up beside her. "Let me guess, free tickets from your job." The woman cackled.

"Isn't there room someplace else for you to go and watch the concert?" His happy mood darkened the moment Trina appeared. "And where I got my tickets from is my business." By then, he had steam shooting out his ears. Like the Trina he'd always known, she couldn't take a hint and leave.

Flashing her rings that nearly blinded him and Joi, Trina couldn't wait to throw the doctor she had an affair with while they were married in his face. "Where are my manners? Cedric, I'm sure you remember my biggest mistake, Wyatt." Cedric stood arrogantly with his ten-pack protruding in front of him. "And Baby, meet his little girlfriend." She pointed down at Joi.

The uppity doctor seemed a little shaken when Trina directed his attention to Joi. He seemed to recognize Joi from the surprised look on his face, but he tossed the thought out of mind. Just because she worked at the hospital doesn't mean that she knew every doctor.

Wyatt held his breath and from the look in Joi's eyes he knew the claws were about to come out. "I'm nobodies little girlfriend, Lady. I'm his fiancé and soon to be *new wife*." She put emphasis on, new wife.

He was completely blown away by Joi's words. She was standing up to his ex-wife in his defense.

"Besides, I like six-packs, not kegs." She shot a disgusting look at Cedric's stomach.

"How dare you?" For the first time Trina was at a loss for words.

"Well I did. Can you and fat boy please move out of our way, so my man and I can get back to enjoying the Jazz Fest."

Shocked by Joi's insult, Trina huffed and grabbed her doctor by the hand and scurried from their sight. When Trina turned to look back at them, Joi laid a hot, steamy kiss on Wyatt's smiling lips. He would have paid thousands if he knew that today was going to end on such a high note.

Chapter Thirty-Seven

"It's time to pay up, Ma'am," Wyatt demanded as Joi placed and paid for their orders. "I take you to an expensive restaurant and you treat me to Taco Bell. What a cheap date." He laughed, reaching for the tray while she led the way to the table.

"I spend my money wisely, Mister." She dug her forefinger into his arm and headed to the condiment section, grabbing packages of hot and mild sauces.

"I learn something new about you each time we're together."

"Like what?" she inquired, batting her long lashes at him.

"Like the way you handled Trina and her new beau, today." He opened and squirted a couple of packages of mild sauce inside his taco. "I didn't know you had all that fire rolled up into that tiny body of yours."

"It's a lot you don't know about me." Wiggling her eyebrows, she gave him a devious smile.

He would love to delve deeper into her statement and discover just what she meant? The woman was full of surprises and he would love to stick around for the long haul to learn what was next. Today couldn't have been more perfect if he had planned it. Joi confessed— involuntary— her feelings for him at the Jazz Fest, which gave him, hope for a future with her. And he looked forward to the day to give himself to her without restraints. She was a good woman, but she had one flaw— learning how to let go and forgive. He had to somehow bring up the subject about Rebekah, why Joi refused to extend the olive branch to the young lady bothered him.

"Seeing you in action today was priceless," he grinned, trying hard to figure out how to approach the subject about the young girl who killed her family. With ease, he politely changed their conversation. "Joi, have you spoken to Rebekah, yet?"

"Why are you bringing up her for?" The resentment in her voice told him that he had hit a nerve. "When I told you my story, I didn't expect for you to throw it back into my face."

"Ho-oo-ld on, Joi," he stuttered, holding his hands up in his defense. The last thing he wanted was for his question to cause her to walk out on him. "I just need to know have you prayed for strength and guidance concerning the matter."

"Wyatt, please. Don't spoil tonight."

The way she tore into her taco, giving him the cold shoulder made him uncomfortable. Was she thinking of him when she grinded it between her teeth?

"I'll drop it for now. But you need to take your mother's advice. She's telling you the right thing."

Because he cared for her, Wyatt had to tell her the truth when she was wrong. When it came to ignoring Rebekah, she was dead wrong. He believed that the young girl was in her own personal torment as well. Joi needed to open the lines of communication and hear the young girl out. She may never love him the way he wanted her to, but he owed her the truth when it came to her unforgiving spirit.

"Thank you," she said; her tone sharp.

He made one last effort to appeal to her spiritual side. "It's funny how we want compassion and forgiveness for our wrongdoing? And we can't forgive or show compassion to those who have wronged us?"

Tears filled her eyes as she stared across the table at him. Grateful his words had gotten through to her, he reached for her hand a gently squeezed it. An old eighties tune played through the overhead speakers, drowning out the silence between them. She buried her face into her hands and sobbed. It wasn't his intention to hurt her, but she was wrong, no matter how she tried justifying it.

"Let's get out of here. I'll go get a bag to put our food in." He handed her the keys to his truck as he headed toward the register.

*****

Joi unlocked the door to her house as Wyatt stood next to her with his hands in his pants pockets. The ride home had been an awkward one. His words back at Taco Bell had stung. She had been so caught up in her own grief that she failed to realize Rebekah was hurting just as much as she.

Once inside, she gestured for him to have a seat. "Would you like something to drink?" she asked, because she didn't know exactly what else to say. She felt ashamed of herself. Here she was, going to church every Sunday, professing to be a Christian and at the same time harboring vengeance in her heart.

She'd always ignored her parents' advice to forgive Rebekah. Their words fell on a deaf ear. Then, today Wyatt had said the exact same thing. Only his words cut her like a two-edged sword. What made his argument penetrate her heart when her parents' words went over her head? Maybe, because she was ready to surrender and stop fighting a fight that she could no longer win.

In Joi's mind, no one understood how losing her entire family affected her. Bouncing back from a serious blow as that wasn't easy. She needed time to process what had happened. And Wyatt's words had been the wakeup call she needed. The fog she'd been lost in for the past two years was lifted, because Wyatt had taken the time to care.

"Water will be fine."

She disappeared into the kitchen, and then quickly returned, handing him the bottled water wrapped in a paper towel. The deafening silence between them caused her to fidget with the hem of her shirt, although, the love that shone in his eyes at that moment calmed her. He patted at the seat next to him on the sofa, hesitantly she obliged. "You can place your drink on the coffee table," she said, after finding her voice.

"We need to finish the conversation that we started earlier." He caressed her shoulder when she sat down, and then turned on the sofa to face her. "Why can't you forgive Rebekah, Joi? People make mistakes."

With her eyes squeezed shut, she shook her head from side to side. She fought hard to control the pain. "I wanted her to suffer just as much as I have," she gulped, taking in a deep breathe. "Because of her stupid mistake, a mistake that didn't have to happen; Rebekah ended my world."

"Your life hasn't ended Joi." With the back of his hand, he stroked the side of her face. "You gave up and stopped living."

"That day was like a bad nightmare that I have tried waking up from, but can't." She lifted her head to face him. "It put me in a cold, dark place, causing me to feel pain and hate at the same time."

"I'm not trying to tell you to move on and forget your family, but if you continue reliving that day, instead of the good times that you shared with them, the pain will never go away."

"It hurts so bad," she muffled through the tears that had begun to spill down her cheeks."

He pulled her close to him, cradling her with his strong, yet gentle arms. If ever there was a time she needed him, it was now. Wyatt was willing to put their friendship on the line to show her the error of her ways. The pain was still there, but his words spoke volumes to her heart.

"I know it does," he said as she lay against his chest and cried. "God never puts more on us than we can carry. You have to trust and believe that."

Chapter Thirty-Eight

"I was surprised when you called to invite me to workout with you." Tara said, running on the treadmill. "Which could mean only one thing; that fine fireman you've been dating has had a positive influence on you."

"He has, Joi agreed. "But I think he's moving a little too fast."

"Are you listening to yourself?" Tara huffed, taking deep breathes between words. "The man adores you. He's good for you, Joi. You're blessed to have found two good men. Some women can't find one." Taking one of her hands off the treadmill handle, she pointed at herself. "Michael wouldn't want you to spend the rest of your life alone. You've been given a second chance at love. Take it. Heck, if you don't I will."

"Girl, you are crazy. I was waiting for that sassy attitude of yours to show up." Joi hopped off the treadmill, toweled dried her face and waited for her friend to finish her run.

"You know it's the truth. The man wants to spend time with you and you keep pushing him away." Tara hoped off the treadmill, huffing and puffing. "You are going to end up sending him right into another woman's arms if you don't open your eyes."

Horrified at the thought of Wyatt with another woman, Joi thought on her friend's words. Although she wasn't ready for a serious commitment, she sure as heck did not want to lose him either.

"He wants me to meet his parents. And you know what that means." She gave her friend a knowing look. "He has marriage on his mind."

"A-nn-d," Tara sang, sporting an annoyed look. "You are blessed and don't even know it."

They continued their talk as they headed towards the sauna room. "I can't give him what he wants." Before entering the steam room, they towel wrapped their hair.

"And what is that?" She watched as Tara leaned her head back against the wall as steam worked its magic on their aching muscles.

"I can't give him my heart. Not completely. At some point and time he's going to want more than I can give."

With a frown on her face, Tara tore into her. "Girl, I don't have time listening to your foolish talk about not able to give this God sent man your heart. That is fear talking." She cut her eyes at Joi.

"You haven't loss a husband and kids."

"No, I have not. But I do know that a sign from above is telling you to move on with your life." Tara closed her eyes, putting earplugs in her ears to tune out Joi.

Was she that closed minded and out of touch with what the Lord was doing in her life? Maybe it was time to do some serious soul searching. Seek God, to find direction and understanding, because everyone made her feel as though her thinking was way off when it came to starting over. Wyatt was everything and more that she could have asked for in a man. Any other woman would count themselves blessed to have such a level headed man. Why was she being so closed off when it came to loving him? A part of her felt guilty, which made loving Wyatt even harder.

She wanted a new life, kids and husband, but thinking those thoughts made her feel horrible inside. Her husband and kids were dead and she wanted to start over. Guilt had taken over her and she needed some spiritual guidance to get her back on track. Before meeting Wyatt, living meant nothing to her. Now she wanted a fresh start and owed it all to him.

If there was any man perfect to settle down with, it was Wyatt. But each time she looked into his eyes, she saw Michael and the life they would never have. Call her silly, but it wasn't right to lead him on. What man wanted to be with a woman who thought about another man when she was with him? None that she knew of and Wyatt wasn't the type of man who would put up with such behavior either.

She glanced at Tara who continued to ignore her, bobbing her head to whatever she was listening to, leaving her to further reflect on where her life was heading. On one hand, she wanted to give herself totally to Wyatt. And on the other, she wanted to keep him at a distance. Sooner or later he was going to grow tired of her indecisiveness and leave her for a woman who would give herself completely to him.

In the middle of her thoughts, the sauna door opened and in walked Trina. Her day of pampering and relaxation had just ended. The first thing she noticed when Trina walked in was her pointy noise, sticking straight up into the air.

"Look who we have here," she crooned, scooting beside Joi. "My leftover's new fiancé."

By that time Tara had opened her eyes, taking out her earplugs she had used to tune Joi out earlier. She knew that Trina was going to wish she had never stepped foot into that sauna. Joi tilted her head up at Wyatt's ex-wife and said, "Lady, I don't know what your problem is, but I suggest you bring that attitude of yours down a notch. And keep your sly remarks to yourself."

"Is this woman bothering you Joi?" Tara now sat in defense mode staring over at Trina.

"This is Wyatt's ex-wife, Trina. And no, she's no problem as long as she doesn't come in here with that uppity talk."

Trina gasped, and slid down to the other end of the bench. She wasn't so mouthy without her doctor on her arm. She folded her arms, looking snooty as ever. Joi should have known better than to think that Trina was going to sit there quietly.

"What do you see in Wyatt?" she asked in a superior manner. "You know he doesn't earn much as a fireman."

Is this woman for real? Joi thought.

Tara jumped to Joi's defense before she could respond to Trina's cut below the belt remark. "You were married to him once. What did you see in him?"

In a fake, proper voice, Trina shot back. "Excuse me…but who are you?"

"Joi's best friend, that's who I am." Tara had risen from her seat. "Don't come up in here flashing those cubic zirconia rings in our faces, trying to act bougie."

"How dare you speak to me in that tone." She clutched her chest.

"I will speak to you however I wish Miss. Gold Digger."

The showdown between the two was causing the temperature in the sauna to rise, but Trina did ask for it. One thing about Tara, she didn't back down from anyone. Feeling like she had to be the peacemaker, Joi intervened. "Stop it you two!" She stood between them, which wasn't a great idea. Standing only five-foot-five to their tall statures made being heard that much harder. So, she stood on the bench to get their attention. "She's not worth it, Tara."

"No, she's not worth it," Trina countered, pointing at Tara. She tossed her hands in the air and headed to a bench in the far corner to put some distance between them.

It took a minute before Tara returned to her seat. Then, she overheard Trina murmuring the words, cubic zirconia, as he stretched her hands out admiring her rings. She twirled them around on her fingers and said, "These are the finest diamonds money can buy."

"Right!" Tara blurted under her breath, which caused Trina to shoot her a dirty look.

"Girl, get over there and sit down," Joi commanded, pulling her friend close to her and away from Trina.

Inwardly, Joi smiled. With the towels wrapped around their heads and bodies, they looked like two boxers ready to spar. *What did Wyatt ever see in Trina? Granted, she is beautiful and has a nice figure. But she fails in the personality department.*

"Trina, as for your question earlier, Wyatt's a good man. You were a fool to let him go."

Trina snatched her head to the side, while Tara kept a blood thirsty look plastered upon her face. Wyatt was a decent man. Where on earth did he meet a woman like his ex-wife?

Chapter Thirty-Nine

"Have you given any thought on going to see Rebekah?" Joi's mother asked over the telephone.

A day never went by without her talking to her parents. She couldn't have been happier that Joi was dating again. The two years she had been on her own were rough. "No, Mother, I haven't." Glad that she could hide her facial expression over the phone, she frowned.

"Well...when do you plan on going, Joi? Rebekah's parents are worried about her mental state." Her mom's voice appeared to be more shaken than usual.

"I have to pray on it."

In the midst of their conversation, warm liquid flowed down her cheeks. How was she going to face the teen? Her mother and the others just didn't understand. What was she going to say to the girl?

"Pray? Pray to forgive?" Her mother's words vibrated through the telephone. "Joi, if you don't stop with that silliness. You know better, forgiving should be second nature. What if Jesus had changed his mind about going to Calvary to wash away our sins? I think it's time for you to do some serious soul searching, Missy."

Joi could hear the disappointment in her mother's voice, but she had to do things at her own pace. She wasn't ready to talk to Rebekah. So, everyone could just leave her alone. Nothing was going to take place until she was good and ready. Even after her talk with Wyatt, she found herself backsliding into her old ways. It was as if two voices were controlling her. One wanted her to forgive and show compassion, while the other voice kept reminding her of her loss.

Before she knew it, Joi had tuned her mother out, until she heard her repeatedly calling her name through the phone. "Joi. Joi... are you still there?"

Like a brooding child she moaned, "Yes, Mama."

"I hope you heard what I said. You are thirty-three -years old and in the prime of your life. Don't allow an unforgiving spirit to take you under. I've seen it enough to last a life time. It will cause you to shut everyone out. You're too young and beautiful to allow that to happen to yourself. You hear me?"

"Yes, I hear you."

"I don't mean to rush off. But this is your father and I date night." Love you and think about what I said, you hear."

"I love you too, Mama. And tell daddy hello for me," she said and disconnected the call.

Retiring for the night, Joi continued her same night time ritual. She picked up a family portrait, ran her hand across it and called it a night.

Everyone keeps telling me the same thing. Forgive. Forgive. Forgive. It is easier said than done. I have held on to hating Rebekah for so long that it's hard to do anything else. Lord, help me with this battle within. The only way that I can do what others' are suggesting, is with help from above. I want to live again. I want to love again, but I just don't know how.

Even in her dreams, her family memory haunted her. She had many dreams of them doing family things together, but this one was different. Michael and the boys were playing football in an opened field as she looked on from a distance, trying to get their attention. She began to run towards them, but the faster she ran the further off they became. She screamed and waved her hands so that they could see her, but they did not.

The grass was the greenest she'd ever seen. The boys' laughter could be heard from afar off, but they couldn't hear her. This time, she ran with all her might to catch up to them, until a huge gulf opened, separating her from them. As she neared the gulf, miraculous they recognized her. She screamed, trying her hardest to find a way around the abyss.

They were speaking at the same time, which made it hard to understand them. She strained with everything within her to read their lips, but the more confused she became. Within seconds, as if the volume had been turned on, she heard them chanting, *"Set us free us. Set us free us. Set us free us."*

"Nooooooooooooooooo!" She yelled. Her echo was so powerful that it knocked her to the ground. *"I will never let you go."*

She continued to search for a way around the gulf. Each time she thought she had found an entrance, the gulf widened to block her from passing. Exhausted, she collapsed to her knees, begging God to allow her to cross over with her family. Screaming out in anger, she asked, *"Why Lord…why can't I be with my family?"*

A gentle voice sounding like her husband, responded, *"Because it's not your time."*

"I don't want to live without you and the boys," she cried, refusing to accept his words. She stood on bended knees, balling her eyes out.

"You have a lot more living to do, babies to be born and a husband to grow old with."

She shook her head. The last thing she wanted to do was create a new family without them. *"Please, don't leave me Michael. Come across the gulf to get me. Please."* Tears streamed down her distraught face as she looked over at them, smiling and rejoicing without her. Had they forgotten about her and moved on?

"We will see each other again, my love. But the boys and I have to go. The others are waiting for us."

"The others? What others?" Perplexed, she stood, and then walked closer to the Gulf separating them. Michael, the twins and people she didn't recognize turned and headed to the light. She screamed as loud as she could to get their attention.

He and the boys turned back one last time to wave, blew her a kiss and walked hand-in-hand into the light.

The gulf separating them had closed, and she stood alone in the beautiful green pasture, sobbing. If only she could have gotten to them, she knew she could have stopped them from leaving. Then, her thoughts turned to what Michael had said about her having babies and a husband. Was he giving her his approval to move on without him? She could never imagine replacing her boys with other children.

Joi woke up in a cold sweat, fighting the covers. "What kind of dream was that?" she said out loud. "Whew... I haven't had a dream about Michael and the boys in months."

The thought of remarrying scared Joi, but she did not want to spend the rest of her life alone.

Chapter Forty

In need of some sound advice, Wyatt visited his friend Paul. He was close in age and more level headed when it came to life and relationships. So, Wyatt thought it best to consult him when it came to matters of the heart. His and Joi's friendship was turning into something more than he could have ever imagined. She told him on several occasions that she only wanted friendship, but from the way she kissed him and her action when other women came on to him, told a different story.

He and Paul played a round of pool in his den to pass the time. "What do you want to talk to me about, Wyatt?" Paul asked, hitting his ball into one of the side pockets.

"You know Joi and I have been spending quite a bit of time together." He propped against the billiard table with pool stick in hand and continued, "She's the type of woman who I should have settled down with years ago."

"What are you saying?" Paul stood to face him after ensuring that his ball had dropped into the hole. "You're going to ask her to marry you?"

He took in a deep breath, and then exhaled. "Yes. I love everything about her."

"Does she know how you feel?"

"I've tried everything, but she can't seem to move pass the death of her family." Wyatt laid his pool stick down on the table. He took a seat in the leather, tan sofa in the far corner of the room. Paul followed him.

"That's not something easy to bounce back from, Man," Paul responded, taking a seat in the recliner in front of Wyatt.

"What do you suggest that I do? Sit around and do nothing? I'm thirty-five. I want to start a family before I'm too old." Wyatt scooted to the edge of the sofa, hoping his friend had the answer to his dilemma. "Man, I don't want to be getting around on a walker to play with my kids."

"Not the way you work out. You'll probably be the only elderly man throwing passes and making tackles."

They both laughed.

Paul turned the television on football, but Wyatt had no interest in watching his favorite sport. "I may get shot down, but I'm going to pop the question, and soon. This waiting until the right moment is about to drive me crazy."

"It seems like you've made your decision. Joi must be an exceptional woman to make you want to jump back into holy matrimony for a second time. All I can say is, go for it, and trust me when I say; marrying the *Bride of Frankenstein* would be better than what you had in Trina."

"You're telling me." Wyatt picked up the remote control to turn the station, looking for nothing in particular. His nervous energy was getting the better of him. The battle in his mind to propose or not propose made him a nervous wreck.

He didn't know what type of man Joi's decease husband was, but, from the way she spoke of him, he sounded like a saint. How was he going to compete with that? If only he could get her to see that in him. His only mistake was marrying the wrong woman. Well, make that two mistakes, both he wished that he could go back in the past and erase.

"I'm not trying to change the subject, but we need to go out on the town and have some fun," Paul suggested, heading to the mini-fridge to retrieve two bottles of water. He had the best bachelor pad ever. Thirty and never been married, he seemed to be enjoying the single life.

"We haven't done much since Jett began his anger management counseling." Anything was better than lying in bed at night, driving himself crazy with thoughts of Joi. "What's on your mind?"

"Bowling," he proposed. "You can ask Joi to bring her friends and all of us can hangout, and then grab a bite to eat afterwards."

"Why didn't I think of that?" he asked, smiling.

"Because your mind is on how to catch a wife."

*****

Wyatt headed home, glad that he had stopped by Paul's house. The bowling idea was a great one. The only person he worried about was Jett. Hopefully, his ninety days of counseling had tamed the savage beast inside him. No doubt, Joi's friend Tara would be there, and he wanted the eight of them to have a great time without Jett doing or saying the wrong thing.

Pulling into his drive way, he noticed a car parked on the curb. To his surprise, it was Trina, in a new black Lexus. He figured that she wanted to stop by and flaunt it in his face. Somebody better inform her doctor boyfriend that lavishing her with expensive gifts would eventually send him into the poorhouse. She had expensive taste and did not take no for an answer. When her new beau stops supplying her with what she wanted, he would be left to pay the bills, just as Wyatt had.

He shut off his engine and exited his truck with caution. Her showing up at his doorsteps at this late hour wasn't a good sign. *What is she up to?* He'd bought Trina out of her half of their house, immediately taken her name off the deeds. It nearly bankrupted him when she took money without his knowledge from their joint banking account. Then, she transferred it into a new one that she opened before their separation. Thankfully, the judge ordered her to return portions of it when their divorce was final.

He walked over to where she stood propped against her new Lexus. "What do you want Trina?" he demanded, showing no warmth in his voice.

"Hello to you to, Wyatt."

If Wyatt didn't know any better, Trina appeared stressed from the look on her face. Any other time, she would have been slanging nasty insults at him. Or, trying to belittle him about the expensive gifts her new beau had given her. "It's late, why are you parked outside my house?"

"It used to be our house, remember," she said in a soft, more humbled tone, which set off the alarms in Wyatt's head.

"Cut the crap, Trina," he ordered, knowing that she was after something. "You left me for another man. Do you remember that? So, save the trip down memory lane, because I'm not in the mood for it." He stuffed his hands inside his pant pockets, waiting on her to get to the real purpose of her visit. "What do you want?"

She seemed troubled. For Trina that was odd. With a tongue for a whip, it surprised him when she didn't cut him down. The way she stood defenseless beside her car, warned him that something wasn't right.

"Wyatt, I know that I have a lot of nerves to ask this of you." She shifted her stiletto heels in the grass. "But," she paused. "I need to borrow some money."

The wind was knocked right of out of his lungs. He bucked his eyes at her. "Are you serious?" The way she flaunted her doctor in his face every chance she got, and now, she stood before him asking for money was a slap in the face. "You left me with well over $50,000. What have you done with it?"

"Wyatt, please," she begged. Her attitude more chastened than he'd ever known. "I just need it to tide me over until an investment that I made comes through."

"What investment, Trina?" He raised a doubtful brow and shook his head in disbelief. He knew that one day her fetish for expensive things was going to catch up with her.

"I can't go into details, but I'm being truthful."

Unable to look him in the face as she explained herself told Wyatt that she was lying. As flimsy as her story sounded, it didn't stop him from reaching into his back pocket for his checkbook. He wrote her a check for a thousand dollars. His gut feeling told him not to do it, but he did it anyway. He guessed he was still under her spell.

"This is a loan," he said, handing her the check. "What I can't understand is why you didn't ask your rich doctor for the money?"

"I don't want to start out our relationship asking for money," she said, folding the check and stuffing it inside her purse.

"Really? You sure didn't have a problem asking me for money when we met." There was something that she wasn't telling him. She lived and breathed money. He should know after being married to her for five years. "I want my money back when your investment comes through. Noticed that I put loan on the check, so if you don't pay it back, I will take you to court."

Her eyes widened when he said that he would take her to court. Something smelled fishy about her investment deal. If it wasn't for his financial sense during their marriage, Trina would have spent every dime he saved. She divorced him, leaving their marriage with a nice nest egg because of his wise investment.

"You will get your money back. I promise." She rounded to the driver's side of her Lexus and hoped in. "Well, I have to go. Thanks."

Before closing her door, Wyatt thought he'd heard her say, "Bye Sucker." Like lighting, she sped off into the street and disappeared. Call him stupid, but that was exactly how he felt. He scratched his head and went inside his home. The home he'd once shared with one of the most selfish women he had ever met. His mom had warned him that Trina wasn't the woman that God had for him. Instead, he ignored his mother's words and paid the price for it ever since.

Chapter Forty-One

"Thanks Joi for asking your friends on such short notice to join me and the guys tonight," Wyatt said, unhooking his arm from around her waist.

"No problem. Trust me. I didn't have to twist any of their arms to get them here." They laughed as they strolled towards the table where the others were waiting on them.

Amazingly, Tara and Jett seemed to be getting alone. After taking an anger management class, he appeared more at peace, and Wyatt hoped that it stayed that way.

"Hey everyone, sorry we're late," Wyatt apologized as he and Joi took their seats.

"Hump...we know why the two of you are late," Jett said, chewing gum with a big grin on his face. "You needed more smooching time."

Wyatt waved a playful hand at him. "No. We are late because, this beautiful lady beside me couldn't make up her mind on what to wear to a bowling alley." Joi punched Wyatt on the arm.

"Did not," Joi said in a babyish tone. "He was trying to catch the ending of some football game on television."

"Okay, okay, okay." Wyatt tried quieting her down to keep her from telling the truth on him. "So, what's it going to be, girls against boys or mix it up?" Wyatt asked.

The ladies yelled, "Girls against boys!" They started whispering as if trying to come up with some kind of strategy to beat the men.

Hopping from their seats, they paired off into males versus females. The men laughed as they watched the women, trying to hold on to the bowling ball. "Oh yeah," Wyatt said. "We have this game won."

Paul burst into laughter when Becky clumsily dropped the ball on the floor. "I declare the men the winners." He stretched his arms in victory as they prepared themselves for an easy win against the ladies.

The guys' voices faded in the background as Wyatt watched Joi's every move. He wished that the teams could have been mixed-up, instead of the same sex. He wanted to teach her how to hold the bowling ball in her hands. He could have had the pleasure of showing her, up close and personal with his arm around her waist. He had to get himself together and get his head in the game.

If everything goes well, he planned to ask Joi to marry him. Playing by the rules wasn't working for him anymore. He had to bend them a little to get what he wanted. If she said yes, his first plan of action would be to sell his house. He wanted a fresh start with new memories. Joi deserved better than to be moved into a home that he'd shared with another woman.

The girls were over in their section, carrying on about whipping the men's behinds. Jett, being the competitor he was said, "Don't let your mouths get you in trouble. The four of you are getting ready to take a serious beating." The men slapped hands in agreement.

Waving for them to prove it, Albre hollered over to the men, "Well, bring it on, then."

"Okay, you girls asked for it. The losers pay for dinner," Paul said, giving his buddies a high-five.

"Those girls don't have a clue what they have gotten themselves into," Wyatt said, being the first man up to bowl.

Doing their best to distract them, the ladies hollered and chanted in their direction. But it didn't work. Wyatt bowled a strike. The men snapped their heads over at the women who became more rowdy than before.

Albre bowled first for the women. She tossed her long raven hair back and sent the ball sailing down the lane. "STRIKE!" The women hollered, laughing and pointing at the men. It was then that Wyatt and the others knew that they had been duped. The women made them believe that they knew nothing about bowling.

"You got lucky on that one," Wyatt said, hoping the other women were horrible at the game. Albre said something to him in her native tongue, Chinese. Whatever she said, the girls understood and burst into laughter.

"I guess she told you," Seth said as he headed up to bowl.

The ball rolled down the lane. Not a single eye blinked. The girls' crossed their fingers, hoping for the worst, while the men held their breaths, frozen as the ball made its way down the lane.

Cheering roared from the girls' section. Seth only knocked over two pins. What a dud. He normally hits strikes. If Wyatt didn't know any better, he'd thought Seth was trying to help the girls win. Not him. He was a natural born competitor. He cared about Joi, even loved her. Forfeiting the game for her, never, she would have to fight to the death to win this game.

"What was that?" Jett asked Seth in disbelief.

Wyatt jumped in. "You did that on purpose." Paul gave his opinion on Seth's disastrous move as well.

"Don't be coming down on Seth," Tara yelled over to the guys.

"Yeah," the other ladies screamed.

The men watched as the ladies showboated, making strike after the strike. The guys had been bamboozled. The ladies waltzed to their seats earlier acting like they didn't have a clue when it came to bowling. Now the men were wiping egg off of their faces. This was the last time they would underestimate the power of a woman.

Now, the men would have to listen to their trash talking the entire night. Glad, he'd brought plenty of cash, because Wyatt was going to need it. Joi's turn came up to bowl. In his heart, he wanted her to do well, but the other part of him; his competitive side wanted her to fall flat on her face. Silence fell among them. He couldn't help but to notice her asset in her jeans. Her sleeveless shirt shone off her glistening, toned brown arms.

The sound, plop, plop, plop, ten times, broke Wyatt out of his trace. She'd bowled a strike. Now he knew those ladies were not amateur bowlers. Joi turned after she scored and winked at him. He waved it off as if it was nothing, but inside he had to admit defeat, and if the other guys were smart, they'd do the same.

"We won. We won," the girls sang, dancing and cheering over in their area.

"It's time to pay up. So get your wallets ready fellas' because we have built up a huge appetite," Joi advised, rubbing her stomach.

"You girls were just lucky," Jett commented, rubbing his hands together, but Wyatt knew better. The girl's had earned their win fair and square.

*****

"Girls, did you see their faces," Becky said, fixing her makeup in the restaurant bathroom mirror. "We should have told them that we use to play on the nurses' bowling league." The girls giggled about their victory and the men's defeat.

"Joi, you and Wyatt's relationship seems as if it has passed the friendship stage." Albre turned her back to the mirror and faced her.

The other ladies were all ears. How was she going to worm her way out of this conversation. Wyatt had begun to grow on her. Whenever she stared into his gorgeous brown eyes, her inside turned mushy. The same way she'd felt when she began falling in love with Michael.

In love! No way.

"Are you going to answer her question, Joi? Because I'm tired of being left in the dark," Tara asked, playing with her braids as she looked in the mirror.

"How many times do I have to tell the three of you, we are just friends?" *There, she said it. They were just friends.*

"Friends? Yeah, right," Becky added. "Keep telling yourself that lie. He's your friend, but from the look on his face, says that you are his woman."

"Stop giving me the third degree," she pleaded, trying her best not to let them see her sweat. She wanted to scream from the mountain top that she loved him, but their timing was all wrong.

"Any fool can see that the man loves you," Becky replied. "You are so busy pushing him away until you can't see it for yourself."

Joi dropped her head. Was she that transparent? Maybe God was trying to tell her the same thing through the dream she had the other night. Even her husband and boys begged her to set them free.

"We better get out of here before the guys think that they have gotten out of paying for our dinner," Albre said, applying a fresh coat of lipstick on her paper thin lips.

"Yes… we better go," Joi agreed as she brushed passed a lady who had just entered the bathroom.

"This conversation isn't over," Tara yelled behind Joi. "You're in love with Wyatt. Why can't you just admit it?"

Confusion flooded her mind. She had no time to sort things out. Everyone was coming at her from every direction with what they assumed she was feeling. Her mother was on her about making amends with Rebekah. Now her friends were on her about confessing her feeling to Wyatt. She needed some time to breathe and to get her head straight. If not, their persistent meddling in her business might cause her to snap.

As she exited the bathroom, Joi watched the guys who appeared to be in a deep conversation. Were they cross-examining him as the ladies had her in the bathroom? The lighting over their table caused Wyatt's beautiful teeth to sparkle when he laughed. Joi did want him, but she had no clue how to start over.

Lord, help me. I'm so confused.

Wyatt spotted her spying on him and the guys. He looked delicious in his baby blue polo shirt and tan cardigan shorts. Was she able to give herself to this man, completely? She'd never been the type to lead a man on. Sooner or later, he might grow tired of waiting for her and seek the love and comfort he desired from another woman. Just the thought of it caused her heart to ache.

Chapter Forty-Two

The ER had been standing room only today, causing Joi to work a double shift. Working non-stop without a break, she finally had a minute to dash off to the cafeteria for a late lunch when she spotted a familiar face. She closed her eyes, and then reopened them, hoping they were playing tricks on her.

The man buffing the hallway floors of the hospital resembled Trina's boyfriend, the doctor. She did her best not to spook him just in case she was correct. So, she tried being as discreet as possible. She ducked around the corner to get a better view of his face.

You got to be kidding me, she told herself. *Trina left Wyatt for a janitor. I can't wait to tell Wyatt. He is going to get a kick out of this.*

Ever since seeing him at the restaurant and Jazz Fest with Trina, her new beau had looked familiar, but Joi had a hard time placing where she'd seen him, until now. That explained why he turned his head or looked off into space each time Trina flaunted him in her and Wyatt's faces. She left a man like Wyatt for a guy who was broker than he.

Wyatt's snooty ex-wife was going to feel like a fool when she learned that the man, she thought was a doctor and loaded with money had conned her. God does have a sense of humor. Tara was right. The rings Trina flashed in their faces at the gym could have very well been cubic zirconium. She would soon be knocked off that imaginary high horse she'd been riding on.

Careful not to let him see her, Joi took the back hallway to the cafeteria. Her head still spun from the new revelation she had just discovered. As soon as she contacted Wyatt, Joi had to tell him the truth about his conniving ex-wife's, new lover.

What if they are in cahoots together to drain Wyatt dry? Or, what if he is scamming Trina with plans to dump her once her money train runs out of gas.

As soon as she arrived in the empty cafeteria, Joi pulled out her cellphone to call Wyatt. His telephone rung a couple of times and then went straight to voice mail.

Darn!

Hunger seemed to have left her. The only thing that consumed her was getting in touch with Wyatt and fast. Her mother had spoken a great truth when she had warned that a person reap what they have sown. Trina had used Wyatt for her benefit. Now she'd met her match. The con artist had been conned.

Her cell phone vibrated on the table.

Wyatt. Thank goodness.

She answered, second guessing herself, now that he was on the other end. "Hello," she answered with reservation in her voice.

"Hey," he responded. "Sorry I missed your call... anything wrong?"

"No," she responded. "I saw something... uh, someone rather."

"Someone? Someone like... who?"

"How far are you from the hospital?" She thought he needed to witness it for himself, instead of telling him over the phone.

"Joi, what's wrong?" She could hear the concern in his voice.

"Do you have time to stop by the hospital?" With her being an outsider between him and his ex-wife's bitter break up, it was best he saw the man whom Trina been parading around as a doctor.

"Yes, I'm on my way."

"Wyatt, do not come through the emergency room doors. Come through the back entrance." She disconnected the call and waited for him. She had twenty minutes left on her lunch break and hoped Wyatt hurried.

*****

"You must have run every red-light in Shreveport to get here?" Joi tried joking, but it didn't go over too well.

"The sound of your voice had me worried," he said, huffing. "So, what is it that you want me to see?"

She led him down the back hallway of the hospital, and then cautioned him to be discreet. He was confused as to why, but followed her command. Upon approaching a wall that hid them from oncoming traffic, his mouth flew opened.

"Is that who I think it is?" he asked in shocked, jaws floored. "That's Trina's, doctor boyfriend wearing that janitor's jumpsuit."

"Yes, that's him. I knew that I recognized him. I just couldn't figure out where, until today."

If Wyatt's feet could reach his backside, he'd kick himself. She had been playing him. He had given her money out of his savings account. The blood seemed to rush to his head. "I'm glad you called me. As soon as I see Trina, I'm going to let her have it. I gave her that loan in good faith and she used me." He shook his head, mad about the bad choice he'd made in helping his selfish ex-wife.

"I'm sorry Wyatt," she said. "I didn't want to get in the middle of you and Trina's problem. But you deserve to know."

"Don't be sorry." He kissed the top of her head. "You did the right thing."

Wyatt had a mind to go and sucker punch the man. Instead, he watched in anger as the so-called doctor buffed the hospital's floors. He'd probably scammed Trina out of the $50,000 she was awarded in their divorce settlement, which explained why she came to him begging for money. Big investment she told him. She was broke because her so-called, wealthy doctor had swindled her out of it.

He escorted Joi back to the ER, kissed her good night, and then left. His next detour was Trina's home. Furious wasn't the word to explain how he felt. This woman had walked over him their entire marriage. He was not going to allow her to continue wreaking havoc in his life now that they were divorced. Tonight, she was going to stop meddling in his life once and for all.

*****

Slowing his speed, because the last thing he needed was another run in with the law. Jett had bailed him out the first time, and he'd regretted it ever since. Hopefully, after his anger management classes, Jett would stop throwing that night in question up in his face. He wasn't proud of his actions that night, but he never asked Jett to cover for him either.

"Good, her lights are on," Wyatt said out loud. He pulled into her drive way. Jumping out of his truck, he headed up her steps. He knocked on the door, and then second guessed himself for showing up at her home.

Trina opened the door. She looked the worse he'd ever seen her. One of the things he did admired about her was that she took great pride in her appearance. "What do you want?" she scowled, her breath reeking of alcohol.

"Trina? Are you drunk?" Was all he could say. Black smudge spots from her mascara had smear around her eyes. Her matted hair caused him to believe that it had been days since she last combed it.

"Wy-a-ttttttttttttttttttt." she slurred and then fell into his arms.

He picked her up and laid her down on the couch. Wyatt covered her half-dressed body with a blanket and went into the kitchen to brew some coffee to sober her up. His first intention for coming over to Trina's place was to let her have it, but his heart softened watching her drunken body lie in a pitiful stupor.

Entering back into the living room, the man that he'd seen earlier buffing the hospital floors had entered the house. "What are you doing in my woman's house?" the man asked with balled fist.

"Look, I don't want any trouble," Wyatt said, watching the man's every move. "I came over here to discuss you, actually."

"Me? You don't know anything about me." The man's husky voice sounded threatening.

Wyatt sat beside Trina on the couch, trying to wake her up. Desperately, he wrestled with her to drink the coffee. He stood once she was able to hold the cup in her hand. He couldn't believe that this was the woman he had once loved. Although, she had done some low-down dirty things to him, he still cared about her well-being.

"Look, she's drunk," Wyatt announced to the unconcerned man. "What is going on here? I have never seen her like this."

"Trina is my concern now," the man said, moving in Wyatt's direction.

"If you cared so much about her, then why is she drunk?" Wyatt asked; irritated how things were playing out. "I'll tell you why. She's drunk because you conned her out of her money."

"Man, who do you think you're talking too? You don't know me." The man, short in height approached Wyatt, causing Trina to jump from the couch and staggered between them.

"Stop it! Stop it!" she screamed, nearly bursting his eardrums. "I'm broke." Spit flew from her mouth as she spoke. "And you're the reason for it Cedric."

"Woman, you better go and sit back down before I knock you down." He threatened.

She did as she was told, which shocked Wyatt. Never once had he'd known Trina to back down to anyone. What hold did this man have on her? "If you put a hand on her, I will call the cops."

The mention of the cops caused Cedric to take two-steps back from Wyatt.

"You are a janitor," Wyatt said, wanting to gloat in what he'd found out about Trina's boyfriend, but couldn't. Watching the misery on her face made his heart ache.

"JANITOR!" Trina eyes nearly popped from their sockets. "You are a doctor. That's what you told me. And what about the money you were investing for me?"

"The investment fell through," he said with an attitude, and then slithered out the door like the snake he was.

Trina ran behind him, grabbing what she could find off a nearby table and threw it at him. When she returned inside, she collapsed into Wyatt's arms and sobbed. "How could I have been so stupid? I'm so sorry Wyatt for all the mean and cruel things that I've done to you. You were a good husband to me. I was too stupid to see it, then."

Wyatt didn't say a word. His only thoughts were on Joi. Thanks to her, he would have never found out that Cedric wasn't the man that he claimed to be. He was the weasel behind Trina's sudden disappearing funds.

Not wanting to leave Trina to her own devices, he stayed with her until her mother arrived. Trina walked him to the door. She was wrapped in the same blanket he'd covered her with earlier. He kissed her on the forehead, smoothing down her disheveled hair, and then said his goodbyes. He had promised to stop by the next day to check in on her. He'd also advised her to file a complaint with the police department about Cedric stealing her money.

Chapter Forty-Three

Joi decided to grab a burger and fries before heading home. Her appetite was ruined today after she had shown Wyatt the man that his ex-wife had left him for. She took a different route through the subdivision, instead of getting back onto the interstate. It slowed her down a bit with the speed limit being twenty-five miles per hour, but she didn't seem to mind. She was in no hurry to return to an empty, lifeless home.

Glad that the neighborhood streets were well lit put her mind at ease. It wasn't her usual route, although she was somewhat familiar with the roads. As she drove, the sounds of easy listening music played on the radio, which always put her in a mellow mood after pulling a grueling double shift at the hospital. She hummed along with the radio as her mind drifted to happier times of her and Michael. The memories put a smile on her fatigued face.

Just when she decided to get off the back roads and head back to a main street, she slowed her vehicle. The man standing on a porch with a woman wrapped in a blanket resembled Wyatt. She shook her head, believing her sleepy eyes were playing tricks on her. The man gave the woman a loving kissed. From the way her hair stood over her head, it looked as though they had been doing more than just kissing.

The man began to turned and head to his truck. "Wyatt!" Joi screamed as his face came into view, and the woman wrapped up in the blanket was Trina. She sped away quickly to keep from being seen. "I've lost him." Tears began pouring down her face, making it impossible for her to see where she was going. Thankfully, the streets were empty. "Trina had won him back."

The last time she spoke with Wyatt, he was going to confront Trina about her lying doctor/janitor boyfriend. From the looks of Trina's hair and the blanket covering her 'nude' body, they did more than just talked. They had slept together. "Wyatt had made love to his ex-wife. Which meant only one thing; he was still in love with her."

Her playing the friend's card had now blown up in her face. She'd lost him. Had she known that exposing Trina's boyfriend for the crook that he was would have caused them to get back together; she would have kept her mouth closed. Pounding her hand on the steering wheel as she searched for the quickest way back onto the interstate, she cried out to God. "Lord, help me. I have been so caught up in my own grief that I failed to see the man that You sent to me. Now, I've lost him forever."

Pulling into her drive way, unable to get out, she reflected back on the days when Wyatt kept expressing his love for her. She continued to push him away and made excuses as to why they should remain friends. It took seeing him in the arms of another woman and not just any woman— his ex-wife— to realize that she loved him.

"What a fool I have been. I let a good man slip through my fingers," she cried, laying her head on the steering wheel, wallowing in self-pity.

Her heart felt as if it had burst into her chest. She hasn't experienced pain of this magnitude since losing her family two years ago. At that defining moment, she realized that Wyatt had indeed found his way into her heart. But it didn't matter now, because he and Trina were back together. "What am I going to do?" she sniffed, trying to get herself together. She lifted her head from the steering wheel and went inside. The burger she hungered for earlier did not look so appealing. Her appetite had left.

To her surprise, she wasn't angry with Wyatt. He was a man with needs and desires. How long did she expect to string him along?

Maybe his feelings for Trina were always there? And it took another man to invade his territory to realize it.

*****

Joi woke up with a headache the size of Texas. Glad to be off for three days, she decided to use it to do some much needed soul searching. Her life was beginning to spiral out of control. If she didn't do something about it and soon, she just might lose her mind.

Strolling toward the shower, her thoughts roamed on Wyatt. After seeing him with Trina last night, how was she going to face him? The way things stood now, avoiding him would be her best out. Her heart couldn't take rejection and since he and Trina was back together; rejection was inevitable.

She dressed and headed over to her parents' home to keep from being alone. Today was the lowest she'd been in a while. Wyatt had returned to his ex-wife and she was back to living her boring life. Tara had warned her that she would lose him and that was exactly what had happened. If only she had listened to sound advice. Instead, she thought she knew everything.

As she pulled into her parents' driveway, she found her mother outside tending to her flowerbed. She stood off her bended knees and strolled to the car. "What brings you by today?" she asked, wiping the sweat from her forehead. "You usually call before stopping by."

"I was in the neighborhood and decided to drop in," she lied. The walls were closing in on her. If she hadn't left home, she swore that she would have gone stir crazy. She followed her mother inside and into the kitchen.

"Do you want a cup of coffee, Baby?" Her mother washed her hands and pulled two cups from the cabinet.

"Yes, and make mine super strong. I need the caffeine." She pulled out a stool from the kitchen island and took a seat. Her mind stayed on Wyatt. She hadn't heard from him today, which was unlike him, but it wasn't like she didn't know why. He probably was with his, ex.

The sound of her mother calling her name jerked her out of her thoughts. "Joi. Joi, did you hear a word I've said?" she asked, standing in front of her.

"Huh." Joi answered, looking up at her mother with a blank stare.

"I asked if there is something wrong. You seemed preoccupied ever since you arrived." She placed Joi's cup of coffee in front of her.

"I have a lot on my mind, nothing serious." The heck it wasn't.

"Child, you have to get up early in the morning to fool me," she said, arching her gray brows at her.

She blew her coffee, and then took a sip. "I messed up, Mom. I've messed up really bad this time." she gulped, trying to keep from crying. "I've lost Wyatt."

"Lost him... how?"

"He's gone back to his ex-wife. I saw him last night coming out of her home." Her voice began to quiver.

"Oh my. Baby, I so sorry." She rounded the counter to comfort her daughter. "There. There, Darling. Let it all out," her mom said, cradling the back of Joi's head against her body.

"I love him so much," she cried. "It hurt so bad, knowing that I pushed him away." She wept in her mother's arms.

Whenever she was troubled about anything, Joi knew in her mother's arms, she could find comfort. If she was granted a do over, she'd tell Wyatt just how she felt, and give him the love and affection that he longed for from her.

She whimpered in her mother's embrace. When he wanted her, she wanted no part of him. Now that he had moved on, she wanted another chance. Maybe she was getting what she deserved. He was a good man and she knew it, but at the time she was too blind to see it.

One part of her wanted to find him and beg him to give her a second chance, but, she had her chance and refused to go groveling to him. She was warned in advance that this would happen.

Her mother pulled her back. Joi's face soaking wet. She could only imagine what she must have looked like.

"Joi, you have a lot of things you need to set right in your life. Starting with Rebekah, and then making things right with Wyatt. That young lady needs your forgiveness. You walk around as if you are the only one hurting. She is eighteen-years-old now and should be enjoying college, but she's stuck in the past... just like you."

"Mom...what does that girl have to do with what I'm going through with Wyatt?" She snapped her neck back with a confused look.

"Girl, I swear sometime you act like you don't have the sense that God gave you." Her mother had a disapproving frown on her face. "Things are never going to go right in your life until you go and see that young lady. She's hurting too. Go and see her, so she can move on with her life. Free her Joi and yourself."

"Mama," she pouted, whining as she had when she was a child who didn't want to do what her parents' had instructed.

"Don't mama me. God is not pleased with your hateful heart."

That got her attention. She was a lot of things but hateful she was not. At least she didn't believe that she was. Those words stung. "I'm not hateful, Mother."

"Then what do you call it?" She placed a hand on her hip. "Rebekah is a child...a baby."

"I hear you, Mama." She dropped her head into her mother's bosom. She had a gift for getting Joi to see the error of her ways. Caught up in her own pain, Joi couldn't see anything else. Between working long hours and keeping Wyatt at bay, took up most of her time. She had no room to focus on Rebekah or her issues.

Joi knew she had to pray for clarity and set thing right with Rebekah. She was ready to live again and she should allow

Rebekah to do the same. She deserved to enjoy her college years and the rest of her life. How had her life gotten so far off course that she had lost compassion for others?

"Well, what are you going to do about it?"

"Will you call Rebekah's parents' and tell them that I will come by tomorrow?" she asked, trying to sound as humble as possible. "Since you're always checking in on her."

"Sure, Baby. But we're not going tomorrow, we're going today." her mom ordered. She kissed Joi on the cheek and gave her a big hearty hug. "Then, after you take care of this problem, go to Wyatt and find out for sure what is going on before jumping to conclusions. Everything is not always what it appears."

Chapter Forty-Four

Joi, with her mother by her side made the overdue trip to visit Rebekah and her parents. She was sweating bullets. She hadn't laid eyes on the young girl ever since the judge sentenced her with five years' probation.

This place looks like a castle, Joi thought as she and her mother ogled the outside of the home, in awe.

With each step, her stomach twisted and turned from fear of the unknown. The red brick winding pathway leading to the front door reminded her of the Wizard of Oz's yellow brick road, Instead of chanting, "There's no place like home." Joi wanted to scream, "This was where the person lived that took away her happy home."

Her mom led the way. Confidence and pride were in each step she took. Joi wished that she could be half the woman her mother was. She didn't know the meaning of backing down from a fight or a challenge, and coming to visit Rebekah was definitely a challenge. Only a godly woman could forgive and show compassion for the person who killed her grandkids and son-in-law, but her mother was that woman.

Finally, they were at the door that stood lofty and majestic. A tall, slender black man dressed in a starched black suit, crisp white shirt and shoes that shined so bright that she could see her own reflection, greeted them when he opened the door. His stance was refined as the house itself. "Good evening, ladies." He spoke with class. "Mr. and Mrs. Harrington are expecting the two of you." He escorted them inside and led them down a hallway with antique paintings that lined the spacious walls. Money screamed at them from every direction of the house. The Harrington's were indeed loaded to say the least.

Even the butler's walk was dignified. Joi whispered to her mom as they followed behind him. "It's not too late to turn around and leave." Now, regretting that she allowed her mother to talk her into facing her family's killer, Joi legs threatened to give way.

"Shh," her mom hissed, shaking her pointed finger at Joi to behave.

With an enormous house of that size, a person needed a scooter to get from one end to other. *Where is he taking us...to the dungeon?* She prayed her mother was right about them coming there. A person could go missing with no hope of ever being seen or heard from again.

On their last turn, they entered a grand room decorated with exquisite figurines and furniture that looked to cost a fortune. The chandelier caused the room to sparkle with an elegance she had only seen in the movies. Once inside, they came face to face with the Harrington's. The immaculate dressed couple stood when Joi and her mom entered the room.

Before anyone could say a word, Joi's eyes scanned the room for the teenager. Rebekah wasn't there, giving Joi time to gather herself.

Mrs. Harrington broke the awkward silence and stepped toward them. Joi became light headed at the sight of them. Her nerves were running wild. "Come in ladies," she welcomed them with a stiff smile. "Have a seat." She gestured towards two chairs that probably cost more than Joi and her parents' home put together.

"It's nice to finally meet you and your husband in person," Ester said with dignity and warmth in her voice.

Mr. Harrington stood in place as the ladies formally introduced themselves. Afterwards, he walked over, shaking each of their hands. "It's nice to finally meet you too, Ester." He held on to her mother's hand as if she was going to disappear. "Thank you for calling each week to check on Rebekah." He turned and gave Joi a faint smile.

The temperature in the room began to drop under Mr. Harrington's cold stare. It made Joi uneasy. *How dare he look at me with such contempt*? She wanted to blurt out and tell him that his daughter was the reason for putting them in this situation. She and her mother wouldn't be there if it wasn't for Rebekah. But, she kept her thoughts to herself.

Joi sat quietly as her mom spoke with the Harrington's. If she didn't know any better, she'd thought they had known each other for years. The servant poured them each a cup of tea and some sort of expensive snack cakes, but anxiety had taken over, zapping her appetite. Her eyes probed around the room, trying to think of what she was going to say to those people.

Her mother tapped her on the arm, drawing her attention back to them. "Joi... are you alright?" Her mother gave her one of those, 'get yourself together,' type of looks. Joi recognized that look in her mother's eyes anywhere. She had seen it enough times when she would act out in church as a child. Her mother never had to say a word. All she had to do was look at Joi and she would straighten up.

"I'm find mother," she said, forging a smile on her face. *Lord, what am I doing here?* She fidgeted with the strap on her purse.

Her mother turned her attention back to the Harrington's. "If you don't mind me asking, where is Rebekah?"

That's my mother. Get straight to the point. Joi cringed at her mother's question.

"She will be down soon. My wife and I had to make sure that everyone was rational," Mr. Harrington said with a watchful eye on Joi.

Rational! She screamed to herself. *Just what is he trying say. Your daughter is the killer, not me*. If her mother knew what she was thinking, she'd pinch her arm, but like an obedient daughter, she sat there prim and proper. When, what she really wanted to do was tell those people off. If it wasn't for Joi's father dragging her out of courtroom kicking and screaming, she would have spoken her peace then.

Joi noticed her mother clasping her hands together, which meant, Mr. Harrington had hit a nerve, but her mother kept a pleasant smile on her face. Joi found her voice and said, "Sir, I don't mean to sound rude, but I have every reason to feel the way that I do." She stiffened her body, trying to remain in control. "My family is laying six-feet under the ground." She stopped, as a rush of heat washed over her.

"Calm down, Baby." Her mother patted her on the leg.

She refused to allow the Harrington make light of their daughter's action. Three people were dead because of her. "I'm fine, Mama," she said, taking in a deep, long breath.

"I didn't mean to offend you or make light of the situation, Miss. Campbell," he said with sincerity in his deep voice. Tears welled up in his eyes. "My wife and I have also been through a lot since the accident."

Joi gave him a sidelong glance, as if she hadn't been through anything. His daughter was somewhere upstairs. Where was her family— down at the cemetery?

His wife came and stood by his side as he tried keeping his dignified composure. Clearly, she could see the pain in his face. Something she was all too familiar with. The years had worn him down.

"I know you and your family has been through a lot, Miss Campbell, but we have lost our spunky, outgoing little girl too. Ever since the accident, Rebekah has been in and out of psy ward so many times until we have lost count. Life has left her. Our baby is gone." Mr. Harrington's voice trembled as he tried to speak.

"Peter. Darling, you don't have to go into every detail," Mrs. Harrington advised, fighting back her own tears.

"But I want to Rose," he said. "We're here together, seeking the same thing. Peace. And hopefully closure."

Joi's emotions for the father took her aback. She'd been so wrapped up in her own misery that she failed to realize that Rebekah's parents' were suffering as well. They had all suffered a loss. Instead of placing the blame, it was time for healing and forgiving. It was the only way— God's way.

Mr. Harrington continued to express his thoughts. "For some time now, we have had to keep a watchful eye on her. Rebekah has stopped eating." He had to take a seat. It was obvious to everyone in the room that the stress and worry he was under had taken a toll on him. "I'm sorry for your loss, Miss Campbell—"

She interrupted him. Her heart ached for the older gentleman. "You can call me Joi," she said in a more subdued tone.

"Joi, please believe me. My wife and I are truly sorry." His wife wrapped her arms around him as he pressed his head against her body. It was evident that Mrs. Harrington had been the backbone that kept her family together. "We know it hasn't been easy for you either."

The same butler, who escorted them through the house, came and interrupted their heartfelt conversation. "Mr. Harrington, Sir. Please forgive me for interrupting you and your guests, but Ms. Rebekah is preparing to come down."

Mr. Harrington jumped to his feet and collected himself before his daughter entered the room. "Very good" His voice sounded more spirited than just a few seconds ago. "Send her on down, Frederick." The butler turned on his heels and exited the room.

"You don't think that it's too soon, Darling?" Mrs. Harrington asked, looping her arms through his.

Joi and her mother sat speechless in their seats as the couple seemed to fall apart right before their eyes. Feeling horrible for prolonging a sit-down to clear the air, she mourned inside for the young girl. Over taken by her thoughts, Joi knew that things had to be set right before she left the Harrington's home. Although, it wouldn't bring back her family, at least it would give Rebekah a second chance at life.

"No, Dear. This meeting is long overdue."

As Joi and her mother watched the Harrington's talk amongst themselves, the butler returned with a frail eighteen-year old girl.

She is skin and bones, Joi thought, trying her best not to gawk.

Rebekah stood in the entranceway of the room, holding on to Fredrick's arm for dear life. He released her arm from around his and then he disappeared, leaving her alone.

Inwardly, Joi gasped at the young girl's fragile state. *Oh my, Lord!*

"Hi, Baby," her mother greeted. She rushed to her daughter's side as if she was a toddler just learning how to walk. Mr. Harrington stood with a forced smile on his face. His eyes lit up when Rebekah entered the room. Joi and her mother stayed seated, trying not to stare at the girl's anorexic appearance.

Rebekah's smile lacked luster as she made her way into the room. Like an infant, needing her mother's assistance, Mrs. Harrington guided her to the vacant seat next to her father.

The girl looked nothing as Joi remembered from the courtroom. Her long, shiny blonde hair looked dull and stringy. Her tanned skin had faded into a washed-out pale complexion. The teenager she'd seen two years ago had vanished into the lifeless shell that stood before them. The tragic accident had indeed affected them all.

Rebekah's father kissed his daughter on top of her head, although he was smiling, Joi could see the pain in his eyes. She recognized that look anywhere, because each morning it stared back at her from the mirror. "Rebekah, Miss Campbell and her mom have come to visit with you."

Through her long lashes, the teenager peered up at them. Joi wondered if Rebekah even remembered her.

"Hello, Sweetie," Joi's mom greeted. "It's so good to see you again."

Joi knew her mom meant every word of it by the compassion in her voice.

"Hi Rebekah," Joi said with warmth in her voice. Her instincts as a mother kicked in, she stood and walked over to the young girl. "Do you mind, Mr. Harrington, if I sit next to her?"

Both parents stared at the other as if trying to decide if it was a good idea. With reservations, Mr. Harrington agreed, "Sure." He exchanged seats with Joi.

Joi allowed the Holy Spirit to guide her. She'd lost her family, true enough, but she could not sit by and watch the Harrington's lose their only daughter. "Rebekah, do you remember me?" Joi asked, choking back her tears.

Rebekah shook her head up and down. "Yes," she said in a hushed whisper.

"I want you to know that I forgive you." She stopped and placed her hands over the young girl's hands. "And I need for you to forgive yourself."

As if waiting to hear those words her entire life. Rebekah leaned into Joi and wept, bitterly. Rebekah's parents and Joi's mother stood from their seats and embraced one another. The healing process had begun.

Chapter Forty-Five

"Baby, I have never been more proud of you than I am now," Ester said, rubbing Joi's arm as they drove home.

"Thanks, Mom. I couldn't have done it without you." Joi looked both ways down the street before turning. "The Harrington's seem to have a new lease on life."

"You've handled this problem. So, when are you going to talk to Wyatt about seeing him at his ex-wife's house?"

Her mother was the type of woman who got straight to the point. Actually, Joi hadn't decided how she was going to handle things between her and Wyatt. "I'm not ready to tackle that issue just yet, Mother."

"You can't let something like this go unaddressed for too long."

"I know."

The only thing Joi had on her mind at the moment was going home and taking a long nap. Her day off from work had been far spent, but in a positive way. She didn't have the energy to put out two fires in one day. She was drained. Her situation with Wyatt would just have to wait.

Her mother dropped the subject, which pleased Joi. "Oh shoots...I almost forgot my cellphone!" her mom shouted. They had both silenced their devices, but later decided to leave them in the cup holder in the car. With the serious issue they were about to discuss, the last thing they needed was to be interrupted by the ringing of their phones. Her mother dropped her cellphone in her purse and rode the next couple of miles in silence, which didn't bother Joi one bit.

Meanwhile, Joi dropped her mom off and headed towards the interstate for home. Her mind wandered on Wyatt. Through tired and sleepy eyes, she checked her cellphone. She hadn't received so much as a text message from Wyatt. Within a twenty-four hour period, Joi would have talked to him at least three times or received countless text messages. She feared the worst. He was getting back together with Trina.

Moments later, she entered her home and went straight to the bedroom. Exhausted from today's event and thinking about Wyatt, she collapsed flat on her back in her bed. She stared at the celling, mad at herself for letting him get away. God had given her a second chance at love and she'd blown it.

*****

Against his better judgment, Wyatt left work, driving to Trina's place. He tried calling Joi earlier to let her know, but for some reason she wasn't answering her cellphone. He arrived at Trina's home and knocked on her door for what seemed like an eternity. After several attempts, she finally opened it. "Hi Trina, I stopped by to see if you were okay." A musty odor slapped him in the face as he walked in. The house looked as if it had been burglarized.

A nicer version of Trina who he wasn't used to, greeted him. "Thanks Wyatt, that's nice of you," she said, pushing the clutter on the sofa aside. "Have a seat."

"I'm not staying long," he said. The smell was making him nauseous. "Trina did you file the police report on Cedric like I told you?"

"Not yet." She scratched through her matted hair and sat down.

"Why not?" His voiced rose before he knew it. "The guy has stolen every dime of your money."

"I'm going to file it tomorrow. I promise," she said, pathetically. "Wyatt, I meant what I said last night. I apologize for every mean thing I've done to you. You are a good man. Too bad it took for this to happen for me to realize it."

"Coming from you that mean a lot," he smiled. He'd been called so many awful things by her that her apology took him by surprise. Years ago, he'd given his life for her, but Trina's love for money destroyed the love they once shared. He wanted kids and she was too selfish to even give him one. Now, he stood in the middle of her living room trying to figure out what caused her to be so cruel.

As he turned to head out the door, she jumped from the sofa after him. "Wyatt, I want you back."

He snapped his head around to face her, hoping that she was joking. The love he once had for her was dead, unable to be resurrected. Was she serious? This was the same woman who moved out of their home when he was at work. She didn't even have the decency to tell him she had left him for another man. Instead, she notified him via text message.

"Trina, I'm in love with Joi," he admitted. He wanted to hurt her the way she'd hurt him, but the God in him wouldn't allow him to. "I'm going to ask her to marry me."

Trina only wanted him because she was broke. The man she'd left him for was a two-bit hustler. He'd drained her bank account dry.

"But, I was once your wife," she pleaded, drawing closer to him. "I still love you. Give us another try, please." The smell of stale liquid on her breath and the desperation in her eyes made him sick to his stomach. He cared about her well-being, but she destroyed what ounce of love he once had for her.

She grabbed his arms to prevent him from leaving. "Trina, you left me for another man. And just days ago, you flaunted him in my face, and you think that I will take you back?" He jerked his arms out of her grip and rushed out the door. He knew it was a bad idea coming to her house.

Anger couldn't explain the way he felt at that moment. Trina had slept with another man behind his back. How stupid did she think he was? Let her find another sucker to swindle money from because it sure wasn't going to be him anymore.

After he'd left Trina's home, he tried calling Joi for the umpteenth time. His calls went straight to voice mail. *Where could she be?* Concern began to consume him, because it was so unlike Joi not to return his calls. She'd usually answer her phone on the second or third ring. Without thinking, he veered onto the interstate in the direction to Joi's home. Suddenly, his cellphone vibrated. Unable to make out the caller's name or number while trying to watch the busy road ahead, he answered. He hoped it was Joi.

"Hello."

"Hey man, this is Paul." His voice had a sense of urgency to it. "Wherever you are, you need to turn around and head back to the fire station. And fast."

"What's going on?"

"Several homes in the Martin Luther King area were reported burning out of control, and they need every available fireman to report for duty," he explained. "Those houses are adjacent to each other. It will not take much for them to catch if we can't contain it in time."

"I'm on my way." He disconnected the call and searched for the nearest exit off the interstate. Wyatt sensed danger in Paul's voice. He said a silent prayer for his and the other firemen's safety and headed back to the station.

Lord, please cover me. As soon as this job is over, I plan to tell Joi exactly how I feel about her. And ask for her hand in marriage.

Chapter Forty-Six

Joi awaken to the annoying sound of her house phone ringing off the hook. With sleep in her eyes, she fished around for the phone on her nightstand. Peeking over at the digital clock that read 10:00 pm, she wondered who could be calling her at that time of night.

"Hello," she answered, yarning into the receiver.

"Joi. Where have you been?" Tara asked, sounding winded. "I've been calling and leaving messages on your cellphone for over an hour."

"I've been home all evening." Sleep left her as soon as she turned on the lamp beside her bed. She grabbed her cellphone off the table and checked for messages. "I see why I haven't received any calls today. I have my mother's phone —"

"Whatever," Tara interrupted. "I'm helping the charge nurse call every available nurse to report for duty, immediately. There are multiple fires burning out of control in the Martin Luther King area."

"I'm on my way," she said, jumping from her bed like lightening. "Have you heard from Wyatt?"

"No, Joi," Tara's voice dropped. "But I'm sure he's at the scene."

"Okay…I better get going. See you soon." Fear surrounded her every thought. She dreaded this day. Wyatt was in the midst of danger and she didn't know how the night was going play out.

Lord, watch over him as well as the others.

In a flash, Joi was dressed and on her way to the hospital. Her heart pounded out of control with each turn she made. As danger lingered, she wanted a chance to set things right with Wyatt. She wanted to tell him that she loved him, but she would never get the chance to do so. He and Trina were back together now.

Her playing it safe has left her alone. What she'd give to have him wrap his strong arms around her and never let her go. His handsome face would be forever etched in her brain. Tears rolled down her checks as she drove down the empty streets. She had no one to blame but herself. Wyatt told her he wanted more, but she continued to push him away, content playing the friend role.

As she neared the hospital, sirens were going off in every direction. An ambulance pulled into the emergency entrance. Quickly, she parked her car and rushed into the sliding doors. Spotting paramedics who carried an African American male on a stretcher, she followed them, hoping it wasn't Wyatt. Relieved that it had been someone else, she rushed to the ER.

She clocked in and ran to the lounge area where she had found others watching the reporter on the news giving minute by minute updates on the fires, and from the looks of it, there would be causalities. A knot formed in the pit of her stomach at the thought of lives being lost.

"Hi everyone," she greeted with fear in her voice.

"Hi, Joi," the other nurses and medical team sang in unison.

Tara patted the vacant seat beside her, for Joi to come and sit.

"This is awful." Joi eyes stayed clued to the television set as she made her way next to Tara. Through her peripheral vision, she'd noticed Albre, Becky and Tara eyes were glued on her. Something wasn't right. She could feel it in the depths of her stomach. *Wyatt... has he died in the fire*? Her thoughts were running wild. *Maybe they are trying to find a way to tell me.* She couldn't look at them, so she kept her focus on the television.

"Joi." Tara patted her on the leg to get her attention.

"I don't want to know," Joi lashed out, continuing to look straight ahead. Then Albre and Becky went over to her.

"He's not dead," Tara responded. "But he is in danger. The cameraman caught a glimpse of the first firemen going in and Wyatt was among them."

Joi gasped, covering her face with her hands. The others left the lounge, leaving the four friends alone. For Joi, it had been a lousy two days with the exception of repairing things with Rebekah and her family.

"We need to pray that God will protect them from harm," Becky suggested.

"She's right," Albre agreed.

They held hands in their seats and prayed for the protection of those trapped inside the house fires. As Tara prayed, Joi's mind went back two years ago when two policemen knocked on her door to deliver the devastating news of the death of her family. Now, she found herself back in the same situation, only Wyatt wasn't her husband.

Later, Joi and the others made their usual rounds in the ER as they waited for more possible causalities. Under normal circumstances she would have been sleepy working the night shift, but tonight was different. She couldn't sleep if she wanted too. The man she loved, life hanged in the balance and she would not rest until she knew that he was safe.

Her mother's cellphone vibrated in her pocket. Although there was nothing that she could do with it, she brought it with her anyway. It had been on silent since she'd arrived to work. She retrieved it from her scrub pants pocket to answer it.

"Hi mother," Joi said before her mom could say a word. "And yes, I know that you have my cellphone."

"Hi, Smarty Pants," her mother quipped. "Wyatt has left several messages for you."

Joi couldn't believe her ears. He did try to contact her. "Did you listen to them, Mom?"

"You know I wouldn't invade your privacy."

"Forget about privacy, Mama," Joi said, moving to a quieter place in the ER. Like that was possible with the commotion surrounding every corner of the place. "Playback the messages so I can hear them for myself."

"Are you sure?"

"Yes, Mother. I'm sure." Joi listen to each message. She stepped inside a nearby bathroom because the noise level was deafening. His first call was to let her know that he had left Trina's house rather late and that he would call her the next day. He went into detail about Cedric and something about stolen money.

He and Trina are not getting back together after all. Several other messages played but the only one Joi cared about was that Trina and Wyatt weren't resolving their marriage problems.

"That's the last one," her mother said. "I told you that I didn't believe that Wyatt was that type of man."

"Yes, you did mother. I feel so stupid and relieved at the same time. I have a second chance." Doubt began to cloud her mind. *What if Wyatt doesn't make it and I never get the chance to tell him that I love him?*

"I know they need you in the ER, so I better let you get back in there. I called because I wanted you to know that Wyatt did try to contact you, if that means anything."

"It means more than you'll ever know," she stated, gripping tight on the tiny gadget. "I love you and thanks for everything, Mom."

"I love you too, Sweetheart. I'll be praying on this end."

"Thanks." She hung up and headed where the others were. That call gave her a new sense of purpose; although, Wyatt and the others were in danger, she knew if he came back to her, she was never going to let him go.

Chapter Forty-Seven

Wyatt, along with other firemen worked throughout the night to extinguish the dangerous fires that threatened to wipeout an entire neighborhood, leaving families homeless in its aftermath. The flames seemed to have a mind of their own. As soon as they had one house under control, the strong winds worked against them, reigniting the fires. It threatened to catch the wooded areas behind the homes on fire as well. If they had to go into the woods to fight the ferocious flames, the outcome may prove to be deadly. With nothing but total darkness around them, finding their way out would be like trying to find their way out of a maze.

Jett headed over to Wyatt with a look of concern on his face. "Man, you look beat. You need to take a minute to rest."

"I can't rest with the chaos surrounding us," Wyatt said, viewing the homes that have already burnt to the ground. Paul and Seth along with other firemen helped to evacuate most of the residents to safety, but there were still others refusing to leave their homes, mostly the elderly.

Wyatt took Jett's advice and waved for another fireman to relieve him. He and Jett walked down a graveled road to assess the damages. Soot and debris was everywhere. Exhausted from the grueling night, thoughts of Joi eased the frustration raging inside of him, but the idea of never seeing her beautiful face again pained his heart.

He and Jett stopped in front of a vacant home where the fire begun. It was rumored that the homeless who slept in the empty house at night started the fire while trying to keep warm. "So, this is where the fire started, uh?" Jett observed the barely erected home. "Because of what took place inside there, others could possible lose theirs. What a shame." Shaking his head, he kicked at the pile of rumble lying on the ground.

"These people don't have much, and to think what they did have is gone up in smoke," Wyatt tsk as they headed back where the others were.

"A child is trapped inside one of the houses!" A fireman yelled.

Wyatt and Jett dashed toward the home. A mother thought she had accounted for her four children before rushing them out the burning house, only to learn that her ten-year old son never made it out. The police restrained her from going back inside. She and her three kids huddled behind the barricades, crying and screaming to save the young boy.

Each man suited up with a breathing apparatus and oxygen tanks strapped to their backs. The chief ordered Wyatt to go help to detain the fire threatening to spread in the woods, but he refused. A frightened child trapped inside a burning home took precedence over putting out a bunch of bushes.

A young boy appeared at one of the bedroom windows, screaming, "Save me, please don't let me die!"

From the look in Jett's eyes; he seemed to be having a flashback of the young girl that he couldn't save a year ago.

"What do you think you're doing, Lieutenant Payne?" the Deputy Chief asked.

Bright, orange flames lapping in every direction looked like a scene straight out of the movies. The water from the charged hose only seemed to tease the ferocious fire. If they make it through the burning inferno without any fatalities, it would be a miracle.

"Chief, let me help out here," he pleaded, knowing that he couldn't just stand by battling a fire in the woods while a young child's life hung in the balance.

Without waiting on the chief to respond, Wyatt put on his protective gear and stormed through the front door of the burning home. The child screams were getting the better of him. He knew pulling a stunt like that could possibly cost him his job, but he'd sleep better at nights knowing a life was saved under his watch.

The chief yelled out in a deep, hoarse voice. "Lieutenant Payne. You get back here!"

Wyatt never looked back. A board with flames fell in front of him as he entered the home. He pushed it aside and went to search for the terrified child. His adrenaline had kicked in, causing him to ignore the danger that he had now put himself in.

"Wyatt." A voice called out to him. He turned to find Jett close on his heels, which was a welcoming sight. As always, Jett was there to cover his behind.

The flames seemed to lap up the water as quick as it came from the hoses.

God, help us.

Knowing that he wasn't alone, Wyatt continued his quest to rescue the child.

*****

Patient after patient streamed through the emergency room, suffering from smoke inhalation. The ER was standing room only. Throughout the night, ambulances continued bringing in firemen and residents in on stretchers. Joi rushed to see if any of them was Wyatt. She worked tirelessly throughout the night, hoping and praying that he wasn't among the missing persons that had been reported on the news.

The last update she had heard on the news, reported that a child was trapped inside a burning home. The house was burning out of control and two firemen had gone inside in attempts to save him. Her chest tightened at the report. In her heart, she knew one of the firemen had to be Wyatt.

"Joi!" Tara yelled from the triage desk. "The news is back on."

She hurried and stood in front of the mounted television on the wall. She gasped, "Tara, the fire is burning out of control." If she wasn't scared before, she had reasons to be now. "How are they going to fight a fire of that magnitude? If the fire reaches the woods, it could possibly catch in other neighborhoods."

"I don't know. I just don't know," Tara said solemnly.

Joi felt helpless, knowing that Wyatt was out there in danger and there wasn't anything that she could do about it. A crowd had now formed around the television. No one could believe what their eyes were seeing. How was the small, impoverished community going to rebuild after such devastation?

Joi, along with other healthcare workers, attended to patient after patient. Everyone pulled together to provide a pleasant atmosphere for those who had been injured from the fire. She listened as the victims recounted their stories of being pulled from their burning homes.

Paramedics brought in more burn victims. Most of them, who had not been seriously injured was treated and released. Many were distraught, wondering what they were going to do after losing everything. The Red Cross, along with other voluntary services took names of those who needed assistance.

Tonight had been a living nightmare and still there was no word from Wyatt. Tending to the injured had kept her from going stir-crazy. She prayed to have another chance with Wyatt. He did nothing but love her and she rejected it.

Her cellphone beeped. Joi pulled it from her pocket. Leave it to her mom to have downloaded a local news App to alert her on breaking news around the Ark-LA-Tex (Arkansas, Louisiana, and Texas). They had updated the news about the fires in the Martin Luther King area. And it read, *"Two local firemen and a child's life are in danger as the fire grows worst and the raging winds work against them. Stay tune for more updates."*

Chapter Forty-Eight

Lord, please allow the three of us to get out of here alive. If You delivered the three Hebrew Boys out of the fiery furnace. I know that You are able to deliver us, Wyatt prayed, keeping his cool as the vicious flames grew around them. He turned to check on Jett and hated that his friend had put himself in danger for him a second time.

Wyatt spotted the young boy crouched into a corner of the bedroom. His face was buried between his knees, waiting for death to come and claim him. Wyatt removed his breathing apparatus and called out to the boy. He and Jett had to do some quick thinking because the smoke was filling into the room.

"Son," Wyatt addressed the young boy. "What's your name?"

"Kevin," he cried out in terror as relief shone in his eyes.

The ten-year old looked up at Jett and Wyatt as if he'd seen an angel. His face had new hope as he pulled himself up from the corner of the wall. He ran, grabbing hold to Wyatt's leg. Jett went to the window and waved, to let the others know that they had located the child.

Wyatt turned to inspect the entranceway that they had entered moments earlier. He shook his head. The situation didn't look good. *"Please Lord. Don't let us have made it this far to perish."* He and Jett stared at each other, knowing it was going to take an act of God to get them safely out of the Hell they were in. Both managed to keep a smile on their faces to help the young child to remain calm. If it was the last thing that he would do, Wyatt was going to try to get the boy back to his mother and siblings.

Jett snatched a blanket off the boy's bed and wrapped him in it. He took off his oxygen mask and instructed the child that they would take turns breathing the air. While Jett explained to the child what they must do to make it out alive, Wyatt searched for possible ways out.

Wyatt motioned that it was time to get going. Jett picked the boy up into his arms and followed him. As they made it back to the middle part of the house, the front door came into view. When they rushed towards it, a wooden beam with fire blazing from it fell from the ceiling, preventing them to exit.

Time was not on their side. Pieces of the house had started collapsing around them. They had to find another exit and fast. With just enough oxygen to sustain them for thirty minutes, Jett and the boy couldn't last much longer sharing it.

Wyatt removed his oxygen mask and asked, "Kevin, where is the back door?" He knew time was ticking against them.

The boy turned as Jett held him securely in his arms and pointed over his shoulder, down a hallway. Smoke had begun to snake its way down the dark hall. If they stood any chance of getting out of the house alive, they had to move, and fast. Jett and the boy continued taking turns breathing through the oxygen mask as they searched for the back door.

Things were not working in their favor. At the end of the hallway, flames were roaring out of control. Quickly, they turned and headed back to keep from getting trapped. Wyatt noticed Jett, trying his best to keep Kevin calm. He couldn't have been more proud of his friend. The counseling and anger management classes had really helped him to mature.

"Kevin…is there another way out of here?" Jett asked.

"Ye-ss-ss, Sir," he stuttered, fear growing in his eyes. He jumped in Jett's arms when a loud thump sounded from another part of the house. Wyatt realized then that the house was about to cave in on them if they couldn't think of something and fast.

"Where?" Wyatt tried to act calm and didn't want to scare the boy, but he needed to know where that exit was and soon or the three of them were going to die.

Just when Kevin began to tell where, the ceiling began to collapse.

*****

Everyone in the ER gasped, and then dead silence, as the house collapsed to the ground on television. "Wyatt!" Joi screamed in disbelief. Tara, Albre and Becky stood by her side. "This can't be happening." She stood in front of the television, rocking with her hands wrapped around her.

"Joi." Tara placed her arms around her shoulders and led her to a vacant seat. "You need to calm down."

She was numb. Joi had thought about the things that she would say to Wyatt. Now, she would never get the chance to tell him how much she loved him. She'd never feel his powerful, arms wrapped around her body. Or his lips pressed against hers, sending excitement and intrigue bursting through her loved-starved body.

Tonight, her worst nightmare had come true. Wyatt had been killed doing his job. How was she going to live the rest of her life without him? He'd helped her to jump over some tough hurdles in her life. Without him, she would have never opened her heart to live or love again.

She laid her head on Tara's shoulder and wept. Wyatt, Jett and a young boy was dead, and just when Jett and Tara were getting along so well. Here she was sulking in her loss and her friend was also grieving.

Joi raised her head and wiped her eyes. "Tara...I'm sorry. I've been so caught up in my feelings that I forgot about yours." Just when she uttered those words, tears began to trickle down Tara's face. Joi realized that Tara had been holding herself together to console her. The girls surrounded each other and prayed for the two firemen and young boy who'd lost their lives tonight.

"We're going to get through this," Becky comforted, squatting in front of her girlfriends.

"We always do," Albre agreed as they held on to each other. "It won't be easy, but the four of us are strong women."

Joi rested her head against the wall in a daze. Images of Wyatt and her in the Caribbean months earlier flashed before her face. The unforgettable memories she'd created with him brought a smile to her sad eyes. He'd made a bold move, when out of nowhere he kissed her on the beach. And she thought he was crazy when he'd asked her to go zip lining with him. As scary as it was, she would do it all over again just to have him here with her.

What she would give to wrap her arms around his neck and start anew. Tears trailed down her face at the thought of never feeling his body pressed against hers. Just like Michael had left her, Wyatt had done the same.

She hoped he and the others didn't suffer when they met their fate. Joi pulled herself from her seat. Tara and the others ladies followed her back into the emergency room. She had a job to do and prepared herself for when the paramedics transported Wyatt's body to the hospital. She would say her goodbyes and touch him one last time.

Chapter Forty-Nine

An hour after learning that a burning house had collapsed and killed Wyatt, Jett and a young boy, sirens blared from ambulances pulling into the emergency entrance outside. The doors slid open as paramedics transported several firemen who had suffered from smoke inhalation and burns. Joi noticed a slew of fire trucks lined the streets while she and others nurses assisted paramedics as they brought in more victims. She assumed they had come to support their injured and fallen firemen. A pain rippled through her heart at the scene.

Back inside, she and other healthcare workers started bandaging and taking care of the injured. Joi busied herself, trying not to focus on the chaos surrounding her. There were people needing her assistance. She had learned to turn off her emotions when it came to doing her job.

Joi stayed away from the television set. No need to cause herself more pain after what transpired tonight. An outburst of clapping tore her from her thoughts. She turned to see what all the commotion was about, and in walked Wyatt, Jett and the young boy through the ER sliding doors. She closed and reopened her eyes, hoping she wasn't seeing ghosts.

Before she had a chance to process what was going on. She left a fireman's side that she had been attending to and raced towards them. She cried, "Wyatt!"

God, please let him be real. The closer she got to them; Joi knew her prayers had been answered.

His face and clothing was covered in soot and wreaked of smoke, but she didn't care. With arms out stretched, she jumped into them. There was no doubt, he was just as happy to see her.

******

Joi was the most beautiful sight Wyatt had ever seen. He kissed her with all his might. As hard as it was, he pulled away just to say those four little words, "I love you, Joi" He was grateful to have a second chance at life and love, and he wasn't going to hold back his feelings anymore.

"I love you to, Wyatt," she confessed. Those words were like music to his ears.

He peeled her trembling arms from around his neck and dropped down on bended knee. Although, he didn't have a ring, the timing was right. "Joi, will you marry me. I love you and I want to spend the rest of my life with you?" He held her hands inside his as he stared with great expectation into her eyes. "I know my career is dangerous, and I know that it concerns you. But, if I didn't learn anything else tonight, I've learn that life is too short to live it without the person you love. The time that I have left on earth, I want to spend it with you."

She screamed with joy as tears ran down her tired face. "Yes. Oh…yes Wyatt." She pressed her small palms against his face, bringing him to his feet. Joi kissed him with her entire being. He knew without a doubt that she truly loved him.

Everyone in the ER waiting room cheered as the two held on to each other, neither wanted to pull away from the other. Jett and Tara were seen talking over in a corner and the young boy was reunited with his mother and siblings.

After Wyatt was treated, he had recounted how he, Jett and the young boy escaped from the burning house. Thanks to the plywood covering a gaping hole in the floor, the three managed to escape safety. The family was so poor that the mother placed a rug over the wood in the hallway, which turned out to be a blessing in disguise. The hole in that floor allowed them to crawl underneath the house to freedom. Without it, Wyatt and the others would have never survived to tell their stories.

He never admitted to her, but that was the scariest Wyatt had ever been. Not for his life, but for Jett and Kevin. If his friend hadn't followed him into that burning home, Wyatt probably would have perished trying to save the ten-year-old alone.

Joi took excellent care of him, making sure that he was in tip top condition before the doctor released him. They wanted to keep him over night to run further tests, but he refused. Joi continued to clean and bandage a wound he sustained in the fire.

When she finished treating him, Joi rubbed the side of his face with the back of her hand. She lean in and kissed him as he pulled her into his embrace. Unspoken words transpired between them. Each knew exactly what the other one was feeling and thinking.

"I'm thankful to have the chance to show you how much I love you," she admitted. Her head pressed against his as he sat on the edge of the examining table. "I was going to tell you earlier today, but everything went haywire after I got the call to report to work."

"I was going to do the same, Baby." He held her in place. "I fell in love with you the first day that I laid eyes on you." He kissed her lips. "I knew from that day that you were going to be my wife. But—"

He paused.

Her lively smiled flatlined. "But what?" Joi asked; her voice now cracking.

"I've done something that I'm not proud of. Something that may cause you to change your mind about marrying me." Ashamed, he dropped his head to keep from looking at her.

"I don't understand Wyatt... something like what?" She pulled away, fear mixed with uncertainty shone on her face.

Wyatt confessed to Joi how Jett covered for him a year ago when he wrecked his vehicle, while driving intoxicated. He understood that someone or even himself could have been killed or seriously injured by his lapse in judgment. Jett, being the friend he was pulled him out of the driver's seat before the police arrived and took the blame. Jett realized that Wyatt stood a greater chance to become chief than he.

Under investigation, Jett was placed on paid administrative leave until his blood test came back. It proved that he had no alcohol in his system. Therefore, he reported back to work. His trying to protect Wyatt almost cost him his job. That night put their lives, jobs and friendship in serious jeopardy.

Wyatt explained that he drank heavily that night when he found out that his wife had left him for another man. Although, it did not justify his decision to drive under the influence, the pain of his wife leaving him overruled his better judgment.

"I'm sorry Joi for not telling you sooner. I just couldn't bear the thought of you walking out of my life or hating me."

"I-I," she stuttered. "I could never hate you."

He breathed a sigh of relief. "But?" he asked, waiting on her condemnation.

"There is never an excuse to drink and drive." Her smile returned, putting him at ease. "But, after meeting Trina, I can forgive you."

He pulled her back into his arms. "Thank you for understanding."

"No, thank you for never giving up on me, I am truly blessed. How could I have been so blind?" she paused. "I didn't think that I could ever love another man the way that I loved Michael, but then, you entered into my life, showing me that it was possible to love again."

"I did all of that?" he joked, pointing at himself. "You taught me how to trust again, Joi. I was in love with a woman that didn't love me. I thought that every woman was after something when they approached me. You were different. You saw me." He brushed his good hand across her soft cheeks. "You saw my heart."

Wyatt cupped her face between his hands and vowed to love her for the rest of his life. Never in his wildest dreams had he imagined finding a woman where the amount of money in his bank account wasn't an issue. Joi loved him, for richer and for poorer.

A man who finds a wife finds a good thing. And Wyatt can truly say that he has finally found his good thing in Joi.

Epilogue

"Take a deep breath Mrs. Payne and push," the doctor ordered Joi. "I can see his head."

Three years had passed since that fateful night that threatened to extinguish their love. Wyatt and Joi were happily married with a two-year old daughter, and just seconds away, they would be welcoming their second child into the world. Life couldn't be better for the couple. Wyatt was in the delivery room with his wife, awaiting the arrival of their baby boy and two years earlier he'd made chief at the fire department.

Joi's relationship with Rebekah blossomed. She was now a junior at Harvard University. During her summer breaks, Rebekah taught young teens about the dangers of texting while driving. Life had indeed changed for both women, and learning how to forgive had been the medicine that each of them needed to move forward in their lives.

Jett and Tara tied the knot months later, after Wyatt and Joi had married. They have a one-year-old baby girl. And Jett threatened to put the fear of God in any boy who dared to look at his daughter. Wyatt and Jett's friendship grew stronger and their secret remained between the two. Jett vowed to never bring that day up again.

Trina continued her gold-digging ways. The last Wyatt had heard, she'd set her sights on some banker who was supposed to be loaded. But if he enters into a relationship with her, he'd be bankrupt soon.

And as for the others,' they were happily single.

"Baby, he's almost most here," Wyatt shouted with excitement, holding his wife's hand. With sweat pouring down the sides of her face, the only thing she could think of at that moment was getting it out of her. She took another deep breath and pushed as hard as she could.

She heard the beautiful sound of crying coming from the other end. The nurse rushed to clean him off, but Joi began to feel labor pains again. "Doctor," she cried. "Something is wrong. I'm still having labor pains."

"What?" Wyatt eyes grew, looking down at her. "Baby, are you sure that this is not some sort of aftershock you're experiencing after having a baby?"

Joi stared up at Wyatt, giving him a crazed look. The contractions were hitting hard and fast until she thought she would faint. "Mrs. Payne," the nurse said. "Looks like you're having twins. Get ready to push."

"Twins," she and Wyatt screamed.

She grunted, took in another deep breath, and gave it everything she had. Moments later, another cry came from the other end. "Lord, please let that be the last baby in there." She collapsed back onto the pillowed, drained from the unexpected birth.

"Mr. and Mrs. Payne, you have two healthy baby boys," The doctor announced, smiling at the shocked couple.

Wyatt leaned down and kissed his wife. Joi had become very emotional at the thought of having twin boys again. The Lord had given her back her sons. She had lost so much, but God had given her back much more. The nurse came and laid both her naked boys upon her chest. She and Wyatt caressed their little infants and kiss each other. The two had been through so much pain in their lives and now they were finally experiencing unspeakable joy.

If you enjoyed reading, *Joi and Payne* Please leave a review at the bookseller where you purchased your copy. You can find other books by Sheila L. Jackson at www.sheilaljackson2.com or any online site where books are sold.

Contact Information

To contact Sheila L. Jackson for book signings or speaking engagements, you can email her at: SJ@comcast.net or visit her website, www.sheilaljackson2.com

Discussion Questions

1) When two police officers arrived at Joi Campbell's doorsteps, they delivered the worse new imaginable (her husband and kids died as a result of a teen texting behind the wheel). As you entered into Joi's world, did you feel her pain, shock, and disbelief of losing her family?

2) If you were in Joi's position, could you have easily gone on with your life as if your decease love ones never existed? Oftentimes, people in our lives expect us to get over our hurts and tragedies, but is it that simple to let go and start over again?

3) Why do good men like Wyatt find themselves attracted to the wrong type of women or vice versa? Does the outer appearance/Eros type of love, blind them of their suitor's flaws until it's too late?

4) Although it was hard for Joi to open her heart to love again and start anew. Did her waiting almost cause her, in her mind, to lose Wyatt? Most people think that it is easy to pick up the pieces and move on after life turns your world upside down. That is why in my story, *Joi and Payne*, shows the back and forth battle in Joi's mind of wanting to love again, but feeling guilty each time she tried.

5) Jett was hotheaded, controlling, and a womanizer. After learning about his past (his mother abandoning him as a child and him unable to rescue a young girl from a

burning house) and that he suffered from Post-Traumatic Stress Syndrome, does that justify his abrasive behavior?

6) Rebekah was sixteen years old when she made that fatal mistake of texting while driving. Was Joi being a bit harsh and spiteful for not forgiving the young girl who was grieving and distraught just as she? Even in our own lives, do we sometimes want the people who have hurt us to suffer or feel the same pain?

7) When Joi and Wyatt vacationed in Jamaica, she seemed conflicted concerning her feelings for him. Should she have stop seeing him, if she wasn't sure of how she really felt? Did her actions (kissing, being affectionate, and going out with him) appear to lead him on as to wanting something more than just friendship?

8) Mrs. Ester is a youthful, fun loving, older woman. When Wyatt and Joi walked in on her and her friends' book club meeting, what with through your mind as the women drooled over Wyatt? Why couldn't Joi see what others' saw when looking at Wyatt (the total package)?

9) Trina, the conniving, coldhearted ex-wife of Wyatt, who wasn't worthy of a man like him, lost it all in the end. She learned that the man (the so-called doctor who turned out to be a janitor) who she left him for turned out to be just has cold and calculating as she. The Bible speaks a great truth when it says, "You reap what you sow." Trina brought destruction upon herself. As a reader, what went through your mind when she asked Wyatt to take her back?

10) Jett charged behind Wyatt into a burning house to save a ten year old boy who was trapped inside. This showed Jett's growth and maturity that true friendship doesn't see the risks when helping a friend. When Wyatt and Jett tried to save the young boys life, as a reader, what was going through your mind when there was no exit to escape the burning house?

11) Do you believe that God is a God of second chances? When Joi found love, married again, and gave birth to twin boys, do you believe, like the Bible story, Job that God was restoring back to her several times over what she had lost? Once she learned to forgive, let go, and open her heart to love again, God began to multiply and pour back into her life what she had lost two years earlier.